A MYTHICAL ADVENTURE

MORPHEUS

CHILD OF TIME & SPACE

A MYTHICAL ADVENTURE

MORPHEUS

CHILD OF TIME & SPACE

GAETANO PICCADACI

EXTREME OVERFLOW PUBLISHING

EXTREME OVERFLOW PUBLISHING
A Brand of Extreme Overflow Enterprises, Inc.

P.O. Box 1811
Dacula, GA 30019
www.extremeoverflow.com

Re-Published by Extreme Overflow
Publishing Produced by GP
Entertainment Enterprises
Edited by Jeana Meadows

Printed in the United States of America
Library of Congress Catalog in-Publication
Data is available for this title

For permission requests, contact the
publisher. Send feedback to
info@extremeoverflow.com

PROLOGUE

The story you are about to read unfolds a cosmic symphony, where earthly existence intertwines with celestial realms in a tale that defies the bounds of human existence, time, and the Universe.

Morpheus is an unsuspecting young man chosen by extraterrestrial entities to be the linchpin in an otherworldly legacy. Aliens pick a human family to conceive. Morpheus was born a human-alien race baby. The baby grows up with care, love, and learning like any other human child on Earth. But, when the child turns eighteen, he discovers he has another family from a planet called Achilles, shattering the illusions of the only life he's known.

Morpheus's father and mother from Achilles always had contact with their son from birth to eighteen through dreams used as the conduit to maintain a connection, subtly guiding him towards a destiny entwined with cosmic significance. When Morpheus turns eighteen, his father from the planet Achilles calls him through his dreams and asks him to join him and his family. When Morpheus joins his father and family, he discovers the truth about his existence in the Universe. Morpheus also finds that he was born as a god-king, and his obligation is to planet Earth and its population.

Morpheus visits his home planet, Achilles, and the High Council of Achilles. The High Council agrees that Morpheus has the powers of the first god of the Universe, Vishnu. Morpheus discovers over time that he will have a second planet to protect from evil. A newfound responsibility emerges as Morpheus discovers that he must protect not only Earth but also a second celestial sphere from impending malevolence. As the sands of time shift, Morpheus ascends to the throne, becoming the sovereign ruler of Earth, Achilles, and two universes teeming with diverse civilizations.

CHAPTER 1

A Child Was Born

On September 17, 1964, a baby boy was born to Italian American parents living in Boston, Massachusetts. Giuseppe and Sophia Cappuccino proudly welcomed their son into the world. As they gazed at their newborn, Giuseppe suggested the name "Morpheus."

"Morpheus," he repeated thoughtfully. "It's the god of dreams, from ancient mythology. What do you think?"

Sophia smiled warmly. "I love it. It's perfect for our son," she explained, her voice filled with affection.

Giuseppe nodded, feeling a deep sense of pride. He filled out the birth certificate with the name "Morpheus Cappuccino," sealing the choice for their son.

A short time later, the doctor entered the hospital room, a bright smile on his face. "How's our little one?" he asked, glancing at the baby.

Giuseppe beamed. "He's a healthy boy. We've chosen the name Morpheus for him."

The doctor raised an eyebrow. "Morpheus? The god of dreams?"

Sophia nodded. “Yes, we believe it’s a fitting name. With his little smile,” she continued, gazing lovingly at the baby, “Morpheus already looks like he’s dreaming his dreams.”

The doctor chuckled. “It certainly seems like he is. A very peaceful little boy.”

The family agreed with a quiet laugh. And so, with their new son, Giuseppe, Sophia, and Morpheus were ready to leave the hospital.

As they arrived home, they gently walked Morpheus around their apartment, showing him his new surroundings. “This is your home now,” they told him, their voices filled with joy and pride. They marveled at the baby they had created together, their love embodied in his tiny form.

Morpheus grew into a calm and content baby, adhering to his eating and sleeping schedule with ease. At each doctor’s visit, Sophia beamed with pride as the doctors and nurses praised her son.

“He’s such a healthy boy,” the doctor always said.

“Thank you, doctor,” Sophia replied, her voice filled with gratitude.

“You’re an excellent mother, Sophia. It shows in how happy and well-cared-for Morpheus is.”

“Morpheus is a happy baby,” she said, smiling at her son. “Giuseppe and I take very good care of him.”

The doctor nodded with approval. "He's a delightful baby. You're both doing a wonderful job."

Time passed, and Morpheus's first birthday came. Giuseppe and Sophia threw the biggest birthday party for Morpheus, inviting the entire family. The Italians always make special occasions huge, especially a boy's first birthday. Giuseppe and Sophia invited their grandparents, parents, uncles and aunts, cousins, and friends. Morpheus's party gave him a feeling of security as a baby, meeting and getting to know his family.

Morpheus had three more great birthday parties as a child, and after his fourth birthday, he began noticing things around him. He started remembering his birthdays, his parents, grandparents, and family members. Morpheus also began watching television and hearing his name and people talking.

One night, Morpheus woke up and noticed a circle-like object in the corner of his room. Morpheus stared at this object for a while. He saw swirls and movement in this circle as he stared at the object. The entity didn't harm Morpheus, but he got scared of the object in his room, so he ran to his parent's bedroom. When Morpheus entered his parent's bedroom, he woke them up and told them about the object in his room. Giuseppe left his bedroom and looked for the object in Morpheus's room.

Upon returning to his and Sophia's room, Giuseppe explained, "There was nothing in Morpheus's bedroom."

Giuseppe and Sophia stayed with their son and reassured Morpheus that nothing would harm him in their home. Morpheus was reassured by his parents but then noticed that this circle followed him, and now it was in the corner of his parent's room.

“Do you see the swirling circle in the corner?” Morpheus asked.

“No, we don’t see anything, Morpheus,” Giuseppe said. “So, what do you see, Morpheus?”

“It’s a circle-like object with swirls in a circle,” Morpheus explained.

“Maybe it is an orb or a spirit,” Giuseppe said. “And we can’t see it ourselves, but perhaps only you can see the orb, Morpheus.”

So, Giuseppe and Sophia suggested that Morpheus sleep with them for the night, and they all fell asleep together.

The next day, when Giuseppe got home from work, he asked, “Sophia, how is Morpheus doing today?”

“It was like nothing happened last night to Morpheus,” Sophia responded.

“That is good,” Giuseppe said.

Giuseppe and Sophia had another baby in 1966. They named this child Marcus. Once again, they provided the same love and care for Marcus as they had for Morpheus.

Time passed, and in 1969, Giuseppe got a phone call at work about his father. Giuseppe’s father had died from an accident on the job. The phone call explained that his father was under a cement bucket and the cables broke. Giuseppe was told to go home and take care of his father.

When Giuseppe got home, he told Sophia about his father and the accident on the job. Giuseppe then went into Marcus's bedroom and started crying. Morpheus went into his brother's room and asked his dad if he was okay.

"Why are you crying, Dad?" he asked.

Giuseppe called for Sophia to come and get Morpheus. Sophia came to get the boy out of the bedroom and explained, "Your father is crying because his father was terribly hurt on his job."

Giuseppe and Sophia were an old-fashioned Italian family, and they sheltered their sons from the magnitude of this terrible fatal accident Morpheus's grandfather had been in.

Morpheus overheard bits and pieces of his grandfather's accident. However, Morpheus and Marcus would not hear the full truth about their grandfather's death until they were old enough to better understand. On the day of the wake and funeral, Morpheus and Marcus stayed with a babysitter. Giuseppe and Sophia went to the wake and funeral and then to the reception with family and friends.

Giuseppe told Sophia that he wanted to move out of the city and move to the suburbs.

"I want our children to have a yard and a house we own," he said.

"Owning a house and having a yard for the children would be nice," Sophia agreed.

MORPHEUS

In the summer of 1970, the family moved to North Randolph, Massachusetts. The house had two bedrooms upstairs and a bathroom, a kitchen and dining room, a big living room, and a den/office adjacent to the living room. Giuseppe and Sophia bought a new pool for the family to enjoy in the summer. The family enjoyed living in their new house for a time. But they soon discovered that people were the same in the suburbs as they were in the city.

In 1971, Giuseppe and Sophia welcomed the addition of a baby girl named Maria to their family.

Crime was spiking, and times were challenging for the town and the people of Randolph. One night, the family was out with other family members, and when they returned home, they found that the house had been broken into. The front and back doors were kicked in, and the house was ransacked and turned upside-down. The criminals went through everything in the home, looking for valuables. The police were called to investigate the crime and question the neighbors.

The police informed Giuseppe that the neighbors had not seen anything.

"How can that be when they kicked in the front and back doors?" Giuseppe asked.

"The neighbors must've looked the other way when your house was broken into earlier," the policeman replied. "I don't think they want to get involved."

Later, Giuseppe told Sophia the family needed to move from the house, build their own home, and escape their current neighborhood. Sophia agreed.

By the summer of 1972, the Cappuccino family had moved into a brand-new house in South Randolph. The neighborhood was all brand-new streets and homes. However, the yard was still dirt with no grass, which was the best yard for the two young boys. The yard was the best place to play with toy dump trucks, loaders, and cars. The boys shared a bedroom, and Maria had her own room. Giuseppe and Sophia unpacked the house and set it up. The boys went out in the yard, played in the dirt, and had fun getting dirty. Finally, when the house was together with all the furniture, beds, and belongings, night came, and the family watched television and went to bed and slept.

When Giuseppe went to work on Monday, Sophia and the kids woke up and watched television in the morning.

Then, Sophia asked Morpheus to help care for his sister.

Afterward, Sophia told the kids to get dressed, make their beds, and clean their rooms. Then, the children played in the yard and had fun. Morpheus always had a feeling that something or someone was around him. He never felt scared, but it was a strange feeling. The thought was like someone was watching over him.

Morpheus and Marcus had fun for the day. Later, Giuseppe came home from work to see the boys and talk to them.

Giuseppe walked into the house, said hello to Sophia, and kissed her. Shortly after, they all sat down to have dinner. After dinner, the family watched television together.

Finally, Giuseppe said, "It is bedtime for the boys. It is nine o'clock."

MORPHEUS

The boys kissed their parents and went to bed at nine o'clock. Morpheus tossed and turned in his bed and then woke up during the night. Morpheus noticed the same orb he saw in the Boston apartment. However, Morpheus wasn't afraid. He turned over and went back to sleep.

In the morning, Morpheus thought about the day and night before. He could not figure out what these things and feelings meant, so he kept the situation to himself. The end of summer was coming, and school would soon be starting. Morpheus's birthday was also in September, on the seventeenth. He would be turning eight years old and starting third grade. When Christmas came, the boys received their bikes, and Maria received dolls. The family was pleased with their new home and neighborhood.

When spring began, Sophia was downstairs sitting on the couch playing with the children, when Morpheus said he didn't like the government or police authorities, out of the blue.

"Why would you say that, Morpheus?" Sophia asked.

"I don't know why," Morpheus answered. "I just don't."

Sophia started asking if something had happened, but Morpheus said, "No."

When Giuseppe got home late that night, Sophia waited up to talk to him about Morpheus and tell him what Morpheus had said.

"Did something happen to Morpheus?" Giuseppe asked. Sophia noted that Morpheus had said, "No."

"I will talk to the boy and find out what is wrong," Giuseppe said.

Later, when Giuseppe and Morpheus were alone, he asked Morpheus about the conversation with his mother.

"Can you explain why you don't like authority figures?" Giuseppe asked. "Can you tell me what is wrong, Morpheus?"

"I don't know why, Dad," Morpheus replied. "I just don't like authority figures."

"Okay, Morpheus," Giuseppe said. "But you know you can come to me if you need to and discuss any problems."

"I know, Dad," Morpheus replied.

In 1973, the Cappuccino family was expecting another boy, and he was named Joseph. Morpheus helped his mom and dad with Maria and Joseph. He learned to care for them by feeding them their bottles, changing their diapers, and playing with the younger siblings.

"Morpheus, you are getting older, and it's time to have responsibilities," Giuseppe said. "And helping your mother and me with the children is a good thing you are doing.

"It's time for you to take out the trash on trash day, and I will teach you how to cut the grass."

"Okay, Dad, when will you show me?" Morpheus asked.

"This Saturday," Giuseppe replied

"Okay, Dad," Morpheus said.

So, Saturday came, and Giuseppe showed Morpheus how to cut the grass. Giuseppe took out the lawnmower and showed Morpheus where the gas and oil went, explaining that the blades would cut his fingers and toes off if he were not careful.

Then Giuseppe explained to Morpheus how to cut the grass and showed him how to do it by following the wheels and cutting edge. Morpheus then took over and started cutting the grass, and Giuseppe watched out for him.

When the grass was all done, Giuseppe said, “Excellent job, Morpheus.”

Time would pass, and the children grew older.

CHAPTER 2

Teenage Years

Morpheus had reoccurring dreams - visions of a life that wasn't his, or so he thought. Morpheus couldn't understand his dreams or his visions of the dreams. He never thought of talking to his parents about his dreams and visions. When his 14th birthday arrived, his family and friends threw him a birthday party and he had a good time there. When November came, Morpheus and his best friend Scott discussed buying a bottle of Southern Comfort and some marijuana and going down to the sandpits to waste time and have fun. About a week before Thanksgiving, the two boys went out to have fun drinking alcohol and smoking marijuana on a gloomy Saturday.

When they got to the sandpits, they lit up the marijuana joint and opened the bottle of Southern Comfort. Morpheus was the first to take a drink, and Scott was the first to light up the marijuana.

"I like drinking and prefer it over marijuana," Morpheus said.

"And I enjoy marijuana!" Scott exclaimed.

So, Morpheus drank the bottle of Southern Comfort, and Scott smoked all the marijuana. As time passed, the boys started feeling the effects of these vices. Finally, Scott and Morpheus climbed a hill and sat down. Morpheus opened the bottle and drank the last of the Southern Comfort. After finishing the bottle, he broke it and started licking the glass shards.

"What are you doing?" Scott asked. “Stop it, Morpheus! You’re going to cut your mouth.”

The boys went down to the railroad tracks, and Morpheus sat in the middle of the tracks.

“Get up, Morpheus!” Scott demanded. But Morpheus ignored him and started throwing rocks at something he saw down the tracks.

“Stop, Morpheus! You are throwing rocks at people,” Scott said. “Come on! We’re going to get in trouble.”

Morpheus got up, staggering, and walked across the tracks toward Scott. When he entered the sandpits, Morpheus saw that Scott was up by the tree line. Unfortunately, Morpheus didn’t realize he would blackout from all the drinking.

Morpheus then realized that he was on the tree line with Scott when Scott said, "Let’s go back home.”

Once again, Morpheus blacked out, but Scott was unaware he was experiencing the blackouts. Finally, Morpheus returned to reality from his blackout and saw that he was in one of the houses being built in his neighborhood. The homes were only at a stage of being framed. Morpheus looked out a window and fell backward, hitting the floor hard and vomiting while on his back. Scott ran over and kicked Morpheus over to his side. Morpheus jumped up and started to go home with Scott.

When the boys got to Morpheus's house, Morpheus entered through the back door and proceeded to his bed downstairs. Morpheus collapsed onto his bed and was out cold. Scott was trying to get him into the shower when Giuseppe walked downstairs and saw his son passed out. Giuseppe called for Sophia to come downstairs and see their son's condition.

"Scott, what happened to Morpheus?" Sophia asked.

Giuseppe and Sophia saw that Scott was scared, so they told him to contact his parents. When Scott's parents arrived at the house, they were all shocked that Morpheus reeked of alcohol and had passed out cold.

"Let's take him to the hospital," Scott's father said. "I'll drive."

When Giuseppe went to pick Morpheus up off the bed, something happened to Morpheus. Just before he was lifted up off the bed, Morpheus could hear the conversations between everyone in the room, but he was unable to move his body or speak. In an out-of-body experience, there appeared a bright light, and Morpheus looked down at the room and saw everyone there, including himself.

Morpheus looked up to the light, and a voice spoke from within it, saying, "It's not time to leave Earth and your family, Morpheus. In time, I will explain your quest on your planet called Earth, but for now, you must learn about the people, history, and the world you live in."

Morpheus didn't understand the voice's reasons, but Morpheus returned to his body just as Giuseppe picked him up.

Giuseppe,
Sophia, Scott, and his parents raced Morpheus to the hospital.

They pulled into the emergency room area with the ambulance entrance when they arrived at the hospital. They called for a nurse to come out to the car and explained the situation to her. The nurse pulled out some smelling salts and put them in front of Morpheus's nose. Morpheus awoke briefly and punched the nurse in her face without realizing it before passing out again. The nurse rushed Morpheus into the hospital, and the doctor rushed over to help save the child from dying.

First, the doctor ordered blood samples to determine how much alcohol was in Morpheus's system. Then, the doctor began speaking to Morpheus.

"What is your name?" the doctor asked.

"Morpheus Cappuccino," Morpheus replied.

"What day is it?" the doctor inquired.

"Saturday," Morpheus answered.

"Who are your parents?" asked the doctor.

"Giuseppe and Sophia Cappuccino," Morpheus responded.

The doctor turned to Morpheus's parents and said, "The test results show that there was 98% alcohol in his blood. He should be dead with that count!"

"His friend said he got sick and vomited," Sophia said.

“That might have very well saved his life,” the doctor said. “You can take him home, and he will likely have a severe hangover. Watch over him. If there are any problems, bring him back to the hospital.”

Soon after, Morpheus found himself at home and in his bed. When he fully awoke, his head was spinning, and he had a severe headache. He got out of bed and went downstairs to see his family pacing all over the house, worried about him. When they saw Morpheus up and out of bed, they joked about the drinking.

“How do you feel?” Sophia asked.

"Like shit," Morpheus replied.

“Go lay back down,” Giuseppe said. “And tomorrow, we will discuss this problem, Morpheus.”

“Okay, Dad,” Morpheus said.

When the next morning arrived, Giuseppe asked, “How are you feeling, Morpheus?”

“Okay, Dad,” Morpheus said.

“Why were you drinking?” Giuseppe asked.

“For fun,” Morpheus answered.

“That is the craziest answer, Son,” Giuseppe said. “You are better than that, Morpheus. I hope you learned a lesson from your mistakes and you never repeat them.”

“Yes, Dad,” Morpheus said. “Can I go out and play?”

"Only if you've learned from your mistakes," Giuseppe said.

"Yes, Dad. I did learn from my mistakes," Morpheus said.

Morpheus immediately called Scott and ran over to his house.

"How are you feeling?" Scott asked.

"Better," Morpheus said.

"I hope you won't do this again," Scott's father said.

"No, it won't happen again," Morpheus assured him.

The boys left the house, and Scott began talking about everything that had happened the day before, running down the events for Morpheus.

"I don't remember everything," Morpheus said.

"You must have had a blackout from drinking," Scott said.

"I guess I did," Morpheus added.

The boys agreed never to drink and do that again.

"I could hear all of you while in bed," Morpheus told Scott. "But I couldn't move or talk."

"That's weird," Scott said.

"I was floating and saw everybody in the room," Morpheus said. "I saw a bright light and heard a voice."

"What did the voice say?" Scott asked.

"The voice said it was not my time," Morpheus said. "And I have a mission on our planet."

"That's weird," Scott said again.

"God must have talked to me," Morpheus said.

"I guess?" Scott responded.

"The doctors explained that I had 100% alcohol for blood," Morpheus said. "He said I was lucky that I didn't die from alcohol poisoning. Little did they know I was dead for a time."

"If you saw the bright light, you were dead," Scott said.

After hanging out for a while, Morpheus and Scott went home for the night. When bedtime came, Morpheus went to sleep and started to have dreams again. These dreams were as vivid as Morpheus's everyday life.

A voice entered his dreams and said, "You don't need to be afraid of me. I am here to help you through your life on this planet and explain that you have things to do in the future. When you become eighteen, I will explain everything you need to know. But for now, follow your Earth parent's guidance and learn everything you can for your mission."

"What task?" Morpheus asked the voice.

"When you turn eighteen," the voice replied.

Morpheus woke up from the dream, shook his head, and couldn't believe what had happened.

MORPHEUS

Morpheus continued with his life and dreams, preparing for a future that he didn't understand. He started getting jobs to support himself. First, he helped his dad with his work. Then, he also worked for a convenience store chain called J K Stores.

When Morpheus was working at the store, he saw some kids stealing and breaking things. So, Morpheus reported the kids to the manager, who kicked the kids out of the store and told them not to come back. This occurred just before Thanksgiving Day.

Thanksgiving Day arrived, and the family gathered for a lovely holiday dinner. Nighttime came, and Morpheus said he was going up the street to the store where he worked.

"Okay," Giuseppe said.

"Be careful," Sophia added just before he left the house.

Morpheus started walking to the store, and when he arrived, he greeted Jimmy, the store clerk. Jimmy was also a neighbor on Morpheus's street, and they were friends. Morpheus and Jimmy were talking about the store and work when the kids that the manager kicked out came into the store. There were five of them: two girls and three boys, and they were all about the same age as Morpheus and Jimmy.

They asked Morpheus why he had told the manager. Morpheus said that he had seen them stealing, and it was his job to report them for the crime.

" Well, you will pay for that!" One of the boys said.

Then, one of the girls pulled out a big kitchen knife and threatened Morpheus. Jimmy saw it and was scared.

The boys said they wanted to fight, and if Morpheus didn't go outside to fight them, the girl would stab him.

"We'll carry you out of the store and beat you," one of the boys shouted.

"Okay, we will fight across the street on the grass," Morpheus said. "One at a time"

The boys agreed, and they all proceeded to go outside.

Morpheus started fighting one boy, and one of the store's customers saw what was happening and called the police. As Morpheus was fighting, another boy came over and kicked Morpheus with steel-toe boots in his face. The boy kicked Morpheus three times, knocking him out cold.

At that point, the police were on the scene with guns pulled and told the boys to put their hands up. The police called for an ambulance for Morpheus. The three boys and two girls were arrested for the fight. When Morpheus came to, the police asked him his name and where he lived.

Morpheus told them that he lived two streets down at the end of the street. A police officer took Morpheus home, and the other police officers investigated the complaints with the store clerk and the lady who called the police.

When Morpheus and the police officer arrived at the house, the officer knocked on the door, and Giuseppe answered. Sophia was at the top of the stairs.

"I have your son," the police officer said. "He was in a fight."

The officer moved out of the way, and Giuseppe saw Morpheus. Sophia started screaming and crying.

"He needs to go to the hospital," the police officer told Morpheus's parents. "But he refused to go in the ambulance."

Morpheus walked into the house, past the officer and his parents, and went to the downstairs bathroom mirror to see his face.

"The other children were arrested for this fight," the officer told Giuseppe and Sophia. "When asked, you must go to court and may need an attorney to represent Morpheus."

Morpheus and his parents went to the hospital and discovered that Morpheus had been kicked three times. One kick was to the eye and split the eyelid; another was to the cheek, and the final kick was to the mouth, shattering his teeth.

"He will need x-rays of his head and cheek," the doctor said. "He will also need stitches for his eyelid and a dentist for his teeth."

The kids went free at the end of it all because the witnesses never came forward, and the police didn't push for justice. Morpheus learned another hard lesson about people and how they acted in this world. He now had a perfect memory stored to remember when he needed to in the future.

CHAPTER 3

Eighteen

Morpheus graduated in 1982 and turned eighteen in September. His mom and dad bought him a 1977 Camaro. Morpheus was pleased with his new car and drove it to work. He also drove to the beach to hang out with his friends. One night, while Morpheus was hanging out with his friends, it got late, so he slept in his car at a hotel parking lot. While he was asleep, he started to dream, or so he thought. The bright light returned over the vehicle, and Morpheus was transported to a gray marble room with walls that were curved and smooth. Morpheus found himself on a gray table or bed. He got up, looked around, and noticed that all the walls were identical. He touched the walls, which were cold and smooth, but the air was comfortable and warm.

Morpheus heard a noise and said, "Hello, is anyone there?" He wasn't scared at all. He felt completely comfortable with his surroundings.

He saw a figure in the shadows, and a familiar voice said, "Do you remember my voice, Morpheus?"

"Yes," Morpheus answered. "I remember from when I died."

"You didn't die," the voice said. "This was supposed to happen to you. Do you remember my words about you turning eighteen?"

"Yes," Morpheus replied.

"It's time," the voice said. "My name is Labrum and I am the king of the gods and Earth. I am going to walk to you. Don't be afraid, Morpheus."

"I'm not afraid but curious," Morpheus replied.

"That's good, Morpheus," Labrum said. "You are an intelligent young man, but now you will learn about your true origin and much more. To start, I am your father, and your mother's name is Denab. She is the goddess of beauty. You will meet her later, along with all the other gods on the spaceship *UNIV ORION*. You come from the Andromeda Galaxy and a planet called Achilles. You, yourself, are a god, as well."

"How did I end up on Earth?" Morpheus asked.

"You were sent here to learn and observe the people, history, and the problems on Earth," Labrum said. "You are the key to this planet and what might happen here on Earth. You learned about the dinosaurs, correct?"

"Yes," Morpheus answered.

"Earth was made by nature of the Universe, and the animals, people, plants, and sea life were planted here on Earth by us Achillesians," Labrum explained.

"How did Achillesians come to be?" Morpheus inquired.

"That is a question that no one knows the answer to," Labrum said. "The Universe created us somehow, and there are many civilizations in the Universe."

“How was I born on Earth?” Morpheus asked.

“You were planted in your Earth mother’s body,” Labrum said. “She had trouble getting pregnant, and we helped her to conceive. After your Earth mother’s first pregnancy with you, the other three children came naturally.”

“Labrum, am I here for you to teach me about our race of Achillesians?” Morpheus asked.

“Yes,” Labrum answered. “And there is much more involved to the situation.”

“What is that, Labrum?” Morpheus questioned.

“You will learn over time being with us,” Labrum said.

“Do we have enough time to spare with how things currently are on Earth regarding the people who are in chaos today?” Morpheus asked.

“Yes and No,” Labrum said. “We Achillesians can manipulate time, place, and dimensions. Today, I will introduce you to your family from Achilles, show you the ship location and the spaceship *UNIV ORION*, and teach you how to contact us while you are on Earth.

“All civilizations are peaceful races of people, unlike the human race on Earth. The people on Earth are warlike, ignorant, arrogant, selfish, greedy, power-hungry, and have many other problems. We are the total opposite of Earth’s people. In our culture, we all have our place and a job to do without any negative emotions to alter our purpose or culture. There is no fighting at all within our Universe or on any other planets. We use the spaceship

UNIV ORION to travel only, not for warfare, unlike people on Earth, who live a short distance from each other and want to use nuclear weapons. Somehow, Earth is the only planet infected with these negative emotions."

"We have a council just like Earth," Labrum continued. "But there are no loopholes in our laws and order, and nobody will challenge the High Council. It is time to introduce you to your family and the crew members."

So, Labrum announced that all personnel on the ship would gather in the Meeting Chamber.

"You will meet your mother first," Labrum told Morpheus.

When Denab saw her son Morpheus, she was happy to hold him and talk to him.

Then, Labrum introduced Morpheus as his and Denab's son to the rest of his family and crew.

Labrum explained the names and meanings of each family member to Morpheus, beginning with himself.

Labrum explained he was the king of the gods and an Earth sign. His wife was introduced as Queen Denab, the beauty of the gods. Next, there was Wega, who represented Atlantis and was a water sign, along with his wife, Denebola, who represented harmony.

Then, there was Rasalhague, who represented invisibility and was a wind sign, and his wife, Zaniah, a dreamer. Then Achernar, who represented destruction and was a fire sign, and his wife Capella, the hope of life. Sirius represented strength, and his wife, Terebellum, was a guardian. Kochab, who controlled magnetic waves, and his wife Rastaban, who oversaw time travel.

"Now, the last two of this ship's members are Sadal Suud, who represents new things to come, and you, Morpheus, are the god of dreams," Labrum said. "And when you marry Sadal Suud, you will be the god of dreams and represent new life for the planet Earth. Now that you have met all your family and wife-to-be, we will all have a feast and drink to celebrate your return home."

Morpheus was amazed at everything, especially with Sadal Suud, his wife-to-be, who was incredibly beautiful. Finding out he was a god and meeting a whole new family was unbelievable. His mind was so overwhelmed with all the news that he could hardly believe it was real. His heart beat like a drum for Sadal Suud.

Morpheus was well-liked on Earth among his friends and the girls, but no girl he had ever met could hold a candle to Sadal Suud. When Morpheus looked around the chamber and saw his family members, they all had an aura of beautifulness and were good-hearted people. He was so overwhelmed with everything that he didn't know what to say or do.

Suddenly, Morpheus remembered his Earth family, and he asked Labrum about his presence being missed on Earth in his absence.

"You don't need to worry about that," Labrum said. "I've taken care of that situation with a vacation for you that was explained to your parents."

"You lied to my Earth parents?" Morpheus asked.

"No! I didn't. I gave them a reason not to worry about you," Labrum responded. "Remember, Morpheus, your parents cared for you for eighteen years, and we all respect them as your parents. I appreciate you caring about your Earth family. It shows that you have a heart, and seeing you enjoy yourself here makes me very proud.

"I explained to you that you will be coming here and staying on Earth, that you have a task for all of us, meaning both civilizations. Your Earth parents have taught you the proper way to think, respect for others, and many other qualities I see in you."

"You must get to know everybody here, especially Sadal Suud," Labrum continued. "You will also need to learn the ship while you are here. In reality, you are heading towards a crash course, starting with the spaceship, crew and family, and our history in the Universe. Then, I will show you the power of looking through Earth's history and keeping up your image on Earth. Finally, both civilizations will need to find an answer for what is coming to them and prove their real history about themselves."

Morpheus became concerned with Labrum's information and asked, "What will happen to all of us?"

"I will show you in time," Labrum said. "For now, I want you to enjoy your time and family here."

"Okay, Dad," Morpheus replied.

Labrum corrected him, "No. You call me father and Denab mother."

"Okay, Father," Morpheus said.

The next day, Morpheus woke up next to Sadal Suud and said, “Good morning.”

“Good morning, Morpheus,” Sadal Suud replied. “Is there anything you need?”

“A shower and some clothes,” Morpheus said.

“Would you like me to join you in the shower?” Sadal Suud asked.

Confused, Morpheus wondered if something had happened the night before that he may have forgotten. So, he asked, “Sadal Suud, did we make love last night?”

“No,” Sadal Suud responded. “Would you like to make love now?”

“No, Not right now,” Morpheus quickly responded. “I’m still unsure of your customs and ways.”

“We are forever paired,” Sadal Suud said. “So I will teach you our customs, practices, and marriage rituals. I am your woman, and you are my man for life. This is one of our customs – being paired together for eternity.”

“What happens if we don’t like each other?” Morpheus asked.

“There has never been a couple paired together that didn’t like each other,” Sadal Suud explained. “You will teach me what you like, and I will teach you what I like as a husband and wife. We are both the same age and innocent in life, and we will always be together. The custom of our people is to match us together in ways that complement each other with our skills, strengths and weaknesses, our minds, our style of being, and much more.

"Labrum and Denab have been watching over you since you were born for eighteen years. They know everything about you and me, as well. In your ancient history on Earth, people were selected to be paired and married. We are the people who taught these traditions on Earth. The people on Earth and our people from Achilles are the same. The only difference is that we have kept our old traditions and values, and the Earth's people are modern and warlike with everything. Our people love and care for each other. On Earth, they take advantage of people, harm each other, steal, murder, rape, lie, and just about anything else. Your father, Labrum, is here to try and right the wrongs on Earth with your help."

"I agree with helping both civilizations and preventing the crimes on Earth," Morpheus said.

"You must shower, and I will join and wash you," Sadal Suud said. "Then you will see your father."

Morpheus went to look for his father and mother. When he found them, Labrum said, "Just the man I was looking for. We have a lot to talk about, Morpheus."

So, Morpheus said "good morning" to his father and mother.

"Good morning, Morpheus," they replied. How are you feeling today?"

Morpheus said, "Well."

Denab asked Morpheus to come closer so she could see her "young man." Morpheus went to Denab and embraced her.

"I've missed and love you, Morpheus," Denab said. "Even though I have seen you over the years growing up, I could never hold you like I am now."

"What do you mean, Mother?" Morpheus asked.

"When you were a child in Boston, your father and I watched over you," Denab explained. "We were the orb you saw in your bedroom and throughout your life."

"I understand now about my past," Morpheus said.

"Okay, Morpheus, you have spent time with Sadal Suud and your mother. Now it's time to learn about the history between your two worlds," Labrum said. "I will explain how things work, starting with the spaceship. And how we all work together without any problems, in our civilization or on spaceships. Your mother and I operate and control the spaceship's bridge. Our job is to keep the spaceship behind the moon and out of sight from the human race."

"Why are you and Mother working here on the spaceship?" Morpheus asked. "King and queen of the spaceship never work."

"We all work together, including the king and queen," Labrum explained. "Down on Earth, your kings, queens, and presidents or leaders do nothing but talk and order men to kill. Our race, Achillesians, all work physically, no matter our status or place in society. When we make decisions, we do this together without debating. We all listen to the reasons, pros, and cons of the situation or problems. It is the same as any case of war. We are defenders of the Universe, and we do not take advantage of any planet or people. We know about your wars on Earth, and we didn't interfere, but if a race of beings were fierce creatures, then we would interfere and stop the war."

"We got sidetracked," Labrum continued. "I must take you to the other gods so they can explain themselves. And then we can go over the prophecy of your quest."

CHAPTER 4

Introduction of the Gods

Everyone has a place and job in our society. There are thirteen people to operate the spaceship, and you make fourteen, Labrum told Morpheus. "So, we all have many jobs, and we are glad to help each other with these jobs and our society. Now you have reunited with your family and with the gods of the Universe."

Morpheus asked about his Earth family and what would happen to them.

"You will see them anytime you want," Labrum answered. "But you will have two families you are obligated to and belong to.

"You have much work to do on the planet and throughout time," Labrum explained. "But for now, I will show you around the ship and its people, with their jobs, and teach you how the spaceship operates. This is Wega and his wife, Denebola. They will present their story and information."

When Morpheus saw Wega and Denebola, they greeted each other.

"Welcome Morpheus to the garden and kitchen area of the spaceship," Denebola said. "We take care of the food sources, and our signs of water and harmony help the growth of the plants."

“We only eat fruits and vegetables and drink only water or the juices of fruits and vegetables,” Wega explained. “We also make the most outstanding wine from the grapes.”

Morpheus asked Wega and Denebola what their relationship with each other was to him.

“We are your uncle and aunt, your father’s second brother and sister-in-law,” Wega said. “Now it’s time to go with Rasalhague and Zaniah.”

“Good morning, Morpheus,” Zaniah said. “How is learning about our family, jobs, and culture going?”

“It’s fascinating,” Morpheus said.

“I will take you to life support and show and explain how things are done there,” Rasalhague said.

When they got to this compartment of the spaceship, Rasalhague showed Morpheus the motors that supply and make oxygen and gravity for the spaceship.

“Our signs are wind and dreams,” Rasalhague said. “This is why I’m in charge of oxygen and gravity, and my wife Zaniah is in charge of our dreams and visions.”

“I was the one in your dreams, and I helped your father and mother with the dreams and visions between you and them,” Zaniah said.

“Are you my uncle and aunt?” Morpheus asked.

"Yes, we are your uncle and aunt, Morpheus,” Rasalhague said.

"Rasalhague is the third brother to your father, and I am his sister-in-law," Zaniah explained.

"It's time for Morpheus to go to the engine room and find Achernar and Capella," Rasalhague said.

Morpheus walked down to the engine room to find the pair. When he arrived, he saw them working at the control panel. So, Morpheus greeted them with a "Hello."

They exchanged greetings and politely asked Morpheus to wait, saying, "We need to adjust the engine first; we'll be with you shortly." Once the adjustments were complete, they apologized and explained, "The engine had to come first, Morpheus."

"I am your father's fourth brother, and my wife Capella is his sister-in-law," Achernar said. "Our signs are fire and hope of life. We control the spaceship engines, and my wife gives us hope of life. We support the ship's engines and other parts of life support.

"Here comes Sirius and Terebellum," Capella said. "They will explain their support and description of their jobs."

Sirius and Terebellum said, "Hello" to Morpheus. Morpheus said, "Hello" in return.

"Sirius and Terebellum, where are you on the family tree?" Morpheus asked.

"We are your cousins," Sirius explained. "My father and mother are Wega and Denebola. And Terebellum is the daughter of Rasalhague and Zaniah."

"That would be considered incest on Earth," Morpheus said.

"That's incorrect," Sirius said. "Our ancestry and Earth's ancestry have married within the family lineage over millions of years."

"The doctors on Earth would say it causes congenital disabilities," Morpheus said.

"Earth's kings and queens of past times kept their royal bloodlines," Sirius explained. "We are the Gods of strength and guardians."

"We are the medical team aboard this ship—the doctor and the nurse," Terebellum explained. "It was us who taught Earthlings how to reproduce in this way. Have you ever wondered why, when families marry into others, they often claim their son or daughter is 'too good' for someone from another family? The human race has forgotten the importance of preserving family lineage, rejecting the idea of inbreeding within their families. This was by design—embedded in their genetic programming—to ensure the human race could diversify and grow.

Remember, Morpheus, you are here for many reasons, but one of them is to remind humanity of the origins they've forgotten or abandoned. The practices that humans once followed—our traditions—were the foundation of this world and its population, Morpheus."

Kochab and Rastaban came along and asked for Morpheus. Morpheus was walking toward them and said, "Hello."

Kochab and Rastaban said, "Hello" to Morpheus, then Kochab said, "Come with us, and we will go to our laboratory."

"We are your cousins and the gods of magnetic waves and time travels," Rastaban said.

"We make all machines work with magnetic waves and time traveling," Kochab said.

Kochab and Rastaban told Morpheus they would show him how magnetic waves work with time travels and explain anything he needed to ask about the ship or their race.

"We are trying to prepare you for your time travels on Earth and your quest from your father, Labrum," Rastaban said. "The magnetic waves and time travel work together to carry you through time waves. The properties are the same as space travels between magnetic and time waves."

"Our bodies carry these properties as well, but when it comes to objects, we need machines to create the properties to carry us and our devices through time and space," Kochab explained. "For example, a part of your brain carries the source of the power within the subconscious part of your brain. When we learn about this power source within our brains, we realize we can travel through time and eventually go through space and time."

"Can I travel to Mars right now without any problems?" Morpheus asked.

"Yes, but you must learn how our powers work with time and space travel," Kochab said. Time travel is also different, and you must learn about the procedures. We will show you everything you need to know about magnetic waves and time travel, Morpheus."

"You are young and eager to learn, but you need time and experience to understand all we are to be and more with the planet Earth," Rastaban said. "When you return to your father Labrum, he will explain much more about us and the reasons for Earth's involvement."

Sadal Suud went looking for Morpheus and found him with Kochab and Rastaban."

"Are you hungry, Morpheus, and ready for lunch?" Sadal Suud asked.

"Yes, I am starving," Morpheus replied.

So, Sadal Suud said, "Come with me and get some lunch."

Morpheus was utterly captivated by Sadal Suud. Her striking beauty took his breath away—her radiant face, piercing blue eyes, and long, flowing blonde hair framed her features perfectly. Her lips were enchanting, and her touch revealed a body as tender as it was graceful. Yet her allure went beyond the physical; her mind was sharp, her spirit luminous, and her presence nothing short of extraordinary.

Morpheus often marveled at her, thinking, "There's no one on Earth like her." She was a testament to the idea that beings from another planet, another place, or even another time could embody beauty and wonder far beyond imagination.

Then, Sadal Suud asked Morpheus if he was okay with all the news he was learning about their family in space.

"It is a bit overwhelming to find out I have two families and a quest to help the Earth," Morpheus said.

"Let's eat lunch, talk about ourselves, and get to know each other better," Sadal Suud said.

"What is your job on this spaceship?" Morpheus asked her.

"I create new things to come with everything," Sadal Suud explained. "And you are the new life on planet Earth."

"Why would I be new life on Earth?" Morpheus asked.

"People on Earth need help understanding their origins in the universe and the history of life on both Earth and beyond," Sadal Suud explained. "They lack knowledge of the ancient cultures and the beginnings of existence. Instead, they create stories to align with their own narratives and misconceptions. However, each era and culture from the past holds significant meaning in the history of this planet.

Take, for example, the dinosaurs, the giants, the Anunnaki, and other god-like beings. Consider Atlantis and the Atlanteans, the mysteries surrounding alien life, and so much more. These pieces of the past are not random—they are chapters in the larger story of Earth's history and its connection to the universe."

"How old are you, Sadal Suud?" Morpheus asked. "And how do you know so much about us Achillesians and our history?"

"Your father, Labrum, will explain the beginning of life to you, our ages, your age, and much more," Sadal Suud said. "You need to eat lunch, and you can relax, and we can talk about ourselves."

"Sadal Suud, what things do you like to do?" Morpheus asked.

"It's hard to explain because we are in a spaceship, not on a planet," Sadal Suud responded. "When we get homesick for our world, we have a Hologram Hall to program our fantasies and dreams, an image of our world, and much more."

"Can we go there and see how it works together?" Morpheus asked.

"Of course!" Sadal Suud said.

As Morpheus and Sadal Suud walked to the Hologram Hall, Sadal Suud asked, "What program do you want to use?"

"I want to see our world, Achilles, the people, and how life works there on our planet," Morpheus said.

"It will be nice to do it together, and you'll get to see everything about our civilization," Sadal Suud said.

Sadal Suud set the program, and they explored their world and galaxy. When the program started, it showed them the Andromeda Galaxy first. Then, it showed them the world they came from and slowly descended through the clouds, and finally, they started seeing the land and oceans. As they descended more, the cities and towns became clearer to see. The cities were so beautiful with a future look of a new world. Every building was like a sculpture city, and the towns had a similar look. Finally, they reached the ground. The people were different in many ways.

Some people looked like Morpheus, and others seemed utterly different in many ways. But, when Sadal Suud and Morpheus started to walk around, everyone was friendly.

"Sadal Suud, how many different kinds of people live here and get along with each other?" Morpheus asked.

"I'm not certain, but what we do know is that war has ravaged many worlds and the people on them," Sadal Suud said. "The devastation from these wars, the destruction of our towns, cities, and even entire planets became overwhelming for all involved. It reached a point where we had no choice but to learn how to stop the wars and embrace the richness of each other's cultures. In all of our worlds, there are no crimes—except on your planet, Earth. This is why your father sent you here."

"We all have a purpose in our lives, and yours is to reveal the truth to the people of Earth. But for now, let us enjoy the beauty of our world, Achilles. There is so much to see." Sadal Suud smiled and continued, "We have a vehicle that will allow us to view even more from the air. Once we've seen enough, we can land and explore on foot."

"Are the animals and sea creatures maneaters?" Morpheus asked.

"Yes, some creatures are, and some are not," Sadal Suud replied. "We have a protected shield around us if something were to happen, and we will be safe."

Morpheus and Sadal Suud ventured to the sea, where they were awestruck by the sight of enormous, powerful sea creatures gliding through the waters. Yet, just as remarkable were the smaller, friendlier beings they encountered, who greeted them with a gentle presence. The seas and its inhabitants were nothing short of breathtaking, a world of wonder and beauty that left them in awe.

"You are falling in love with our world, aren't you?" Sadal Suud said.

"Yes, it is so beautiful and wonderful," Morpheus exclaimed. "What are the forests with the animals there like?"

"We are going there now, and you will find out," Sadal Suud said.

The trees were unlike anything they had ever seen, and the animals they encountered were far larger than any found on Earth.

"I love your world and everything about it, Sadal Suud," Morpheus said. "Will we be together someday in our world, Achilles?"

"We will after the ship members finish their job on Earth," Sadal Suud replied.

After that, the synthetic program of the Achilles world ended, and Morpheus and Sadal Suud started talking about their mission on Earth.

"What will my mission on Earth be?" Morpheus questioned.

"Your father will guide you and teach you about your mission—to reveal the truth about their world's history and the future of war to the people of Earth," Sadal Suud said with a reassuring smile. "But for now, let's find your father and mother so you can spend time together and learn more about everything."

Sadal Suud and Morpheus made their way to his parents, where warm greetings were exchanged. Before departing, Sadal Suud gave Morpheus a gentle kiss and said, "Goodbye for now."

CHAPTER 5

Labrum Teaches the History

Labrum and Denab sat with Morpheus to discuss his quest. "The world you've lived in for 18 years is plagued with problems that the rest of the universe has long overcome—chief among them, war," Labrum began. "You see, every conflict starts from something small, a simple word: disagreement, dislike, hate, fight... and eventually war."

Morpheus nodded in agreement with his father. "I understand," he said. "I've never liked aggression or conflict with others—it always feels destructive and unnecessary."

"We understand how you feel, but you are vital to addressing the issues plaguing Earth and its people," Labrum replied with calm determination.

Morpheus, his voice tinged with doubt, asked, "How can an 18-year-old possibly stand up to the leaders of such a corrupt world?"

Denab stepped forward, her tone reassuring. "You won't be alone in this, Morpheus. Everyone here on the ship will guide and teach you how to face Earth's challenges. Each of us possesses unique powers, as do you, and we will share some of our abilities to aid you in your mission. We will also reveal the truth about Earth's ancient history to help you make your case."

She paused, then continued, "Although you are only 18 now, when you leave this ship, both your body and mind will undergo a transformation. You will emerge as a man of wisdom, strength, and knowledge, fully prepared to share the truth with the people of Earth."

Denab picked up where she left off. "You will have the ability to defuse conflicts among Earth's people and seek knowledge from the past, even traveling through time to fulfill this part of your mission. To aid you further, we will provide you with a recording device—an invaluable tool to expose both the truths and the lies to humanity."

"I will explain how this galaxy came into existence and evolved into what it is today," Labrum began. "The origins of the Milky Way are often linked to the Big Bang theory. While part of this theory is accurate, there are gaps in the story. The Big Bang itself resulted from the explosion of a black hole in space. Like everything in the universe, black holes have a lifespan. When a black hole reaches the end of its cycle and explodes, all the matter it has consumed is released, giving rise to the formation of a galaxy.

"This explosion creates a swirling motion in space, and this rotation scatters the released matter, forming individual solar systems with planets, moons, asteroids, and comets. As planets take shape, some rocks contain critical elements such as oxygen, water, and other compounds necessary to sustain life. Over time, these planets undergo a natural process of stabilization, allowing their elements to mature and align with the planet's specific characteristics. Once these celestial bodies are ready, beings from other galaxies intervene to nurture and develop these planets and moons, tailoring their support to meet the unique needs of each world."

Labrum continued, "Your planet has undergone countless changes over billions of years. Earth's formation spans approximately 425 billion years, during which time the air you breathe and the water that sustains life gradually came into existence. Earth also needed to cool down from its fiery beginnings. Only then could plants begin to grow, fueled by the planet's hothouse effects, paving the way for life to emerge—with assistance from beings from other galaxies. The origin of the first people remains the universe's greatest mystery, as no one can recall the beginning of their existence. After the firstborn humans appeared, they began aiding other galaxies and planets, adapting to meet the unique needs of each world's population.

"On Earth, animals like dinosaurs were intentionally introduced to initiate a life cycle that would transform the planet's hothouse conditions. Dinosaurs, along with plants, played a critical role in accelerating Earth's stabilization, making it suitable for human habitation and eventual population. Time, above all, has been the essential factor in shaping every aspect of your planet," Labrum explained. "You live in a solar system with one Sun and nine planets, each unique in its characteristics. All these celestial bodies, including the Sun, possess a core. Let's start with the Sun: its core is a powerhouse of nuclear fusion, converting hydrogen into helium and generating plasma. It serves as the primary source of energy for the entire solar system, emitting gamma rays and solar flares that provide light and heat.

"Mercury, the closest planet to the Sun, has no moons and consists of approximately 85 percent iron, with a molten liquid core. Its surface is rocky, and its temperatures range from a frigid -279°F at night to a scorching 801°F during the day. Venus, often considered Earth's twin in size, is even hotter than Mercury, with a rocky landscape and a core similar to Earth's inner core.

"Earth, the third planet from the Sun, is a unique blend of 70 percent water and 30 percent land, with an atmosphere rich in oxygen. It has four inner cores and temperature extremes ranging from -60°F in Antarctica to 130°F in desert regions. Its diverse landscape includes soil, rocks, plants, and life in many forms.

"Mars, the red planet, features polar ice caps, towering volcanoes, vast canyons, and weather patterns within a thin atmosphere composed primarily of carbon dioxide, nitrogen, and argon. It bears similarities to Earth's topography and geological features. Between Mars and Jupiter lies the asteroid belt, a region filled with debris—remnants of celestial bodies that never formed into planets or leftovers from the planets we know today.

"The first four planets lie within the asteroid belt," Labrum continued. "Now, let me introduce the last five celestial bodies in our solar system. These include four massive planets followed by a small dwarf planet at the farthest edge of the Sun's reach.

"Jupiter, the fifth planet, is known for its faint system of rings and an astonishing 79 moons. It possesses the strongest magnetic field in the solar system and is primarily composed of hydrogen and helium, surrounding a dense core.

"Saturn, the sixth planet, is famous for its prominent ring system. Like Jupiter, it consists mainly of hydrogen and helium. It is the least dense planet in the solar system, with an average temperature of -285°F, and it too has a core.

"Uranus, the seventh planet, is composed of hydrogen, helium, and methane, with the latter giving it its striking blue color. It also contains water and ammonia and has a frigid average temperature of -371°F, making it an icy planet.

"Neptune, the eighth planet, is another ice giant with similar characteristics to Uranus. It features water, ammonia, and methane, with temperatures averaging -370°F. Its vivid blue hue is one of its most distinguishing features.

"Finally, Pluto, the ninth celestial body, is a dwarf planet. It is rocky and icy, with the coldest temperatures in the solar system. Though small, it holds its place as a fascinating part of this cosmic family."

"Your father has covered the start of the galaxies and solar systems," Denab said. "Now it's time to cover the history of Earth and your quest. Before we talk about history, we need to explain our thoughts on what may have happened over millions of years, which would lead to the account of Earth's history. There was a place and time for everything that has been here on Earth throughout its existence.

"For instance," Denab explained, "dinosaurs—whether on land, in the sea, or soaring through the air—had their era on Earth. After them came the Ice Age mammals, like the woolly mammoth and saber-toothed tiger, as well as early humans like cavemen. Each of these groups had their time here. Furthermore, beings from various galaxies across the Universe also spent their time on

Earth, contributing in ways now lost to history. And now, it is the era of modern humanity, both in the past and in the present world.

"This brings us to an important discussion," Denab continued. "It's time to consider where things might have gone wrong for Earth and its people."

Morpheus's parents explained their thoughts, and the family and crew's thoughts drew the same conclusion.

"It has something to do with this solar system, the Sun, and maybe the gamma rays," Labrum said. "The five main stars heat up their areas in their solar system. The first star is the hottest. Its color is blue. The second star is white; the third star is yellow, which is the one here in our solar system of Earth. The fourth star is orange, and the fifth and last star is red and the least hot star. The yellow Sun has gamma rays and flairs that may have contributed to the people's violence but not to the animals or sea life. So here is why you have a quest to fulfill - to find the problems and repair the world as we know it."

"How can I do this for everybody from our two worlds?" Morpheus asked.

"This is for the Universe and not just one species of people. It's for all the species in the Universe," Labrum explained. "The Earth's government has been trying to go into space since the 1960s, and in the summer of 1969, they made it to the moon, or so they say. The government also has rockets with research equipment, cameras, and videos taking pictures of the planets. Then you have this enormous telescope in space that can see into other solar systems and galaxies. The people from our Universe are at peace with each other, except the people of Earth."

Morpheus interrupted his father and asked, "How much more learning will I have to do before the quest begins?"

"You need to understand each god on the ship and their powers," Denab said. "Then you need to understand time travel and magnetic waves before going anywhere and learn other things in case of mishaps or any issues that may arise. Morpheus, we all know this is a lot to take in and understand, but we cannot allow the human race to enter space without harming another world of people. Humans are too self-centered, greedy, and power-hungry. They intentionally hurt one another for no reason and do much more that is wrong.

"Throughout history, Earth's wars have acted as a form of population control," Denab began, her voice steady yet solemn. "But even now, the planet remains overpopulated, plagued by food shortages, rampant waste, and countless other issues. Remember this, Morpheus—we contributed to the population of this planet, just as we have with other species across the Universe."

Denab paused briefly, her expression grave. "We want the human race to thrive, to reach the stars and prosper. But this must happen without conflict in any form or manner. The Universe exists in harmony, free from war. If humanity ventures into space now, that balance will be shattered, sparking battles that could lead to the complete extinction of the human race."

Labrum stepped forward, his tone filled with both pride and frustration. "We have shielded this planet from countless threats—comets, asteroids, and cosmic catastrophes. Yet, the humans' own scriptures and ancient scrolls, which held vital knowledge and guidance, have been lost or destroyed by their hands."

He turned his gaze to Morpheus, a spark of hope in his eyes. "So, we have devised a new solution to these problems. You, Morpheus, are that solution."

"When you learn all the information needed and our powers, you will go back through time and record Earth's history to present it to them. Unfortunately, humans forget all the harm done over the ages by man and Mother Nature. Earth has a margin to live within, and if anything upsets this margin, the Earth will react to the problems. Earth is a live, breathing planet with a list of do's and don'ts, and over the ages, the Earth has shown its fury to the population of animals and mankind. The other issue will be that it's possible to travel through time. The humans will find out this information through your records and videos," Labrum continued. "You will not present recordings and videos directly, but over time through their technology, computers, television, and radio system. Humans cannot see us because their minds cannot handle the knowledge of alien or non-Earthly beings. Earth's government denies the existence of an alien race of people in the Universe. The simple answer is that they fear the unknown. The complicated answer is because that's how the governments rule over the people with fear."

"The issue," Labrum continued, his tone heavy with disappointment, "is that humans lack the ability to keep an open mind. They carry their problems and insecurities not only within their own lifetimes but pass them down to future generations. Even the brightest minds on Earth couldn't advance their current technology without help—help that came inadvertently from our spaceships crashing on their planet. Without those crashes, there would be no cell phones, computers, or technical devices as they exist today."

He paused, his gaze stern. "We have tried to introduce the reality of other lifeforms in the Universe through these incidents, but Earth's governments continue to deny these truths to their people. The knowledge available in the Universe is vast, yet humanity consistently misuses it—just as they are doing now on Earth. They prioritize wealth over wisdom, failing to see that no amount of riches can compare to the knowledge necessary for the survival of their people and their planet."

Labrum's expression darkened as he continued. "As the superior race, it falls to us to correct these problems before it's too late. If we fail, humanity will never be ready to enter space, and their future will be lost forever."

Morpheus interjected, his voice weighted with conviction, "The truth on Earth is deeply flawed—wrong, harmful, hurtful, discriminatory, built on lies and deceit, and so much worse than one might expect. The people are like sheep scattered across the land, while the governments act as their shepherds, controlling them. Trust has eroded entirely; people no longer believe in one another. It's as if everyone is at each other's throats—strangers, coworkers, governments, and, most tragically, even families. There is so much wrong with Earth and its people, and I can't deny the truth in your observations. However, I will give greater attention to your teachings, Father and Mother, with guidance from the other gods on the ship."

Denab placed a reassuring hand on Morpheus's shoulder, her expression softening. "It's time to rest now. Go to Sadal Suud and enjoy the night with her. In the morning, your father and I will continue guiding you on the path of understanding."

CHAPTER 6

Next Morning

Morpheus and Sadal Suud woke together, exchanging soft good mornings. Almost simultaneously, they asked each other, "What are your plans for today?"

Morpheus was the first to answer. "I plan to speak with my father and mother to learn more about my life, my two worlds, and what the future holds for everything."

Sadal Suud observed him closely. "You seem troubled," she said gently. Morpheus nodded. "I am," he admitted.

Sadal Suud reassured him by placing a comforting hand on his. "You will be fine, Morpheus. You must take this time to understand and learn from us. Building your confidence will come from strengthening your heart, mind, and knowledge. Trust yourself to know when to follow your heart, when to rely on your mind, and when to draw upon your knowledge. When the time comes, you'll make the right decisions."

After their exchange, Morpheus rose and went to the bathroom. Catching his reflection in the mirror, he froze and called out, "Sadal Suud, come here! What's happened to my body? It's... different."

Sadal Suud joined him and smiled softly. "You're transforming, Morpheus," she explained. "You're becoming one of us, growing into your true form and filling out your body."

Morpheus stared at his reflection, feeling a mixture of awe and fear. "I like it, but... it's also frightening."

"There's no need to worry," Sadal Suud said with quiet assurance. "Remember the question you asked your parents: how would you, as an 18-year-old man, handle this quest and all the challenges ahead? Now you see the answer. You're growing into who you truly are—a god. Your appearance now reflects your divine nature, along with the wisdom and seriousness of age. When you meet your parents, they will be amazed. You're fulfilling your destiny, Morpheus, and the purpose for which you were created."

She smiled warmly, her confidence in him unwavering. "I am so proud of you, Morpheus. Together, you and I will create a wonderful life—not only for ourselves but for the people of Earth. But for now, it's time for you to meet your parents. Learn all you can about our ways, Earth's cultures, and its history. You are ready to take the next step."

Morpheus made his way to his parents' chamber, eager to learn more about the quest that lay ahead. Upon entering, he greeted them warmly. "Good morning, Father. Good morning, Mother."

They turned to him with welcoming smiles. "Good morning, Morpheus," they replied in unison. "How did you sleep? Did you rest well?"

Morpheus hesitated before answering. "I slept well... but when I saw myself in the mirror this morning, I noticed something had changed. I've transformed physically overnight."

Labrum nodded knowingly. "That's because you're on our ship," he explained. "Your body is adapting, aligning with our physiology, and catching up to our age."

Curious, Morpheus asked, "And how old is that?"

Labrum smiled faintly. "Most of us are around 1,000 years old, while the younger ones are closer to 500."

Morpheus processed this revelation in silence, realizing how much he still had to learn about his heritage and his destiny.

"What will happen when I return to Earth and my family sees me?" Morpheus asked, his voice tinged with uncertainty.

Labrum replied calmly, "You will appear the same as you were before the quest began."

Morpheus frowned. "But what about my family seeing me like... this?" He gestured at himself.

"You will be fine with them," Labrum assured him, with Denab nodding in agreement. "Otherwise, your focus will remain on your quest."

Morpheus hesitated before asking, "And what about the time I've lost on Earth? How will that be resolved?"

Denab leaned forward. “Remember, you have time travel on your side. You can make adjustments if needed.”

Labrum added, “Now, let’s focus on preparing you for your quest. There’s still much to learn.”

Morpheus looked skeptical. “Will I meet anyone significant from Earth’s past?”

“You will,” Labrum said. “You’ll visit people from earlier periods in history, and they’ll guide you. You can also return to us on the ship whenever you need guidance.”

Curiosity sparked in Morpheus’s eyes. “Who exactly will I meet?”

Labrum smiled. “First, you’ll journey to the age of the dinosaurs. Then, you’ll move forward in time, observing pivotal moments in Earth’s history. You’ll record your experiences—video documentation of the cultures, events, and transformations you witness. We’ve mapped specific points in history for you to visit.”

“Won’t time travel risk altering the course of history?” Morpheus asked, leaning forward with concern. “What happens if my interactions change things?”

Labrum shook his head. “We’ve been doing this for millions of years. We’re careful to prevent disruptions. It’s good that you’re thinking ahead, though—it shows you’re grasping the complexity of your task.”

Morpheus pressed on. “Who will I meet from the past?”

“You don’t need to know just yet,” Labrum said. “But let me ask—who would you want to meet? Who do you think would be important?”

Morpheus pondered for a moment before replying. “I’d start with the dinosaurs, then the early humans, and significant civilizations like Atlantis, the Anunnaki, the Garden of Eden, the Egyptians, the Romans, the European empires, and eventually the Americas.”

Labrum nodded approvingly. “That’s an excellent outline. There may be more to observe, but your journey will be invaluable. Once you’ve recorded everything, we’ll analyze it to make informed decisions for Earth’s future.”

Denab interjected, her tone serious. “Do you trust Earth’s leaders—governments, scientists, religious authorities?”

Morpheus shook his head. “Not really. Too often, they speak in circles, contradicting themselves. Add in greed, power struggles, and manipulation, and trust becomes a luxury society can’t afford.”

Labrum tilted his head. “Are you aware of the secret societies?”

“Yes,” Morpheus replied firmly. “They control the government, banks, big corporations—everything.”

Denab nodded gravely. “You’re correct. The tragic part is that people allow these problems to persist, not just for themselves but for the children of future generations. Adults, with their shortsightedness, poison the lives of children. And those in authority? They poison the world and everything within it.”

“You’re a wise young man to recognize these issues,” Labrum said with an approving look.

“What will happen when we uncover the root causes of these conditions?” Morpheus asked, his tone earnest.

“Our people won’t know the full answer until we identify the problems,” Denab explained. “Even the discoveries from Earth’s past remain misunderstood or deliberately obscured. Let’s take the Egyptians as an example—the hieroglyphs hold messages and records from past lives on this planet, yet their true meanings remain elusive.”

Morpheus raised an eyebrow. “A child could make sense of that, but adults seem lost.”

Denab continued, “Exactly. The same applies to the Mayan codes and calendar. When the Spanish Conquistadors and Catholic priests arrived, they destroyed countless codices and decimated the native populations of South America. The Atlanteans? They were a mix of self-destruction and natural catastrophes, all fueled by greed for power. And the generations that followed were no better, perpetuating destruction without understanding the wisdom left behind. Wars came, lands and people were ravaged, and so much was lost—knowledge, culture, history.”

"There are countless reports from military personnel and civilians about spacecraft sightings, even crashes," Morpheus said, leaning forward. "But governments deny everything. When people witness these events, they're threatened into silence. Authorities manipulate every aspect of life for their benefit. Tax systems and judicial systems—are all rigged to favor the few in power. The rich grow richer, and the poor grow poorer. It's all wrong."

Denab's expression hardened. "And that's why we're working to address these issues. These problems cannot be allowed to exist in space, not with other races or planets. Earth is unique in its dysfunction—the only planet plagued by such destructive human tendencies. If we cannot uncover and resolve the core issues, we may have no choice but to agree on a final solution: to end the planet itself."

Morpheus's eyes widened, his breath catching. "End Earth?"

Denab's silence was heavy, the implication clear.

A storm of emotions surged within Morpheus—shock, sorrow, and a gnawing sense of urgency. He had always known change was necessary, but this? The prospect of Earth's annihilation was a solution he had never considered. Something had to be done, but was there still time to save humanity from itself?

Finally, Morpheus turned to his father and mother, his voice trembling with emotion. "Why me?"

Labrum placed a reassuring hand on his shoulder. "Because you are the answer, Morpheus. The key to fixing the problems on Earth. You are a 'new life for the planet.' Everyone here on the ship believes in your success. But you must also understand the stakes—the potential end of Earth if we fail to resolve its issues."

Denab added gently, "We don't want this burden to overwhelm you. Focus on creating a better future—not just for Earth, but for other planets and the entire Universe."

Labrum's tone grew serious. "There's more to your mission. You must find and recover critical artifacts and records: the very first Bible, the Dead Sea Scrolls, the Mayan Codices, the Cup of Christ, the Ark of the Covenant, and anything of similar importance. If you can't physically retrieve them, record their images and details. You'll also gather information about civilizations like the Atlanteans, the Anunnaki, the Mayans, the Egyptians, and the Romans. These records will help us identify the root issues plaguing humanity. Resolving them will make the Universe safer."

Denab stepped closer, her expression earnest. "As much as your focus is on the present, you'll find the past even more captivating. Every culture, tradition, and species you encounter will offer glimpses of a forgotten world—things that were once good but have been lost over time. However, you'll also witness humanity's darker moments, the mistakes, and the destruction."

Morpheus's face grew solemn. "And what if I'm in danger?"

"Remember this," Labrum said firmly. "You do not interfere with the timeline, no matter what. If you find yourself in harm's way, stop time immediately. Remove yourself from the situation, and only then let time resume. Your safety is paramount, and your mission depends on it."

Morpheus nodded slowly, a mix of determination and uncertainty in his eyes. The weight of his task was immense, but he understood its importance.

"You're there to identify the issues and problems," Labrum explained. "Once you've uncovered them, you'll report back to us for guidance. Along the way, you'll meet other crew members who will teach you critical knowledge for your quest. First, you'll work with Kochab and Rastaban. They will guide you in understanding magnetic waves and time travel—an essential part of your training. You'll also learn how to operate the time vehicle and safely transport the artifacts we discussed. These artifacts are vital for preservation. The ignorance of humanity, destroying such treasures, is both unbelievable and tragic. Scrolls, books, cave drawings—all held answers to Earth's greatest mysteries, yet they were neglected, dismissed, or lost over time."

"Could anyone take on this quest?" Morpheus asked, tilting his head in thought.

Labrum's expression softened. "No... and yes," he replied. "But you must remember, we all have a role to play. This is your role, your purpose—as the god of new life for the planet and the god of dreams. You are the god of dreams, not only for the people of Earth but also for the other gods. Now, reunited with us, you've been given a second calling: to bring a new life to the planet.

Though these two callings seem different, their purpose aligns—to bring hope, answers, and a better future."

"You carry all the hopes and dreams for a better world and Universe," Denab said warmly. "Everyone on this ship believes in you, Morpheus, and we will do everything in our power to help you succeed."

Labrum smiled and announced, "It's time for dinner. That concludes today's lessons. Tomorrow, you'll begin your training with Kochab and Rastaban."

The crew made their way to the Dining Chamber, where they gathered around long tables filled with food. Conversations buzzed across the room as people shared stories about their day.

"How is your learning going with your father and mother?" Kochab asked Morpheus, seated beside him.

"I'm beginning to understand the quest and its importance to everyone involved," Morpheus replied thoughtfully.

"That's good to hear," Kochab said with a nod.

Labrum interjected with a chuckle. "Kochab, you'll have plenty of time with Morpheus tomorrow during training. For now, let's enjoy our dinner and relax for the evening."

"Morpheus, what do you plan to do after dinner?" Denab asked.

“I’d like to return to the Hologram Hall,” Morpheus said. “I want to explore more about the Universe and other worlds with Sadal Suud.”

The suggestion was met with approval, and the crew agreed it would be an excellent opportunity for Morpheus and Sadal Suud to learn together and deepen their understanding of the Universe.

Labrum stood, raising his glass in a toast. “To Morpheus and Sadal Suud—may your journey of discovery bring light not just to yourselves, but to the entire Universe.”

The room echoed with cheers as everyone raised their glasses, united in hope and support for the mission ahead.

CHAPTER 7

Another Day of Learning

Morpheus and Sadal Suud woke early the next morning, discussing the wonders of the Hologram Hall and the adventure they had shared.

"I can't believe the Universe is so vast," Morpheus said, his eyes wide with wonder. "There are so many galaxies, so many worlds. And the people we met—they were so kind and welcoming."

"That's precisely why we can't afford to let the human race become a problem," Sadal Suud replied. "Mixed marriages between worlds have existed for a long time, creating children who belong to multiple worlds. If a war ever broke out with humanity, these families would be the first to suffer. History shows how Earth's people were discriminated against based on color and nationality. But in our worlds, we don't discriminate against anyone, and we've avoided wars over such differences. The Universe thrives on unity, not division."

Sadal Suud glanced at the time. "Morpheus, you need to get ready for your training with Kochab and Rastaban."

Morpheus nodded, thanking Sadal Suud before heading off. After preparing himself, he walked to Kochab and Rastaban's laboratory.

MORPHEUS

"Good morning," Morpheus greeted them with a polite smile.

"Good morning, Morpheus," Kochab and Rastaban replied in unison.

Kochab wasted no time. "Are you ready to learn about the physics of magnetic waves and time travel?"

"Yes, I am," Morpheus answered confidently.

Kochab studied him for a moment before asking, "Do you understand the meaning of 'physics'?"

"It's the science that deals with matter, energy, motion, and force," Morpheus replied without hesitation.

Kochab smiled approvingly. "That's an excellent definition. Your father told me you're intelligent, and now I see he was right. Not many grasp the fundamentals of physics, let alone the complexities of magnetic waves and time travel."

He paused, his tone growing serious. "The humans on Earth, for instance, should already be exploring space. But their ignorance, hatred, wars, hunger for power, and greed keep them tethered to their planet. If humanity ever gained access to knowledge about magnetic waves and time travel, they'd destroy not only their world but also the Universe itself."

"If the humans did go into space, their greed alone would kill them for the riches in other worlds," Rastaban added.

"You both don't like the human race, do you?" Morpheus asked.

"It is because the human race could have so much more and be interactive with the rest of the Universe," Rastaban replied.

"You're both right, as is the rest of the crew," Morpheus said firmly. "But if humans fail to understand the laws of the Universe, the consequence is dire—sometimes even death. They fight over money, wealth, land, religion, skin color, and even words. It's a sad reality, but that's why I'm here alongside the crew. We will uncover the root of these problems and fix them to save the world."

Rastaban nodded, a faint smile on his face. "That's a noble mission, Morpheus. You carry the best wishes of everyone aboard this ship."

"Now that we've heard your perspective on Earth and your quest, we can move forward with your lesson," Kochab said.

Morpheus raised an eyebrow. "You're testing me, aren't you?"

"Not exactly," Kochab replied. "But we do need to understand your intentions fully."

Morpheus sighed. "Fair enough. Let's continue."

Rastaban leaned forward. "Have you ever projected yourself into another place, time, or dimension?"

"Yes, I have," Morpheus replied confidently.

“You just traveled through time from Earth, didn’t you?” Rastaban pressed.

“I’ve also been in outer space—on another planet,” Morpheus added.

Kochab frowned slightly. “You might dream of being in outer space, but that doesn’t mean you’ve physically projected yourself there.”

Morpheus stood his ground. “No, I did. I’ve been to another planet.” He paused, his tone growing sharper. “You two seem unusually confrontational. Is it because of me or something else?”

Kochab and Rastaban exchanged glances but said nothing.

Morpheus continued, his voice steady and authoritative. “Now I’m the one testing you—not just as gods, but as cousins, individuals, and as members of this ship. Remember, I’m not only a prince aboard this vessel but also the harbinger of a new world. My powers are part of that role.”

He crossed his arms, fixing them with a piercing gaze. “I thought the people in space had better control over their emotions.”

Kochab and Rastaban lowered their heads, chastened. “You’re right, Morpheus,” Kochab admitted. “We apologize for being confrontational with you and your race. You are indeed the prince of this ship, and your future wife is the princess. We meant no disrespect.”

Morpheus nodded, his expression softening. “Good. Let’s move forward with understanding and unity. There’s too much at stake for anything less. Are there any more problems?”

“No, Morpheus,” Kochab and Rastaban replied in unison.

“Then teach me how to use the knowledge of magnetic waves and time travel to improve Earth and its people,” Morpheus said, his tone resolute.

Kochab and Rastaban exchanged a glance before nodding. “Yes, Morpheus,” they said together.

Kochab leaned forward, his expression thoughtful. “Let’s return to the moment when you projected yourself from Earth and traveled into space, arriving on another planet. Tell us more about that experience.”

“Yes, please elaborate on your projected Earth travels,” Rastaban said.

“I was reading a book,” Morpheus began, “And suddenly, I could see, feel, smell, and touch the things described in it. It was as though I were physically there, experiencing everything—not just reading about it.”

“So, you projected yourself into the place, space, and time described in the book?” Kochab asked, intrigued.

“Yes,” Morpheus confirmed.

“You have the ability to time travel within your own body,” Rastaban remarked, a note of awe in his voice.

Kochab leaned forward. “And what about your space travels? How do you explain those experiences?”

Morpheus thought for a moment before answering. “I was writing a story for school about space and a different world. As I wrote, I began to see the characters I was creating come to life around my table. Then, I found myself in space, surrounded by a protective shield as I flew through the void. I descended onto a planet—a place similar to Earth but far more advanced. The people, animals, buildings, and plants were all beyond anything on Earth.”

“You time-traveled to another world using magnetic waves,” Rastaban said, impressed.

“It reminded me of Achilles’ planet from the Hologram Hall,” Morpheus added. “There was a man there, wearing a blue robe and carrying a walking staff.”

Kochab’s eyes lit up with recognition. “In that time travel, you indeed saw our planet, Achilles. And the man in the blue robe with the staff—that was your father. You have incredible powers, Morpheus. But before you can master them, you must learn to control them. Once you do, we’ll move on to operating the vehicles.”

“Where does the power in our brains come from?” Morpheus asked. “And how do we adapt vehicles to function the same way?”

“Our brains are the power source,” Rastaban explained. “Specifically, the subconscious part of the brain—the cerebellum—activates these abilities. A chemical reaction within the brain triggers these powers, and they can be amplified using specific crystals, elements, and minerals. On this ship, the food we eat is infused with these substances from our home planet, enhancing our abilities further.”

“Is that how my body has changed?” Morpheus asked. “From the food and water here on the ship?”

“Exactly,” Rastaban confirmed with a nod.

Kochab leaned forward, his expression thoughtful. “There are many forms of wealth in the Universe, but the most valuable is the knowledge of life—how it works and how to care for one another across the cosmos. If humans were to venture into space, they would bring their flaws: greed, selfishness, and the hunger for power. Instead of caring for the Universe, they would exploit it, just as they do on Earth.”

“We don’t use currency in our Universe,” Rastaban explained. “Unlike Earth, where wealth is measured in things like diamonds, jewels, gold, platinum, and even paper and coins, we don’t value material riches. The true wealth in our world is knowledge—specifically, knowledge of life and how to care for it. That’s why your quest to uncover and solve the problems on Earth is so vital.”

“Let’s return to the topic of food and how it sustains our people,” Morpheus said.

"The soil we use to grow our food carries all the essential properties," Rastaban explained. "As we mentioned earlier, the plants absorb these properties directly from the soil. Our solar systems also provide energy that enhances our well-being through the suns or stars."

"There are countless benefits in the Universe, from galaxies to solar systems to individual planets, and yet humans on Earth remain oblivious to it all," Kochab said.

"We help one another, and in return, we need other resources to meet our collective needs," Rastaban continued. "This is why each of us has a role to play. We must help guide the people of Earth and correct their course."

"Now, we need you to start practicing time travel," Kochab said. "We'll begin here on the ship. Your task is to transport yourself to the compartment next door. I will stay with you, and Rastaban will move into the next room."

"How do I do this?" Morpheus asked.

"It's all in your mind," Kochab replied. "Focus on what you want to do, and imagine yourself moving into the other room. Remember, you have the power to make it happen."

"We'll guide you through it, so don't worry about making mistakes," Rastaban added.

Morpheus closed his eyes, focused on the other room, and in an instant, he was there. He looked around, amazed at the result. "Did you help me?" he asked.

“No, you did it on your own, Morpheus,” they both answered.

“It’s time to try something a bit more challenging,” Rastaban said. “Now, we’ll try traveling from one end of the ship to the other. I’ll go first, and then you can follow.”

With that, Rastaban vanished, and Morpheus quickly followed. When he caught up to her, Rastaban said, “Now, we’ll stop at Kochab’s location, and then we’ll head outside the ship to walk along its hull.”

“Okay,” Morpheus agreed, and they appeared before Kochab for a brief moment before heading out onto the ship’s hull.

As they stood on the hull, Morpheus was suddenly aware of the lack of oxygen.

“You have a protective shield the moment you think of space,” Rastaban reassured him. “Just like when you visited our planet while writing your story.”

“Was my story accurate when I wrote it?” Morpheus asked.

“Yes, you saw our world as it was,” Rastaban replied.

“Space is beyond incredible,” Morpheus marveled.

“It’s time to return to Kochab,” Rastaban said.

They reappeared inside the ship, and Kochab asked, “How was Morpheus in space?”

"Perfect," Rastaban replied. "Now, Morpheus, it's time for you to try traveling to Earth and returning to us."

"I would like to go to the Earth and experience more time travel," Morpheus said.

"No, there is too much to learn," Kochab responded.

"That's fine," Morpheus agreed.

"You are not afraid of time travel," Kochab said. "That's good, Morpheus."

"Is there anything to worry about with time travel?" Morpheus asked.

"No, we'll make sure that it is safe to time travel," Rastaban replied.

"When do the magnetic waves come into play?" Morpheus asked.

"When you start with time travel," Kochab explained. "The magnetic waves will begin simultaneously."

"When will we try time travel to Earth?" Morpheus asked.

"I changed my mind," Rastaban said. "Yes, we can go to Earth in a few minutes. We need to make some adjustments for the ship."

"We need to ensure the ship is always stable," Kochab said. "This is part of the job on the ship, as well as teaching you about time travel and magnetic waves."

"You need to think of a place and time you want to visit on Earth," Rastaban said.

So, Morpheus thought about a place and time. Then, he decided on the time of the dinosaurs.

"That's an excellent place to start," Kochab said. "Which is also the beginning of your quest."

"Great! Let's go!" Morpheus said.

"Are you ready?" Rastaban asked.

"Yes," Kochab and Morpheus said.

"The time slot that we are looking for is 240 million years ago," Rastaban said. "And if we get separated, you stay at that time, Morpheus, and we will find you."

Morpheus agreed, and the three began their time travel to the dinosaur era. Kochab, Rastaban, and Morpheus arrived in the dinosaur era. When they started walking around, they saw dinosaurs roaming and being delivered to Earth.

"Who is providing the dinosaurs?" Morpheus asked.

"We aren't from that time," Rastaban said.

"What about my father?" Morpheus asked.

"No, Morpheus," Kochab said. "Our people lived for a long time, but this was a different generation from the time we are in now."

Morpheus looked around and saw the enormous plants and dinosaurs. The temperature was hot and humid, and the smell in the air was like animals' smell, but a lot worse being dinosaurs. The Earth was a beautiful planet before humans, at the time of the dinosaurs, but it was also a hazardous planet. Morpheus thought about all he saw and was amazed at the Earth's past, present, and future.

CHAPTER 8

Time on Earth

Labrum asked for a meeting with all the gods for unknown reasons. When they came together, they met in the Conference Chamber on the ship, and Labrum asked Morpheus to join him at the head of the table.

When Morpheus stood beside Labrum, Labrum announced that he would like Morpheus to give his opinion about the Earth and the people with the pros and cons of Earth.

"We all have to share our knowledge and information," Labrum said. "I think it's time for Morpheus to share his knowledge and information about Earth and its people."

After that, all the gods agreed to hear Morpheus's explanation and thoughts about Earth and the people.

"Where do I start with the information?" Morpheus questioned.

"You are very observant with everything," Labrum said. "We need to know things you see, right or wrong, with the people and Earth."

"The numbers just don't add up," Morpheus remarked thoughtfully. "The casualties of wars throughout history, the population figures, and the historical records—none of them ever align properly. Yet, you've all explained that the gods have populated the Earth over time, which does align with my childhood musings about population, people, and the wars they've fought. But there's another issue: no one truly remembers the moment of their own birth, except through stories passed down by their parents. And then there's the mystery of the firstborn on Earth, a puzzle that has baffled scientists for centuries—much like the arrival of dinosaurs and countless other creatures on this planet."

Morpheus began explaining the mysteries of ancient civilizations and the limitations of modern understanding. "Scientists still struggle to grasp the lifestyles of those times," he said. "Despite the wealth of information carved into stone, written on scrolls, inscribed in the original Bible, etched as hieroglyphics, or painted on cave walls, so much knowledge remains lost to us. Wars, deliberate destruction, and the evil intentions of those seeking to erase history have obliterated countless ancient records—records that might have greatly advanced the human race."

He paused, reflecting. "These documents often spoke of beings descending from the skies or space, and yet their cities—Atlantis, the Garden of Eden, Troy, Sodom, Gomorrah, and many others—have vanished through time. Whether lost to natural disasters, wars, or humanity's ignorance, their disappearance leaves a void in our understanding of the past."

Morpheus continued, his voice steady. "I believe everything has its place and time—people, animals, plants, even the unknown from both the past and future. Yet the lessons we teach and the knowledge we pass down are riddled with gaps. School subjects like history, geography, and science never quite made sense to me because they can be misinterpreted, manipulated, guessed, or outright fabricated. The only subject that felt true was mathematics—numbers don't lie. But words, authority, and records do."

He leaned forward, his tone sharp. "People blindly trust what governments and scientists tell them, rarely thinking beyond the confines of textbooks and the systems imposed on them. Leaders exploit this trust in countless ways, especially through taxes and laws that benefit them more than the people. Governments take about a third of most paychecks, varying by wage or salary, and then there are additional taxes, fines, and penalties. It's all about money—not the welfare of Earth's people or upholding laws equally for everyone."

Morpheus's gaze darkened. "In the end, those in power perpetuate this cycle, and humanity remains trapped in ignorance and inequality."

Labrum interjected, "That's precisely why we don't use currency. Everyone has a role to play, and in return, food, clothing, and shelter are provided for all the people of our world."

Morpheus pressed on, his tone filled with conviction. "Everything costs money—land, homes, clothing, food, taxes, and countless other necessities. Governments compel people to pay taxes, buy insurance, and meet endless obligations. While law and order are essential for society, the cost of maintaining this system is often far too high. Leaders and authorities create laws only to break them themselves, all while expecting citizens to follow convoluted, double-edged rules.

“Slavery has existed since the beginning of time, affecting all nationalities across the globe. Today, governments outwardly denounce it, claiming it’s against the law, yet they turn a blind eye to modern forms of exploitation. Corruption thrives because of backward laws and bureaucratic red tape, which frustrates and silences those who dare to challenge the system."

Morpheus’s gaze hardened as he continued. “Major crimes must be addressed decisively to preserve humanity. The first crime is murder, and wars are nothing more than murder on a grand scale. The penalty for taking a life should be equivalent to the crime itself. The second is lying—deceptions that harm lives and distort the truth. Punishments should reflect the extent of the damage caused by the lie. Then there are sex crimes, including rape, sex slavery, and crimes against children. Perpetrators of such heinous acts should be removed permanently from society to protect the innocent.”

He paused, his voice growing heavier. “As for thieves and robbers, there should be proportional consequences. Repeat offenders should face severe penalties, escalating from the loss of fingers to more significant consequences based on the severity of their crimes. These measures may sound harsh, but the world is in chaos, and drastic actions are needed to restore order.”

Morpheus’s tone sharpened as he addressed leadership. “Those in positions of power—leaders, authorities, the wealthy, and the influential—must be held to the highest standards. When their actions lead to the suffering and destruction of innocent lives, they, too, should face ultimate accountability. No one should be above the law, especially not those entrusted with the power to govern.”

Labrum interrupted, “Morpheus, aren’t you being too harsh on humans?”

“How can I be,” Morpheus countered, “when your solution is to wipe out the human race entirely? My plan is to eliminate those who perpetuate harm—the criminals—and see what humanity can achieve in their absence. I’m trying to save countless lives by addressing the root of the problem, ensuring criminals face the ultimate consequence, no matter the crime.”

“You want to protect the human race?” Labrum pressed.

“Yes, Father,” Morpheus replied. “There are good people in the world, but criminals prevent them from thriving under laws meant to uphold righteousness. These criminals infiltrate every aspect of society—jobs, politics, law enforcement, and families—corrupting all levels of human life. Meanwhile, governments manipulate their citizens, instilling fear of aliens and alien races from Earth’s past and its potential future. They keep people trapped in endless cycles of confusion with oppressive laws, taxes, white-collar crimes, political deceit, and divide-and-conquer tactics. It’s a web of dirty deeds designed to maintain control.”

Labrum sighed. “You’re recounting the same issues we’ve known for ages, Morpheus. What we need are the *whys*, the *hows*, the *whens*, and the reasons behind it all.”

“I understand, Father,” Morpheus replied. “But you asked me to share my knowledge of Earth and its people, and I believed you wanted me to embark on a quest to uncover these problems and attempt to fix them.”

"You're correct, Morpheus," Labrum said. "But we must test you—your intentions, your methods—with both the people of Earth and ourselves."

Morpheus nodded. "I accept your reasoning, Father, but I will never harm anyone unless in self-defense or when no other choice remains. Perhaps we could take control of humanity—not with oppression, but by adhering strictly to their laws. We could demonstrate the power of force as their governments do, but with fairness. Then, reveal the truth to both governments and citizens: they are not alone in the Universe. Show them the reality of their origins and alleviate their fear of alien life."

"That might actually help the humans," Labrum conceded.

"I would like to return and share more about the aliens and many other stories from the past and present that I've gathered from human knowledge," Morpheus began. "Humans create movies about their history—real and imagined—and their expectations for the future, including life in space. With all the ancient records, films, and sources of knowledge, you'd think humans would have achieved peace by now. But instead, they remain warlike, driven by power, greed, hatred, jealousy, and countless other destructive emotions. The way humans treat one another, both in history and in the narratives they create—true or false—mirrors how they would behave as they venture into space and encounter other worlds. In their stories of aliens, humanity always casts them as aggressors, a view that military leaders and politicians seem to share."

The four ship leaders—Labrum, Wega, Rasalhague, and Achernar—stood abruptly, their concern evident. “Morpheus, is this true?”

“Yes,” Morpheus replied. “How can you not already know what I’ve just explained?”

“We were aware of some of it but didn’t realize the extent of the issues on Earth,” Labrum admitted.

“That only confirms that if humans succeed in reaching space, they will likely attempt to conquer other worlds,” Wega said grimly.

“What exactly are you suggesting for the long-term future of Earth and humanity?” Morpheus asked.

“If humans are this destructive, we must act now and abandon the quest altogether,” Wega stated.

“You can’t help humans when they can’t even help themselves or resolve their own problems,” Achernar added.

Rasalhague interjected, “We still need to understand why things went wrong on Earth. We have some theories—perhaps the Sun or the planet itself is to blame.”

Labrum raised his hand, signaling for order. “We cannot give up on the quest. Morpheus must continue to uncover the root of humanity’s problems and work to heal the situation. As the superior race, we have both the knowledge and the responsibility to guide and protect this human race. Morpheus is right—there is still hope for humanity, and I support his mission. If we cannot resolve these issues, however, we will have no choice but to end human existence. We cannot allow such an aggressive species to spread destruction across the Universe. That is the final decree from the High Council."

"I agree with my father and the High Council," Morpheus said firmly. "I will do everything in my power to find solutions for humanity's problems, especially for the sake of my human family. May I visit and speak with the High Council directly?"

"That's an excellent idea," Labrum said. "You will gain a deeper understanding of our culture and the Achilles race. You've learned much about humanity—now it's time to learn about your own origins."

The crew unanimously agreed to visit Achilles in person.

"This time, we'll take the entire ship," Labrum announced. "It's not just you who needs time on our planet—we all need to reconnect with our people."

Morpheus hesitated. "I thought all of you were my family."

"Yes, we are," Labrum replied gently. "But, like on Earth, we also have extended family members and friends."

Morpheus's curiosity deepened. "Why did the four brothers allow marriages between cousins?"

"Because that's how it has been for eons, since the beginning of time," Labrum explained. "Our society is structured around the High Council, which holds the highest authority in our culture. Following that is the royal family, which includes everyone here on this ship."

"Are there other influential figures on our planet, Achilles?" Morpheus asked.

"Yes," Wega replied. "We have a system similar to Earth's, but it operates with strict oversight. No one defies our laws without facing severe consequences. The checks in place ensure that order and justice are upheld at all levels."

Labrum nodded in agreement. "This has been an enlightening discussion," he announced. "We've gained new insights and a clearer plan for Morpheus and his quest. But before we proceed, we'll return to Achilles. Morpheus needs to immerse himself in our culture and heritage to fully understand his role."

"It's time for dinner and rest as we prepare for the journey home," Labrum added.

The family moved to the Dining Chamber and began their meal. Morpheus, lost in thought, reflected on the intense conversation they'd had in the Meeting Chamber.

Breaking the silence, he turned to his father and asked, "What would happen if humans used nuclear weapons on Earth?"

Labrum's expression darkened. "That will not happen," he said firmly. "If humans ever reach the point of deploying nuclear weapons, we would have no choice but to intervene. We would disable the weapons, abolish humanity, and save the planet. The

Earth is far too vital to allow its destruction at the hands of its inhabitants. If humans choose to destroy their only home, they will have chosen their own end. We would act decisively, stopping the weapons before they could activate and ensuring the Earth's survival—regardless of the cost to humanity."

CHAPTER 9

The Space Trip

The following day arrived, and the crew diligently prepared to leave the moon's gravity and set a course for Achilles. Labrum, as ship captain, took charge of the flight, while his wife, Denab, served as lieutenant. Wega and Denebola, deck officers, ensured the ship was clear of any flight issues. Rasalhague and Zaniah managed life support and gravity systems, while Achernar and Capella oversaw the engines and supported life systems during transit. Sirius and Terebellum handled radar operations and assisted the captain and lieutenant. Kochab and Rastaban were responsible for managing magnetic waves and time travel functions. Morpheus and Sadal Suud served as versatile assistants, lending support across all departments.

Labrum conducted a final readiness check, confirming that all departments were prepared and had issued a go signal. With everything in place, he invited Morpheus and Sadal Suud to the ship's bridge. He intended to familiarize them with bridge operations and the complexities of navigating through space.

Morpheus was captivated by the intricate controls and systems, and his curiosity drove him to absorb every detail. Sadal Suud, though familiar with the bridge from past journeys, found each experience just as thrilling and new. The entire crew shared an underlying excitement, anticipating a brief return home to reconnect with their families and friends.

As Labrum guided the ship out of the moon's gravitational pull, he slowly maneuvered through the solar system. Turning to Morpheus and Sadal Suud, he instructed, "Pay attention to the planets as we pass them. There's much to learn."

"The Sun's heat could damage the ship," Morpheus remarked.

Labrum shook his head with a knowing smile. "Not at all. I'll navigate us between the Sun and Mercury. Then, you'll see the other planets as we journey out of this solar system."

Approaching the Sun, the crew felt no discomfort. The ship's advanced systems reported external temperatures exceeding 28,259,540°F, but the internal environment remained perfectly controlled. As they passed Mercury, the planet revealed itself as a barren wasteland of rocks and mountains, devoid of water or vegetation. Venus followed, equally desolate and hostile.

"We'll now orbit Earth," Labrum announced. "Morpheus, take a good look. This is the planet you've called home for years. It's the world you must protect and help, should the opportunity arise."

The ship then approached Mars, its red surface stark and lifeless. Labrum explained, "Mars was once a vibrant planet, full of water, foliage, animals, and even people. Now, it's barren like Mercury and Venus."

"Jupiter, on the other hand, is a gas giant. Its surface hosts alien life forms, much like the other gas planets," Denab added. "Each of these planets, and their inhabitants, is unique in its own way. Finally, there's Pluto. While barren on the surface, it supports life underground, where caves and water sources sustain its population."

As the ship prepared to leave the solar system, Denab announced, "Our next destination is the Andromeda Galaxy, Morpheus."

"How far is the Andromeda Galaxy?" Morpheus inquired.

"2.5 million light-years from Earth," Denab replied.

"And how long will it take us to get there with this ship?" Morpheus questioned, his curiosity piqued.

"About two weeks of Earth time under normal conditions," Denab explained. "However, with the time travel method we're using, it's only two days of Earth time in an emergency situation."

As the ship began to accelerate, Morpheus gazed out the bridge windows, marveling at the vast expanse of the Universe. Then, the time warp began.

Morpheus turned to his parents, excited. "It's like going to the movies on Earth, but so much better," he said, his eyes wide. The stars in space seemed to stretch out like bright white lines, shimmering in the ship's path. Then, he noticed a tunnel coming toward them, drawing closer with incredible speed. As they entered it, the tunnel seemed to twist and turn around the ship. The sensation reminded Morpheus of his own time travel experiences.

Curious, he turned to his father. "Why does the tunnel twist like that as we travel through it?"

Labrum smiled and explained, "It's like when you're playing a music cassette, and you fast forward or reverse it. Speeding up anything in the Universe causes a turning motion. It's similar to when you shoot a gun—the bullet spins as it exits the barrel. If you were to study it, you'd learn it in physics. It's all about the relationship between matter, energy, motion, and force. The twisting you see is just the way time travel works—everything is in motion, even when you're traveling through time."

Labrum set the automatic controls for the journey and announced, "We're all set for two days of travel. The ship's sensors will alert us to any issues. For now, we can relax unless something arises. Morpheus and Sadal Suud, you two can head to your Chamber Compartment and rest until I call for you."

"Alright, Father and Mother," Morpheus replied.

Turning to Sadal Suud, Morpheus added, "I'd like to see the engine room."

"Okay, Morpheus," Sadal Suud said, taking his hand as they walked together.

When they arrived in the engine room, Sadal Suud asked, "Why did you want to come here?"

"I'm here to learn more about our culture, the spaceship, and time travel. There's much to discover over time," Morpheus explained.

Sadal Suud smiled gently. “Yes, but your father said we could relax together. I wanted to spend time with you before we reach Achilles.”

Morpheus paused, realizing the oversight. “I’m sorry. I didn’t mean to offend you.”

“It’s okay. You didn’t do anything wrong,” she reassured him. “I just wanted to be alone with you. I know you’re curious about everything, but aren’t you curious about me, Morpheus?”

Morpheus looked into her eyes, his voice softening. “Yes, I am very interested in you.”

“Then let’s go to our chamber and relax,” Sadal Suud suggested with a smile.

“Okay, let’s go,” Morpheus agreed, his hand still in hers as they left the engine room.

When Morpheus and Sadal Suud entered their chamber, Sadal Suud smiled and said, “Let’s take a shower together.” Morpheus agreed, and the two of them stepped into the shower, sharing a quiet moment of intimacy before making love and washing away the stress of the journey. Afterward, they dried off and had a light meal in their chamber. Once they finished eating, they moved to the bedroom, where they lay down together, deep in conversation.

Morpheus looked into Sadal Suud’s eyes and confessed, “I’m in love with you.”

"I'm in love with you too, Morpheus," she replied softly.

He smiled and asked, "Sadal Suud, what kind of things do you like to do?"

"I love floating in space, walking along beaches, flying over beautiful countrysides, and I'd love to be your wife," she said, her voice filled with warmth. "What about you?"

Morpheus gently caressed her and said, "I love living life to the fullest, having fun with everyone and everything. I like your ideas, and I would love to have you as my wife."

They held each other close, eventually falling asleep in each other's arms. The next morning, after waking and making love again, the ship's alarm suddenly blared.

Over the intercom, Labrum's voice came through, "Brace for impact—comet collision imminent."

Morpheus and Sadal Suud hurried to the bridge, where they saw the comet approaching at alarming speed.

"What's going to happen, Father?" Morpheus asked, his voice tense.

"We must shoot it down," Labrum replied calmly.

"Has this ever happened before?" Morpheus asked, eyes widening.

"No," Labrum admitted.

In an instant, Morpheus stepped onto the ship's bow. In a strange moment of clarity, he felt a surge of energy. Using his powers, he somehow pushed the comet away, averting disaster.

When Morpheus returned inside, Labrum, both astonished and impressed, asked, "How did you do that?"

"I don't know," Morpheus answered, his voice filled with wonder. "It felt like it came from my mind and heart—just a deep instinct to protect us."

Labrum then ordered, "Morpheus, can you destroy the rogue comet?"

Morpheus returned to the ship's bow, closing his eyes and focusing his mind and heart on the comet. With a powerful surge of energy, he destroyed it in the vastness of space.

Labrum and Denab stood in stunned silence, their amazement palpable.

Labrum called for the entire crew to gather on the bridge.

Once everyone had arrived, Labrum shared the news, "Morpheus has destroyed the comet."

The crew stood in awe, looking at Morpheus.

"How did you do that, Morpheus?" one of them asked, wide-eyed.

"I don't know," Morpheus admitted, his voice filled with wonder. "But it felt like a surge from my mind and heart—

something took over. I just moved the comet away from us and then destroyed it."

"The prophecies were true about Morpheus," Achernar said with reverence. "The prediction spoke of an Achillesian born to be the Universe's protector, especially Earth. He would act only for the good of the Universe and all its inhabitants."

Earth was a critical stronghold for the Universe in many ways, and the family beamed with pride. Morpheus had become the living embodiment of the prophecy, the protector of Earth and the Universe.

"How did the comet end up in our path?" Morpheus asked. "We have advanced instruments to detect any potential hazards to our ship's trajectory."

"A rogue comet is a natural phenomenon in space," Wega explained. "It's like a rogue wave in Earth's oceans. That's why your father asked you to destroy the comet—it's how we've protected Earth from comets and asteroids for years. But we've never had anyone destroy a comet like you did, Morpheus."

"When we use time travel and magnetic wave powers, we focus our minds and hearts to project our energy," Rasalhague added. "But your powers go beyond ours. You destroyed the comet with the strength of your mind and soul."

Morpheus paused, deep in thought. "Is it always a good thing to have such powers?"

"Yes, Morpheus," Labrum replied with certainty. "You are the one foretold to save Earth."

Morpheus's curiosity grew. "What exactly does the prophecy say? What is its message?"

"The prophecy speaks of an Achillesian who will save Earth and its people," Rasalhague said. "This person will belong to both Earth and Achilles."

"The prophecy describes him as tall, powerful, both mentally and physically," Denebola added. "Intelligent, protective, humble, charming, fearless, self-aware, and confident in everything he does."

"Nothing can stop him," Zaniah said. "He is loyal, honest, responsible, reliable, sincere to all, and genuine in every way."

Finally, Capella spoke, her voice rich with admiration. "He is the essence of a ruler, a king, and so much more than just a man."

Sadal Suud smiled, her eyes soft with love. "He's the man I love. I'll marry him when we reach Achilles."

Morpheus was deeply moved by their words and asked, "Are you sure I am the person from the prophecy?"

Everyone nodded in agreement, their pride in him evident.

"It's time!" Labrum announced. "We've arrived at Achilles. Prepare the transport ship for departure to the planet."

"Will everyone be coming to the planet?" Morpheus asked, his curiosity piqued.

"Yes," Labrum replied.

"Who will watch over the ship while we're on Achilles?" Morpheus inquired.

"Nobody," Wega said with a reassuring smile. "The ship will remain stable, with sensors monitoring everything. If anything happens, the ship will alert us. It will be docked safely."

"The ship will remain docked in space, above the planet's atmosphere," Labrum added.

"Wait until you see our planet, Morpheus," Rasalhague said with excitement. "It's incredibly beautiful."

Labrum instructed Morpheus and Sadal Suud to prepare for the trip to Achilles. The family and crew members boarded the smaller spacecraft, readying the ship for departure.

"As we enter the atmosphere, take a look at our planet from the air, Morpheus," Denab said. "The planet's sensors will detect a spaceship in its orbit above Achilles, and it will recognize the ship's unique signature. The people on the planet will know the crew is returning, and they'll be prepared to welcome us home. The small craft will land on the surface, where people will be waiting to greet us."

CHAPTER 10

The Family is Home

Labrum landed the small craft and opened the doors, allowing everyone to exit. The Achillesians greeted the travelers warmly, with families reuniting, exchanging "Hello's," and sharing heartfelt hugs and kisses. The leaders of the Achillesians were present, offering their greetings to Labrum and his crew.

One of the leaders, Zeus, approached Labrum, and they exchanged a cordial greeting. Then, Zeus turned to Morpheus and asked, "Who is this new face among us?"

"This is my son, Morpheus," Labrum replied. "He is the prophecy figure we've spoken of in our stories."

"Greetings, Morpheus," Zeus said with a smile.

Morpheus nodded and asked, "Are you the king of the gods on Earth?"

"Yes, Morpheus, that's correct. How did you know?" Zeus asked, intrigued.

"I read the history books and heard the tales of the past," Morpheus answered. "Are all the gods from that time here on Achilles?"

"Yes, they live here," Zeus replied.

Morpheus paused for a moment, then asked, "Zeus, where are your father and the Titans?"

Zeus' expression shifted slightly, and he replied, "If you know Earth's history, you would know that I killed them back on Earth."

Morpheus raised an eyebrow. "Where are their graves?"

Zeus hesitated for a moment before saying, "Can we discuss that subject another time?"

"That would be fine," Morpheus said, "And I will be eager to learn about the Titans and the beginning of the gods."

Zeus chuckled softly and turned to Labrum. "Labrum, you have a fine son, but he's clearly eager to learn about the past."

"Morpheus is the one who will correct the wrongs on Earth before humanity ventures into space," Labrum said solemnly. "The evil on Earth is too great, and if left unchecked, it will destroy our Universe and the peace we've worked so hard to establish."

"Now I understand why Morpheus asked about the Titans," Zeus said, nodding in understanding.

Labrum turned back to Zeus. "Our mission for Earth has always been to fix the problems before they reach space."

"You're right, Labrum," Zeus agreed.

The people of Achilles prepared a grand feast to celebrate the return of their people from Earth. As the banquet unfolded, filled with food and drink, Zeus turned to Hades and said, "We need to discuss Morpheus, his mission on Earth, and his role in the prophecy."

Meanwhile, Morpheus turned to his father and asked, "Would you betray me?"

"No, Morpheus," Labrum replied, his voice calm. "Why would you ask me that?"

"I sense there's more going on with Zeus and his family—his grandfather, his father—and something to do with Earth," Morpheus explained, his tone thoughtful.

Labrum's brow furrowed. "What do you mean?"

"I'll explain more clearly once I speak to Zeus and get his answers about the Titans and where they're buried on Earth," Morpheus said, his curiosity growing.

"Do you think they might have something to do with the hatred and problems on Earth?" Labrum asked.

"Yes, I do," Morpheus replied, his tone heavy with concern.

"For now, slow down and enjoy yourself," Labrum suggested. "You're rushing too fast with your investigation."

Morpheus turned to Sadal Suud. “Do you want to take a boat ride?” he asked, eager for a change of pace.

“Yes, Morpheus,” Sadal Suud answered with a smile. “I’ll need to teach you how to operate the boat controls.”

Morpheus attentively watched and listened as Sadal Suud guided him through the controls. While doing so, his thoughts drifted back to Earth, Zeus, the Titans, his two families, and the greater good of all.

“Morpheus, is something wrong?” Sadal Suud asked, sensing his distraction.

“No, but I’ll explain later,” Morpheus replied, his mind still grappling with the weight of the mysteries he had to unravel.

Sadal Suud, noticing his tension, gently added, “You need to enjoy your life with me and have some fun.”

“I am having fun,” Morpheus said softly. “Just being with you here on Achilles and seeing our planet is enough.”

Meanwhile, Zeus called for a private meeting with the High Council members, ensuring Labrum was not present.

“We cannot allow Morpheus to uncover any problems on Earth,” Zeus declared, his voice tight with urgency. “Morpheus threatens our civilization, from the past to the present and into the future.”

One of the High Council members spoke up, "Where is Labrum? He should be here. Zeus, you're talking about his son."

Another council member chimed in, "You're breaking our laws to protect yourself from the past, Zeus. You're mistaken about Morpheus. He is the prophecy—of our people and Earth. You agreed with Labrum to send his child to Earth to help humans. And now you want to change your mind? If you do, the blame will fall squarely on you as the one who allowed evil to persist."

A third council member added, "The beginning is the beginning. We must correct the problems on Earth, even if it means confronting the past. Times are changing, and humans are trying to reach space in corrupt ways. We must stop them before they can do any more harm."

The council made it clear to Zeus: Do not interfere with Morpheus or Labrum. The consequences will be severe if you do.

Meanwhile, Sadal Suud continued to show Morpheus their planet, introducing him to different cultures and revealing objects that connected to those on Earth. She also led him to the pyramids and showed him the secret mechanisms that could open them.

"The pyramids are both tombs and sources of power," Sadal Suud explained. "Some act as markers for spaceships. Back on Earth, the pyramid in Atlantis was used as a power source, and it was responsible for the destruction of the Atlantis continent. Something is wrong with Earth. So much bloodshed has been shed for no clear reason."

Morpheus turned to her, searching her eyes. “Can I trust you, Sadal Suud?”

“Of course!” she said, her voice steady and sincere. “I’m your wife-to-be. Our words are our bond in life and marriage.”

Morpheus’ expression softened, but the weight of his thoughts remained. “I think I’ve found a piece of the puzzle regarding the problems on Earth.”

“What do you mean?” Sadal Suud asked, her curiosity piqued.

“I think Zeus is part of the problem. From the past to the present, and maybe even the future,” Morpheus said, his voice filled with uncertainty but conviction.

“I don’t understand,” Sadal Suud said, furrowing her brow. “What do you mean, Morpheus?”

Morpheus took a deep breath, his mind swirling with more questions than answers, but his resolve firming. “I’m not sure yet, but I will find out before we leave Achilles and explain everything when the time is right. But I need to know the truth about Zeus and his role in all of this.”

“You better make sure you’re right about the accusations against Zeus and others,” Sadal Suud cautioned.

Morpheus met her gaze, his resolve firm. “I’ll be okay with the outcome.”

Later, Morpheus noticed his father and Zeus engaged in a heated discussion, their disagreement apparent. He approached them and said, "Can all three of us go somewhere private to talk?"

Labrum nodded, "Sure, Morpheus." But Zeus, with a hint of irritation, responded, "I have things to do, Morpheus."

"That's not true," Morpheus countered. "You're just making excuses, Zeus."

Zeus fixed him with a steely gaze. "How would you know, Morpheus?"

"Because I know," Morpheus said, his voice steady. "You've been avoiding me since I arrived, and I know about the secret meeting with the High Council without my father there."

Zeus' expression darkened. "Again, how do you know?"

"I would like to talk with you, my father, and the High Council Members," Morpheus insisted.

At this, Zeus' temper flared. His powers surged, and he began to grow, his height and muscles expanding before their eyes.

Morpheus remained calm, his voice unwavering. "Do you want to fight, Zeus, or do you want to talk about the problems?"

Morpheus' words were deliberate. "Remember where I lived for eighteen years—among your father, Cronus, and the other Titans."

As the words hung in the air, Zeus' powers began to recede, and his size shrank back to normal. He took a deep breath and said, "We will talk with the High Council Members without any incidents, Morpheus."

"Zeus, go ahead and call the meeting," Labrum said, his tone steady. "Morpheus and I will join the Council."

Zeus walked away, and Labrum turned to his son, his brow furrowed. "Morpheus, why did you challenge Zeus like that?"

Morpheus sighed, his thoughts weighing heavily on him. "You asked me to help with Earth's problems, but I see something more. The problems didn't start with Earth; they started here—with Zeus."

Labrum's expression softened. "You're right, Morpheus." He paused, then asked, "Tell me about the meeting with the Council without me."

"The Council met without you, Father," Morpheus replied. "They asked Zeus where you were, and they warned him not to interfere with us on this mission."

Labrum's anger simmered beneath the surface. He clenched his fists. "This isn't good," he muttered, troubled by the news his son had revealed.

The meeting convened with all members present, including Morpheus. Labrum wasted no time. "Was there a meeting held without me?" he demanded, his tone firm.

A council member spoke up. “Yes. Zeus did not want you present because of Morpheus—since you are his father.”

Labrum frowned. “What does that have to do with anything? When we hold meetings, all Council Members are required to attend.”

Another council leader interjected, “Morpheus is a threat to Zeus—specifically to the truths about Earth’s ancient history, the Titans, and what came after their demise. Furthermore, Morpheus possesses a power he hasn’t explicitly declared to us—or even to you, as his father. However, we have assessed that Morpheus poses no threat to our culture in any way, shape, or form. On the contrary, he embodies the prophecy you spoke of, Labrum.”

The leader continued, “Morpheus possesses a unique ability—he can perceive truths across time telepathically or through an advanced sixth sense tied to his powers. This gift grants him knowledge beyond Zeus’s control, positioning him as a formidable figure. Zeus fears losing to Morpheus, especially given the insights Morpheus holds about him, Earth, and the underlying causes of its problems.”

The council member leaned forward, his voice steady and commanding. “Yet Morpheus demonstrated wisdom and restraint. Instead of resorting to conflict, he sought dialogue—a stark contrast to Earth’s penchant for violence. Morpheus is not merely the prophecy; he is the supreme being destined to bring balance and truth to the Universe.”

The Council Members collectively congratulated Labrum and Morpheus. They praised Labrum and Denab for bringing Morpheus into existence, his Earth family for their influence, and Morpheus himself for his exceptional character and promise to unite all beings in the Universe.

Finally, the Council turned their attention to Zeus. "You must reveal everything to Morpheus," one leader demanded. "He needs the complete truth about Earth's ancient history to help humanity."

Labrum stepped forward. "I propose that the Council be present when Zeus explains these events. The truth of the past should be shared with all of us so we can prepare Morpheus for the challenges ahead."

The Council agreed. "We will reconvene tomorrow," a council leader declared. "For now, let us spend the evening with our families."

As the members left the Meeting Chamber, Denab and Sadal Suud hurried over to Labrum and Morpheus.

"What happened in there?" Denab asked, her voice tinged with concern.

Labrum smiled reassuringly. "Everything is fine. The Council affirmed Morpheus's greatness and the importance of his mission. Zeus has been tasked with explaining Earth's ancient history in a formal meeting tomorrow so we can all learn the truth."

"We saw Zeus grow larger, but then he backed down," Denab noted.

"Morpheus confronted Zeus for a private conversation, and that's when things escalated," Labrum explained.

Morpheus added, "I only wanted to understand the truths about Earth's ancient history. Zeus's reaction confirmed my suspicions."

Labrum continued, "Zeus fears Morpheus, not just for his knowledge but because of his telepathic or sixth-sense powers. Zeus likely saw Morpheus as a threat long before today."

"Do you think Zeus will attack Morpheus in the future?" Sadal Suud asked, her voice filled with worry.

"No," Labrum assured her. "Morpheus has the upper hand, both with his abilities and his composure."

Turning to lighten the mood, Labrum asked, "How about we all go for a boat ride and relax for the evening?"

Everyone agreed enthusiastically. As they glided across the water, the tensions of the day began to fade.

"Morpheus, you're still thinking about Zeus, aren't you?" Sadal Suud asked with a knowing smile.

Morpheus chuckled. "Am I that obvious?"

"Yes," she said, leaning closer. "But I'm incredibly proud of you, Morpheus, in more ways than you know."

Labrum brought the boat to a stop and turned to the group. "Who's up for a swim?"

The unanimous cheer of "Yes!" was followed by laughter as they dove into the cool waters. They spent the rest of the evening swimming, laughing, and enjoying one another's company under the stars. For a brief moment, the weight of the Universe's problems lifted, leaving only joy and hope for the journey ahead.

CHAPTER 11

Council Members

The next day, Morpheus and the Council Members convened in the grand Meeting Chamber. The air was heavy with anticipation as the Council entrusted Morpheus to lead the inquiries with Zeus.

Morpheus addressed the gathering with a composed authority. "I will begin by retracing events from the day of your arrival, Zeus, and proceed from there," he said before turning his gaze to the God of Thunder. "Zeus, in your own words, what issues have you had with my family and me?"

A stern voice from the Council interrupted before Zeus could reply. "Do not perjure yourself before the Council, or there will be consequences," one member warned.

Morpheus inclined his head respectfully. "Thank you for upholding the laws," he said before redirecting the question to Zeus. "Do you have an answer?"

Zeus hesitated but finally spoke. "I knew you were the figure of prophecy foretold in our culture, the one described in our ancient stories."

"Am I a force for good or ill in your eyes and for our community?" Morpheus pressed.

Zeus's response was candid. "Good for the community, but bad for me."

"Why am I bad for you, Zeus?" Morpheus asked, his tone calm but probing.

Zeus's expression darkened as he delved into a painful history. "At the beginning of Earth's time, my father, Cronus, was a tyrant—a cruel god to his children and the Earth alike. Under the laws of that era, no one could hold him accountable. Cronus ruled unchecked, tormenting and killing the people of Earth when they disobeyed him. That is why my siblings and I rose against him, ending his reign forever."

"And where was Cronus banished?" Morpheus inquired, his voice steady.

Zeus nodded gravely. "We imprisoned him in a cavern beneath Tartarus after a war that lasted ten years. Cronus was the creator of the monsters that plagued Earth's lands and waters."

"What kind of monsters?" Morpheus asked.

"Terrifying beings like Chimera, Hydra, Cerberus, Minotaur, and the most fearsome of all, Typhon," Zeus listed, his voice heavy with the memory. "Yet, he also created a few good creatures, such as Pegasus, the winged horse. Despite this, Cronus's tyranny drove the people of Earth to rebel, rejecting the gods. In time, we faded from their world and returned to Achilles."

Morpheus tilted his head. "Was Cronus truly dead when you left Earth?"

Zeus replied with certainty. “He was banished to the depths of the Earth, presumed dead, leaving only his bones as a grim reminder of his tyranny.”

Morpheus shifted his line of questioning. “How loyal are you to the planet Achilles and its people?”

“I am deeply dedicated to Achilles and its citizens,” Zeus affirmed.

“If that’s true, why did you convene a meeting without my father, one of the Council Members, being present?” Morpheus challenged.

Zeus lowered his gaze. “I was wrong. But I knew you were the one god who could see through me—through my faults and the burdens I carry from the past.”

Morpheus turned to the Council Members, his voice firm and resolute. “Since Zeus’s return from his time on Earth, has he conducted himself as a proper god and citizen of Achilles?”

“Zeus has been an adequate citizen since his arrival,” a council member confirmed.

Morpheus turned to Zeus and the Council Members. “Would it be possible for Zeus to return to Earth with me and assist in my quest?” he asked.

“That is a sound idea,” another council member replied. “Zeus will accompany you and take orders from both Labrum and yourself.”

Zeus's expression softened, but his voice carried the weight of time. "I would be honored to return to Earth, but my time is nearing. Soon, I must pass on to the stars."

Morpheus met his gaze earnestly. "When the time comes, can I return to Achilles to seek your counsel?"

"Yes, Morpheus," Zeus assured him. "I will help you however I can."

Morpheus turned to Labrum. "Father, when should we return to Earth?"

Labrum's reply was calm and reassuring. "We have all the time in the Universe, Morpheus. The situation is much like your absence from Earth with your human family. Time aligns with purpose."

Morpheus smiled. "That's perfect for what I have planned. And we have the recording devices to document everything."

Labrum nodded. "Yes, Morpheus, they'll be invaluable for your journey."

Turning back to Zeus, Morpheus declared, "Zeus, you and I will work closely together. We'll record our conversations so I can revisit them whenever needed."

"That's a wise plan," a council member remarked. "Through Zeus's experiences, you'll gain insights into the past and the challenges that shaped our worlds."

A different council member leaned forward. “Morpheus, what do you believe is wrong with Earth?”

Morpheus hesitated, carefully considering his response. “I’m not entirely certain, but I suspect three or four key factors. First, I think Cronus’s buried evil might be leaking into the Earth, corrupting its people with wickedness. Second, there could be something involving the sun, comets, or space dust disrupting Earth’s balance.”

The council exchanged surprised glances. “That’s an angle we hadn’t considered,” one admitted.

Morpheus continued. “The third possibility involves the ancient transfer from the original planets the people came from. Perhaps something was lost—or carried forward—that is now destabilizing their existence.”

The Council Members nodded thoughtfully. “We grant you safe passage on your quest, Morpheus,” one member said.

With that, the Council dismissed Morpheus and Zeus, though they requested Labrum remain behind for a private discussion. “You both may leave now and take time to prepare,” another member added.

Once Morpheus and Zeus had left the chamber, a council member addressed Labrum. “You have a remarkable son, Labrum. What is your perspective on him?”

Labrum smiled fondly. “When we first brought him from Earth, he was a quiet young man. Over time, he opened up and adapted to our ways. Morpheus understands more than we initially expected, and he blends seamlessly with our family. It's as though he has always been one of us. He also embodies the prophecy from our cultural stories. What stands out most is his aversion to conflict and aggression. He prefers resolution and understanding, as you saw in his interaction with Zeus. He handled that situation with wisdom and grace."

The Council Members murmured their agreement. "He is the promise of two worlds and the Universe, Labrum," one member said solemnly.

Meanwhile, Morpheus and Zeus walked together, reflecting on their earlier confrontation.

"I was wrong about so much," Zeus admitted. "Especially as my power grew, I allowed arrogance to cloud my judgment. I owe you and your family an apology, Morpheus. I should have shown more respect. You handled my aggression with wisdom, without causing harm to anyone."

Morpheus nodded. "You're forgiven, Zeus. On Earth, we learned your story through history books, but hearing it from you gives it so much more depth. The trauma of your experience is lost in those written accounts. That's why I needed to speak with you directly. You once fought your father to save Earth and its people. Now, it's my turn to save Earth before humanity expands into space and the Universe."

Zeus looked at Morpheus with newfound respect. "What can I do to help you, Morpheus?" he asked.

"Will you explain more about your family and the challenges you faced?" Morpheus asked.

Zeus sighed, his gaze distant. "My father, Cronus, had no self-control. He ruled through chaos, and his actions quickly spiraled out of control, affecting not just our family but the other gods as well."

"How strong were his evil ways?" Morpheus inquired.

Zeus's expression darkened. "When he grew angry, the sky would vanish, replaced by the darkest clouds. Lightning emerged from the shadows around him. Cronus had the power to make the Earth bleed in a single moment or erase an ocean in the blink of an eye. His wrath was unmatched."

Morpheus regarded Zeus carefully. "Can you be loyal, honest, and trustworthy in this quest?"

"Yes," Zeus replied firmly. "I've told the Council Members the same thing. We're on good terms now, aren't we?"

"You'll be needed on Earth to confront your father's lingering evil spirit," Morpheus said.

Zeus hesitated. "I'm not in good enough health to help you fight him—neither his spirit nor any physical remnants he may have left behind."

Morpheus leaned forward, his tone resolute. "Don't you want to be remembered as the god who saved Earth not once, but twice?"

Zeus considered this for a moment, then nodded. "It would be an honor to have that legacy."

"In our culture," Morpheus explained, "It is better to die for the right reasons than to fade away quietly."

Zeus suddenly stood, his voice booming with determination. "Yes! It is always better to die in battle for a just cause."

"Then we have an accord," Morpheus said, his eyes locking with Zeus's. "But remember, Zeus—do not break your word to me."

"Never," Zeus vowed. "We are Achillesians to the end."

Morpheus smiled faintly. "I will fight for you and all those involved in this mission. Do not forget the truth I speak, Zeus."

As their conversation continued, Morpheus's mind raced with plans. He needed to uncover the full truth—both from the stories of humans on Earth and from Zeus's accounts. But first, he had to locate the cavity in the Earth's crust where Cronus had been banished and uncover its secrets.

"Zeus," Morpheus said at last, "You will serve as my guide, pointing out the locations tied to your stories."

Zeus inclined his head in agreement. "I can do that for you, Morpheus. I will help you find what you seek."

“Will Cronus’s spirit try to take control of our minds and bodies?” Morpheus asked, his tone serious.

“If he still retains his powers, it’s entirely possible,” Zeus replied grimly.

“We must prepare for this possibility and ensure it doesn’t happen to us,” Morpheus said with resolve.

“I agree, Morpheus,” Zeus said, nodding.

“A god banished to the Earth’s bowels would harbor a grudge that could last an eternity—and beyond,” Morpheus added thoughtfully.

“You’ll see the chaos Cronus has sown, along with everything else that might come our way,” Zeus said.

The two of them reflected on the challenges ahead, particularly those tied to humanity and Earth. Morpheus also revisited the ideas he had shared with the Council Members, and even Zeus seemed to be pondering those same concepts.

“Do you think the Sun, comets, and space dust might have an influence on how humans behave toward one another?” Zeus asked, his brow furrowed.

“It’s possible,” Morpheus said. “And let’s not forget that humans have migrated from their original planets. That movement could be another factor. Can we visit those original worlds and learn more?”

"Yes, but the answers you seek might not be easily found," Zeus cautioned.

"Why not?" Morpheus asked.

"Because those worlds are nothing like Earth," Zeus explained.

"Let's consult the Council Members for their wisdom and insights," Morpheus suggested.

The two returned to the Council Chamber to discuss the conditions of the worlds humans had originally come from.

"For eons, the planets and humans lived together in harmony," a council member explained. "There were no wars, crimes, discrimination, power struggles, or conflicts over resources."

"Would it be possible for Zeus and me to visit those worlds and see firsthand how humans lived in their original environments?" Morpheus asked.

"That's an excellent idea," a council member agreed. "Go and investigate for yourselves."

Morpheus and Zeus journeyed to several worlds, observing how the inhabitants coexisted. These planets were home to mixed cultures where peace and cooperation had endured for countless years. Morpheus meticulously studied the waters, lands, and solar systems, noting differences such as the color of the suns and stars, as well as the comets passing near each planet. They recorded extensive data to analyze later.

When they returned to the Council, they presented their findings.

"You've done well to gather this information," a council member said, impressed by the detailed recordings. "Did you notice any significant differences between the planets?"

"Not yet," Morpheus admitted. "But we still have the issue of Cronus poisoning Earth's land and waters."

"Could Cronus be the root of the problem?" another council member asked.

"As a god with immense power in both life and death, it's plausible," Morpheus said. "Cronus was defeated by his children, but the bitterness and hatred he carried were immense. It's possible that he left behind a legacy of poison—hatred, resentment, hostility, and more—that continues to infect Earth."

"You've raised an excellent point," Labrum interjected. "It also explains why Zeus was reluctant to face you, Morpheus."

"Your next mission is clear," a council member declared. "Return to Earth with Zeus. Find Cronus—alive or dead—and resolve this once and for all."

CHAPTER 12

Return to Earth

Morpheus met with the High Council Members one final time before departing for Earth with his family. After the meeting, a farewell banquet was held in their honor.

Later, Morpheus and Sadal Suud took a last ride around Achilles, taking in the planet's beauty.

"I'm going to miss Achilles and its people," Morpheus admitted, his voice tinged with emotion.

"I'll miss our home, too," Sadal Suud replied. "But we can always return for a visit."

As the departure drew near, Morpheus, Sadal Suud, and their family bid heartfelt goodbyes to their friends and loved ones on Achilles.

Finally, the family, along with their crew members and Zeus, boarded the small shuttlecraft that would transport them to their spaceship, the *UNIV ORION*, and ultimately, Earth.

Once aboard the *UNIV ORION*, the crew began unloading supplies from the shuttle and conducted thorough inspections of the ship's systems, including the computers, instruments, departments, and hull. After the inspections were complete,

Labrum ordered everyone to report to their stations and await further instructions. However, he asked Zeus, Morpheus, and Sadal Suud to remain on the bridge with him.

“Are all computers and instruments ready for departure?” Labrum asked.

“The bridge systems are fully operational,” Denab confirmed.

Labrum then initiated a final check with all departments. Voices reported in sequence:

“Engine room ready.”

“Time-travel and magnetic wave systems ready.”

“Life support systems ready.”

Satisfied, Labrum turned to Denab. “Begin departure—start slowly, then proceed to full speed ahead. Are the ship’s coordinates loaded into the system?”

“Yes, Father,” Morpheus confirmed.

“Sadal Suud, double-check Morpheus’s work,” Labrum instructed.

Sadal Suud quickly verified the information. “The coordinates are correct, Labrum,” she said.

“Good. Denab, proceed to time-travel speed,” Labrum ordered.

"Engaging time-travel speed now, Labrum," Denab replied.

Labrum then turned to Zeus. "Zeus, stay here on the bridge with Denab. I need to show Morpheus and Sadal Suud something important."

Labrum led Morpheus and Sadal Suud to his private chamber and closed the door behind them. His expression grew serious.

"You must keep a close eye on Zeus at all times," Labrum said. "I've instructed the rest of the crew to do the same."

"Why, Father?" Morpheus asked, concerned.

"I don't trust him," Labrum admitted. "Zeus is a double-faced being—one side shows kindness, but the other harbors darkness. You saw how he behaved when we arrived on Achilles, and let's not forget his private meeting with the Council Members—without me. Then there was his confrontation with you, Morpheus. You've seen enough to understand that Zeus's motives aren't always pure."

Morpheus and Sadal Suud exchanged uneasy glances, realizing the gravity of Labrum's concerns.

"You're right, Father," Morpheus said. "But during my long conversations with Zeus, I didn't sense any ill intentions from him."

Labrum frowned but replied, "We'll discuss this more privately later with your mother."

With the ship's coordinates set for Earth, Labrum instructed everyone to relax but remain alert for any travel issues. Shortly after, he called for a meeting with the crew.

When the crew gathered, Labrum began, "I want to remind everyone of the ship's rules. First, Zeus, do you have any familiarity with operating modern ships like this?"

"No, Labrum," Zeus admitted. "But let me assure you, I won't harm the ship or its crew. My only purpose here is to help Morpheus and atone for the mistakes of the past."

Labrum nodded, though his expression remained skeptical. "Very well, Zeus." Then he turned to Denebola and Wega. "I want you both to keep an eye on Zeus while keeping him occupied. The rest of us need to convene privately."

In Labrum's chamber office, Labrum addressed Morpheus, Sadal Suud, and Denab. "Morpheus, what is your plan for Earth and handling Zeus's situation?"

Morpheus replied, "I'll address it as we proceed to Earth."

"No, Morpheus. You're heading back to Earth now. I want an answer now," Labrum pressed, his voice firm.

"Why are you so upset, Father?" Morpheus asked.

"I'm troubled by what happened on Achilles—Zeus's secret meeting with the Council, his confrontation with you, and the way he challenged your authority," Labrum said.

"I understand your concerns," Morpheus said calmly. "Back on Achilles, I assessed Zeus's abilities. His powers are tied to the old ways of the gods, and they're limited. The Council Members themselves said he's no threat to me. I've proven I can overpower him in every way. When Zeus tried to assert himself on Achilles, nothing came of it. Father, as long as we remain vigilant, we'll be fine. Besides, whether I'm awake or asleep, I'll know if Zeus tries anything."

Labrum sighed, his tension easing slightly. "All right, Morpheus. I'll trust your judgment. But what's your plan for handling Zeus once we're on Earth?"

"I've been considering traveling back through time," Morpheus said. "I want to witness Cronus's actions firsthand. I don't want to rely solely on stories. I need to evaluate the truth for myself."

Labrum, Denab, and Sadal Suud exchanged glances and nodded in agreement.

"That's the right approach," Labrum said. "But you might face resistance from Cronus and his family in that era."

"I'm not going there to fight," Morpheus said firmly. "I'll be there to observe and gather answers. But if a conflict arises, I'll be ready to defend myself, the Earth, and our mission—even if it means dealing with Cronus, his family, or both versions of Zeus."

The meeting concluded with Labrum, Sadal Suud, and Denab reassured by Morpheus's confidence.

Later, as Morpheus and Sadal Suud strolled through the ship, Sadal Suud asked, "Can you sense it if Zeus does something wrong?"

"Yes, Sadal Suud," Morpheus replied. "I can see the truth in a person's eyes, their heart, and their thoughts—but I have to be present to sense it fully. Of course, with you, I don't need to guess. Your eyes always reflect the truth, my love."

Sadal Suud smiled, comforted by his words as they walked together through the ship, preparing for the challenges ahead.

"How many powers do you have, Morpheus?" Sadal Suud asked, her voice curious yet thoughtful.

Morpheus considered the question. "Since we've been on this ship and then on Achilles, I've noticed changes—within my body, my mind, and even my heart. They feel like they're evolving constantly."

Sadal Suud smiled. "I noticed those changes too, especially in your physique when you first came aboard. Your body has transformed drastically."

"I don't know exactly how many powers I have," Morpheus admitted. "But they seem to appear when I need them. It's as if my abilities respond to the moment, but there's a strange balance. I can't hurt anyone or anything without a deeply justified reason. It's as though I instinctively check myself, ensuring I don't act wrongly."

Sadal Suud tilted her head, intrigued. "If I were to harm you, would you defend yourself?"

Morpheus shook his head gently. "No, I wouldn't. It's the same way I handled Zeus on Achilles. Even when he threatened me physically, I knew in my heart it wouldn't escalate to true harm. With Cronus, though... that might be different. Cronus represents a force beyond personal relationships—one tied to chaos itself. I need time to figure out how to confront him while managing everything else with Earth."

Sadal Suud placed her hand on his arm, her gaze steady. "I'll keep an eye on Zeus. Take the time you need to think and prepare."

"Thank you," Morpheus said, his tone warm with gratitude. "If anyone needs me, they can reach me over the intercom."

He grabbed a notepad and pen before retreating to a quiet corner of the ship. There, in solitude, he let his thoughts flow. He wrote notes for his father, mother, and the crew, reflecting on their journey, their purpose, and the challenges ahead.

His mind wandered to the peaceful worlds they had visited—worlds where harmony and order prevailed. By contrast, Earth was a cauldron of turmoil, fractured from its leaders down to its everyday citizens. Why did such stark differences exist?

Morpheus also pondered his newfound powers. Since reconnecting with his family on Achilles, they had changed him in profound ways, both physically and spiritually. Yet his connection to Earth and its people remained deeply rooted in his being. These thoughts swirled as he sought clarity on his path forward, not just for himself but for the future of both his worlds.

Morpheus reflected on the data from the other planets he and Zeus had visited. On each of those worlds, peace and order prevailed, but Earth remained an outlier, plagued by turmoil. Determined to find answers, Morpheus gathered samples of land, water, air, and even orbital data from those planets. After analyzing them, everything appeared normal—the land, water, air, and orbits were stable and harmonious. But Earth was different. He knew that before he could confront Cronus, he needed samples from Earth itself. While Morpheus wanted to protect everyone involved, he understood that difficult decisions might lie ahead. If it came to it, he would be forced to make the impossible choice—sacrifice some for the greater good.

Returning to the crew, Morpheus found Zeus and asked if they could speak privately. The two of them retreated to the Meeting Chamber, where they sat down to discuss Zeus's past.

"Zeus, is there anything else you can remember about your past?" Morpheus asked, his voice steady but tinged with urgency.

Zeus hesitated, furrowing his brow. "Let me think, Morpheus."

"You've been on this ship for a week now," Morpheus said. "I expected you to have thought things through by now. The reason you're here is to help your people—on Earth and Achilles. Nothing more."

"I'm trying, Morpheus, but I just can't remember anything else from that time," Zeus explained. "If anything comes to me, I'll tell you. I want to help you prepare for Cronus—or anything else that might come from the past."

Morpheus nodded. He understood Zeus's position but felt the urgency weighing on him. Returning to the ship's bridge, he briefed his father and mother on the next course of action.

"We're going to Earth to collect samples, just as we did on the other planets," Morpheus said.

Labrum raised an eyebrow. "What's the purpose of these samples?"

"To rule out any potential problems that we might have overlooked," Morpheus replied. "I've already taken samples from the other planets for comparison."

"Then you should do the same here—take the samples, analyze them, and compare the results," Denab added.

"I'll be back soon," Morpheus said, a slight grin on his face.

Labrum chuckled. "Very funny, Morpheus."

Morpheus and Zeus headed to Earth, retrieving samples from the planet's land, water, and air. Upon their return, the analysis revealed troubling results. The Earth's samples contained high levels of chemically inert radon—a radioactive gas produced by the decay of radium and released through rock, brick, and other materials. These emissions posed significant health risks to humans. Additionally, Morpheus observed solar flares erupting from the Sun, sending bursts of gamma-ray radiation toward Earth. In contrast, the other planets showed no such flares, and their suns had different colors altogether. The yellow Sun of Earth, compared to the blue stars of other worlds, seemed to affect life in ways that were not immediately obvious.

Labrum spoke first. "What does this mean for the humans?"

"If these people originated from a blue Sun and are now living under a yellow one, it means their bodies are undergoing a chemical change," Morpheus explained. "And then there's the radiation—how it affects the land, the water, the air, and the people. Humans from different parts of the universe may not be able to adapt as easily as they think. Add to that the ignorance of Earth's governments, scientists, and doctors—they're unaware of the dangers, or they're deliberately hiding the truth from the people. These authority figures are either clueless or deceptive, and the people, unfortunately, don't want to know the truth or take action to protect the planet for future generations. Even those who seek the truth are silenced by the very powers meant to guide them."

Morpheus's voice hardened, a mix of frustration and resignation in his words. The truth was clear to him: Earth's problems were not just physical but systemic, rooted in lies, ignorance, and deliberate neglect. He knew that solving these issues would be far more complicated than simply confronting Cronus.

"You discovered differences between the Suns of various systems and the radiation from a yellow Sun star?" Labrum curiously asked.

Morpheus nodded and explained, "It's a chemical reaction between the Suns, the people, the land, the water, the air, and even the space orbits. The effects are interconnected. He continued. "Would you like me to research and report back to you and the family on everything I'm doing for everyone involved? All of these samples are intended to shed light on any known or overlooked problems."

Then, with a serious gaze, Morpheus asked Labrum in front of the family and crew, "Father, do you trust me?"

"Yes, Morpheus," Labrum replied, his tone laden with unspoken concern. "Why do you ask?"

"I don't understand why you're so upset with the mission," Morpheus said, his voice reflecting a quiet frustration. Turning to the rest of the family and crew, Morpheus added, "How do you all feel about me taking on this quest?"

Without hesitation, they answered in unison, "We all believe in you, Morpheus."

Morpheus turned back to Labrum, a solemn expression on his face. "Do you trust me and believe in me, Father? Have I proven my love for both my families and the Universe?"

Labrum paused, his expression softening. “I’m sorry, Son. I do believe in you—and in this quest,” he said, his voice now full of understanding and support.

CHAPTER 13

Cronos

The spaceship once again docked behind the moon, and Morpheus called for a meeting with the crew members and Zeus.

Labrum's voice echoed over the intercom: "Morpheus has requested a meeting in the chamber with the crew members."

When everyone had gathered, Labrum addressed Morpheus, saying, "You called for this meeting, Morpheus. Please, explain yourself."

Morpheus stood before them, his voice steady but full of gravity. "You asked me to handle this quest, and I agreed," he began. "I was told to report everything to you and discuss the issues I've uncovered. I apologize if I haven't shared my thoughts or information sooner. I needed time to process and plan how best to approach all these problems. Now, I'm ready to share my ideas and plans on how to address them."

Morpheus turned to Labrum, his gaze firm. "You told me that I am your son and that I am a god, just like all of you. I am also the king of Earth and the god of dreams while I remain unmarried. When I marry Sadal Suud, I will become the god of new life for this planet. When we visited Achilles, all of you told me I was the prophecy of your culture's stories. I am a man who belongs to two worlds, and I love both of them equally. I have listened to and respected the stories of both worlds and their people, striving not to violate or disrespect them. Now, I need you to understand me and the quest you've given me to handle—without any doubts."

Labrum's expression softened, guilt in his eyes. "I didn't realize the burden I was placing on you, Morpheus," he admitted. "I'm sorry. I trust you and your judgment."

A fellow god spoke up, "We are all sorry for the pressure we've put on you, Morpheus."

Zeus, his voice filled with empathy, added, "You face a challenge unlike any other, and I see the weight you care for both worlds. I will follow your lead, no matter what happens. You have my loyalty."

Denab stepped forward, her tone sincere. "You have our loyalty as well, Morpheus. Don't ever think we're against you."

Morpheus took a breath, his voice steady but resolute. "Mother, I know you all love me, but you must understand—I will not harm either world unless I have no choice but to protect the other. I hope I never have to make that choice. Now, let's discuss the plans for investigating Earth. As you all know, I grew up on this planet and spent the first eighteen years of my life here, learning from these people and the world itself. I interacted with them, experienced their struggles, and then had to learn about Achilles. I evaluated both worlds, and I've taken samples of where humanity originated from so we can assess them, too. Now, we need to understand what went wrong on Earth and see if we can change things for the better. We've already analyzed the chemical changes caused by the interactions between space and Earth elements, and we've received some answers. Next, we need to look into the corruption that Cronus left behind and how long evil has poisoned both the people and the planet. I believe it all started with Cronus and the dark stories involving Zeus, the humans, and the scriptures."

The next day, Morpheus and Zeus prepared to experience time travel, hoping to uncover the truth of the past. They entered the time travel machine, which was equipped with all the necessary tools and supplies for their journey. Morpheus checked the instruments and computers, inputting the coordinates for their destination. Finally, with a hum of the machine's engines, they left—heading to a time long forgotten, a past that no one would remember.

"Zeus, is there anything else you can reflect on from the past?" Morpheus asked.

Zeus paused, thinking. "I will try, but I've already told you everything I remember so far."

"We need to make a stop at Cronus' time, but there are other stops we'll need to make as well," Morpheus replied.

"Where else are we going?" Zeus asked, his curiosity piqued.

"You need to remember everything from the past, Zeus," Morpheus urged.

"I do remember, Morpheus," Zeus answered, his brow furrowing.

"Think about other times and places, and tell me what you know about those moments when we arrive. For example, the Roman Empire or other significant events," Morpheus said. "This is why I need you to recall your knowledge of different times and places."

Zeus' eyes widened as understanding dawned. "Now I see. But what other times and locations are you planning to visit?"

"I need to know everything without you knowing where we're going next," Morpheus explained. "For instance, I can tell you everything about Earth's history and human development, but the question is: Is that knowledge the truth, or is it simply distorted, exaggerated, or false?"

"You're talking about the long passage of time and whether the knowledge we have is the actual truth or just embellished stories," Zeus said.

"Exactly," Morpheus replied. "Pretend I know nothing about history, our people, humans, or the Achillesians. Now, tell me what you've learned throughout all of history, Zeus."

Zeus took a deep breath, reflecting. "I know about Atlantis, its destruction, and how it all happened. I was there with Cronus, and I remember my time with the Greeks. I also know about the monsters that ruled this world across various eras. And, of course, there was the ten-year war with my father, Cronus."

"Alright, Zeus," Morpheus said. "When you remember more, let me know before things take a turn for the worse. Remember, you're guiding me through the past. We're here only to observe—no interference. We'll report back to the crew, but we can't disrupt the timeline."

As the time machine approached the moment Cronus appeared on Earth, Morpheus slowed its speed. The machine could hover over a time slot for as long as it was moving simultaneously within time, allowing them to observe without being noticed.

The landscape of Earth was barren, devoid of life. It was a time before any living being had set foot on the planet. Morpheus and Zeus watched, silent, as Cronus began to shape the world.

Cronus created the waters, the land, the trees, the grass, the animals, and the people. The creatures and humans came from other worlds, just as the planet itself had. At first, Cronus crafted a beautiful world, yet beneath it all, his thoughts were tainted with greed, selfishness, hatred, and the horrors of oppression. Slavery, violence, and numerous other atrocities took root in this new world.

Cronus brought forth a malevolent force that couldn't be fully articulated, a king of destruction whose cruelty was beyond comprehension. As Morpheus and Zeus observed, they saw the devastating effects of Cronus' reign on the first humans who populated Earth.

Zeus turned to Morpheus, his voice somber. "I'd heard stories of these horrors, but people never truly understood how bad it really was for the first inhabitants of this world. You were right about Cronus. We need to try to save this world for the better, Morpheus."

"We knew Cronus was wrong, but we still need to pinpoint the exact moment when everything became irreversible," Morpheus said, his voice thoughtful.

"What do you mean, Morpheus?" Zeus asked, puzzled.

"I'm not entirely sure," Morpheus admitted. "That's why we're here—to uncover the truth and resolve the problems. We must stay focused on our quest and our observation of Cronus. Once we have enough, we'll report back to the ship and the crew. For now, we need to glide through time and follow Cronus, seeing where he and his actions lead us."

As Morpheus and Zeus continued their journey, they witnessed something that left them in disbelief—Cronus was banished from Earth. His parents, Uranus and Gaia, had disapproved of his behavior and, in a decisive moment, banished him from the planet. They punished Cronus by stripping him of his god-like powers and exiling him to a desolate, faraway world. And just like that, Uranus and Gaia vanished from Earth.

In the time that followed, Earth began to flourish—plants and animals thrived, civilizations rose, and countries were born.

On the desolate planet where Cronus had been exiled, his parents allowed him to marry his sister, Rhea. Together, they had five children. However, Cronus grew fearful of a prophecy that foretold one of his children would overthrow him. Driven by fear, Cronus swallowed each of his children upon their birth. But when

Rhea became pregnant for the sixth time, she devised a plan. She tricked Cronus by wrapping a stone in cloth and presenting it to him as the newborn child. Believing he had swallowed the sixth child, Cronus unknowingly spared Zeus, who was hidden safely on the island of Crete. Eventually, Cronus and Rhea returned to Earth, where Cronus resumed his rule.

Years passed, and this time, his children sought vengeance for their father's tyranny, just as Cronus had avenged his own father, Uranus.

Morpheus and Zeus observed a disturbing pattern: each generation's parents were cruel, and in turn, their children sought to overthrow them. Zeus, the third generation, was destined to claim the throne of Earth. He freed the monsters Cronus had created and rescued his siblings from Cronus' stomach—an act of revenge for the suffering his father had caused the family.

Morpheus reflected on this cycle of harm. Whether gods or mortals, the pattern of cruelty persisted. The gods of the universe and their families suffered at the hands of their fathers, just as today, governments and systems of power inflicted chaos and betrayal on the people they were meant to serve. Lies, deceit, and the brutality of wars against humanity had marked both ancient and modern worlds.

Morpheus wondered if this destructive cycle was rooted in something deeper—perhaps a chemical imbalance caused by the sun's gamma rays or something he was failing to see.

"Morpheus, is something wrong?" Zeus asked, snapping Morpheus out of his thoughts.

Zeus repeated his question, and Morpheus finally acknowledged him. “I’m fine, Zeus.”

“You looked lost in thought,” Zeus remarked.

“I was thinking about all the problems, Zeus,” Morpheus admitted. “What we saw doesn’t align with the stories I knew. The truth seems far more complex.”

“You’re right,” Zeus agreed. “Something’s wrong here. There’s more to this than we’ve seen.”

“Starting with Uranus and then Cronus… You were abused by your fathers,” Morpheus said. “I’m trying to piece together the answers. Where did it all go wrong? How do we stop this cycle of abuse?”

Zeus hesitated before speaking. “Uranus and Gaia weren’t from Achilles. They came from a planet that no longer exists. It exploded.”

“What happened to the people from that planet?” Morpheus asked.

Zeus paused. “I don’t know. It was before my time.”

“We need to return to the ship,” Morpheus said. “We’ll explain what we’ve learned and ask Father and the crew about Uranus and Gaia. We need more information before we can move forward.”

When Morpheus and Zeus returned to the ship, the crew greeted them warmly, relieved to have them back.

Morpheus then requested a meeting with Labrum to present the recordings and ask questions about the past. Labrum immediately instructed everyone to gather in the Meeting Chamber.

Once everyone was seated, Morpheus began, “Where were Uranus and Gaia born, or which planet did they originate from?”

Labrum paused before responding. “That’s an unknown answer. All we know is that their planet burned up and exploded. After that, they were on Earth with their children.”

Morpheus pressed on, “How far back do the wars in the Universe between its planets and galaxies go?”

Labrum thought for a moment. “As far back as we know, these battles have existed since the beginning of time—before the civilizations we understand, both alien and human. The wars have been a part of the Universe for as long as we can trace.”

“When did the wars start or end?” Morpheus asked. “Did it coincide with the time of Uranus and Gaia?”

“Perhaps, but we can’t say for certain,” Labrum answered. “It’s like asking who was the first-born baby in the Universe—an answer we can’t definitively give.”

Morpheus nodded. “The beginning of evil can be traced to Uranus, and it’s persisted through time. Gaia was the start of goodness in the Universe. Now, in the middle of the Universe's existence, ninety-nine percent of the world works for the good of humanity, but Earth remains the one percent—a place of evil where it all began."

Morpheus then instructed the crew to watch the recordings and reflect on the events. He would return later to discuss the findings.

Once the recordings were complete, Morpheus returned to the Meeting Chamber, where he waited for the crew's questions.

"Morpheus, you did an excellent job documenting Cronus's past and the origins of evil in the Universe," Labrum said. The crew nodded in agreement.

After a brief silence, they asked, "How can we fix Cronus's problems and the evil he unleashed upon the Universe and Earth?"

"I didn't get that far," Morpheus admitted. "My role was to observe and report back to you."

"We know you, Morpheus," Wega said, "And we know you're already thinking of a solution to this problem."

"You're right," Morpheus replied, "I've been considering the possibilities. But this time, I wanted to hear your thoughts before presenting mine."

CHAPTER 14

Cronos and Evil

Labrum informed the crew that it was time to reflect on the recordings and Morpheus's work in order to find an answer and a solution. But for now, they would take a moment to celebrate Morpheus's return and honor the hard work he had put in for the good of humanity.

"We'll clean up and prepare for dinner," Labrum said, signaling the crew to begin.

Morpheus and Sadal Suud retired to their sleeping quarters. They showered together, and their connection deepened as they made love.

"Morpheus, how bad are things from the past with Cronus?" Sadal Suud asked softly.

Morpheus hesitated, then responded, "If you don't mind, I'd like to hold you right now and not talk about the quest." He kissed her gently. "If you'd prefer, we can talk about anything else, My Love."

Sadal Suud smiled and settled into his arms. "Okay, Morpheus. Let's just hold each other."

Eventually, Morpheus fell asleep, but Sadal Suud couldn't shake the feeling that something was troubling him. As he slept soundly, she quietly used her powers to probe deeper into his mind and emotions, hoping to understand what weighed heavily on him.

At first, the surface thoughts she encountered were unsettling—an undercurrent of anxiety and distress. But as she delved deeper, the horrors of Morpheus's visions began to surface: cruelty, pain, betrayal, and unspeakable crimes against humanity. The sheer negativity overwhelmed her, and the intensity of the emotions she encountered made her powers strain to their limit. Unable to bear the weight of it any longer, she severed the connection, leaving Morpheus's troubled thoughts behind.

When Morpheus woke up, he found Sadal Suud staring at him with concern.

"Are you okay?" she asked softly.

"Yes, I'm fine," Morpheus replied, his voice steady, though a hint of something lingered beneath. "Why do you ask, Sadal Suud?"

Sadal Suud hesitated before confessing. "I noticed something was bothering you before you went to sleep. I could feel your emotions, and I used my powers to look into your thoughts about the quest and Cronus. I hope you're not upset with me."

Morpheus smiled gently, brushing her hair from her face. "No, Honey. I'm not mad at you. I know you care about me." He paused, his expression turning serious. "But why did you go into my thoughts and feelings?"

“I could feel it, Morpheus,” she said quietly. “Your emotions were heavy. I needed to understand what was troubling you. But… the things I saw… it was too much for me to handle.”

Morpheus sat up, his mind racing. “You saw the cruelty from Uranus, Cronus, and Zeus, didn’t you?”

Sadal Suud nodded solemnly. “Yes. The pain, the torment—it was overwhelming. I had to stop before it broke me.”

Morpheus’s gaze softened. “I wonder if the crew saw the recordings the same way.”

“We’ll see,” Sadal Suud replied, offering him a gentle smile. “And we’ll find out if it’s time for dinner.”

The two of them left their quarters and made their way to the Dining Chamber, where the family had already gathered.

Achernar looked up as they entered. “Did you sleep well, Morpheus?”

“Yes, I did,” Morpheus answered, his voice calm but carrying an underlying weight.

“We watched the recordings, Morpheus,” Achernar said, his tone serious. “The problems are... not good.”

“I know the problems,” Morpheus said gravely. “I had to live through them myself, just as Zeus and countless others have relived them.”

Labrum, overhearing the conversation, stepped in. “That’s enough for now, Achernar. We’ll discuss the recordings after dinner,” he said firmly. Turning to Morpheus, he added, “These recordings are deeply troubling. We will address them properly, but only after we’ve had our meal.”

“I understand, Father,” Morpheus replied, his voice subdued.

The family then gathered for a grand feast. They ate and drank heartily, momentarily setting aside the weight of their discoveries. Once the table was cleared and everyone had settled, Labrum rose to address the group.

“Now that everyone is here,” he began, “It’s time to address these issues. Morpheus, we need answers.”

Morpheus stood and faced them. “I don’t have a definitive solution,” he admitted. “I’m struggling to fully comprehend how everything unraveled. What we saw is both horrifying and difficult to process.”

Labrum nodded solemnly. “We are all deeply concerned about the abuse we witnessed—the harm inflicted on people and Earth. It’s like a slaughterhouse, far worse than anything we’ve ever seen.”

“It’s no different from my present time, 2023,” Morpheus said. “The stories of the past—told in books and through the memories of people—echo the same patterns of suffering, generation after generation.”

"What do you mean, Morpheus?" Wega asked, leaning forward.

Morpheus sighed. "Throughout Earth's history, there have been endless tragedies. One of the closest examples in time is World War II."

"What happened during that time?" Wega pressed.

"One man sought to exterminate the Jewish people across Europe, aiming to become the sole ruler of the world," Morpheus explained. "He orchestrated the deaths of millions in concentration camps, stole wealth from banks, museums, and homes to finance his war, and conducted monstrous experiments on humans, treating them like subjects in a twisted laboratory. It was cruelty on a scale that still haunts humanity."

The gods exchanged uneasy glances, shocked by the gravity of the events Morpheus described.

To refocus the discussion, Morpheus asked, "Did you notice in the recordings that there were two distinct times involving Cronus?"

Labrum nodded. "Yes, we did. What was that about?"

"Cronus was banished from Earth by his parents, only to return later in time," Morpheus explained. "In both instances, he perpetuated cycles of abuse."

Labrum leaned forward. "So, we have two pivotal figures—Uranus, the father of Earth, and Cronus, his son—who both inflicted suffering upon their children. Yet, their wives stood as symbols of goodness and nurtured humanity."

Rasalhague chimed in. "The cycle began with Uranus and passed to Cronus. To break it, we may need to change Uranus's role in the past to fix the present and future."

Morpheus furrowed his brow. "Are we in a rush to address this? It's a delicate matter."

The gods exchanged a thoughtful look. "No," they said in unison, "But we must act as soon as we can."

"We need to consider all possible solutions carefully," Morpheus cautioned. "If we interfere with Uranus, the father of Earth, the consequences could ripple across time. Changing his role might lead to positive outcomes—or it could create even greater harm."

"Good point," Achernar said. "The question is, will the change bring about meaningful improvement across the ages?"

Morpheus took a deep breath. "If you destroy the root of the problem, the branches may flourish. But we must be certain—there is too much at stake."

Labrum nodded thoughtfully. "Morpheus is right. This requires deliberation. The actions we take regarding Uranus and Cronus carry profound consequences. We must weigh the pros and cons carefully."

“There are only two outcomes for dealing with Uranus and Cronus,” Morpheus said, his voice resolute. “The first choice is force—if they choose to fight, we’ll have no option but to defend Earth with all our power. The second choice is reason—to convince them of the destruction they’ve caused, spanning their time and ours, and persuade them to cooperate with us. Either way, we must be prepared.”

Labrum nodded thoughtfully. “We need to rest and reflect individually. Tomorrow, we’ll reconvene to share our ideas and discuss them collectively. Together, we will determine the best course of action.”

Morpheus continued, “Uranus ruled without law or order, wielding unchecked power. Cronus, driven by vengeance, repeated his father’s mistakes. Both tore their children from one another by force. If it comes to that again, we must be ready. But resolving this—saving the Earth—ultimately falls on me as the bearer of a New Life for the Planet.”

The room fell silent as the weight of Morpheus’s words sank in. Labrum and the other gods exchanged solemn glances. They understood the unspoken truth: Morpheus might have to end the lives of Uranus and Cronus to break the cycle of destruction. Denab and the goddesses, too, realized the gravity of the situation. They remembered how Morpheus had protected them from the comet and stood by Zeus on Achilles. He was the fulfillment of prophecy—a savior not just for Earth but for their culture and the entire Universe.

“It’s time to rest,” Labrum finally said. “We’ll revisit these issues tomorrow. Until then, carry out any tasks needed for the ship and take the time to think of answers. Share your thoughts at the table when we gather again."

Turning to Morpheus and Sadal Suud, Labrum added, "I want you both to rest and enjoy each other's company. If you need to talk, my door is always open."

Before anyone could respond, Morpheus spoke again. "Sadal Suud and I have an announcement. We want to get married before the quest resumes."

The room brightened with joy as the gods celebrated the news. Denab, smiling warmly, declared, "The wedding will be held in honor of Morpheus and Sadal Suud."

Labrum raised his hand for quiet. "But first, we need answers and solutions. The mission must remain our priority." Everyone agreed and began to disperse.

As the others prepared to leave, Morpheus approached Labrum. "Father, may we talk privately?"

Labrum looked at him with a knowing expression. "Of course, Morpheus."

"Let's meet in your Office Chamber," Morpheus said.

Labrum nodded. "I'll be waiting."

When Morpheus and Labrum entered the Office Chamber, Labrum gestured to a seat and asked, "What's on your mind, Son?"

MORPHEUS

Morpheus settled into the chair, his expression heavy with thought. “I lived among the humans and learned their ways—their laws, their thinking, and their culture. But the evil that Uranus and Cronus unleashed in their time has only grown worse. Humanity is now consumed by greed and a hunger for power so profound that people will betray even their own families. Governments exploit their citizens, sending them to fight wars rooted in greed while the powerful sit safely behind desks. This poison of hatred, selfishness, and destruction flows through the blood of humanity, and it all stems from Uranus and Cronus. If we’re to save Earth, we’ll have to destroy them. They’re gods without law or accountability, and their legacy has festered unchecked.”

Labrum nodded solemnly. “And what of Zeus? Do we need to be concerned about him?”

“Zeus made mistakes during his reign,” Morpheus said. “But from what I’ve learned through the stories and records of his time, he’s changed. He now serves on the Council, striving for balance. Still, we should keep a watchful eye on him until the quest is complete.”

Labrum’s gaze sharpened. “So, this course of action—destroying Uranus and Cronus—you’ve already made up your mind, haven’t you?”

“At first, I hoped for a different solution,” Morpheus admitted. “At the meeting, I plan to reason with them. But if they resist—if they refuse to see the destruction they’ve caused—we’ll have no choice but to end them.”

Labrum exhaled deeply, his shoulders heavy with the weight of Morpheus's words. "I knew before this conversation that it would come to this. So did the other gods. The blood of gods and mortals has soaked the Earth for too long, tainting its soil and its people. We'll explain your decision to the Council tomorrow."

The two exchanged a quiet "Good night" before retiring to their chambers.

When Morpheus entered his room, Sadal Suud leaped into his arms, her embrace warm and eager. "I love you, Morpheus," she said softly.

"I love you too, my lady," Morpheus replied, holding her close.

"Everyone is so happy about our decision to marry," Sadal Suud said, her eyes glowing with joy.

"You complete me," Morpheus said. "As both a man and a god, I feel whole because of you. I love everything about you—your independence, your devotion, and the perfect balance you bring to life. You are beautiful in every way: your heart, your mind, your spirit, and your power. You are a goddess like no other."

Sadal Suud smiled, her voice tender. "And you, Morpheus, are brave, intelligent, and endlessly charming. You are more than a man or a god—you are my universe."

After a pause, Sadal Suud asked, "What will happen with Uranus and Cronus?"

Morpheus sighed. “Let’s wait until tomorrow. I’ll explain everything to the gods during the meeting.”

“Just tell me this,” Sadal Suud said. “Will you go to war with them?”

“Yes,” Morpheus said, his voice firm. “If reasoning fails, war will be our last resort. To defeat them, we’ll need every god aboard this ship to stand together. For now, let’s rest.”

“Of course, Morpheus,” Sadal Suud replied, her faith in him unwavering.

Morning came, and Sadal Suud woke Morpheus with gentle kisses. He returned her affection, and soon they were lost in each other, making love. Later, they showered together, their passion reigniting under the warm water.

Their quiet moment was interrupted by the ship’s intercom. “Attention, gods. Please report to the Dining Chamber for breakfast, followed by the Meeting Chamber for today’s council session.”

Hand in hand, Morpheus and Sadal Suud prepared to face the day ahead, their bond stronger than ever as they braced for the challenges to come.

CHAPTER 15

Plans for Marriage

The following morning, the gods gathered for breakfast before assembling in the Meeting Chamber. Labrum began the discussion with a somber tone.

"We are here to address the pressing issue of Uranus and Cronus," Labrum said. "These two gods are at the foundation of Earth's creation and much of the life on this planet. Through Morpheus's research, we've uncovered troubling truths about their past actions.

"Uranus, the first god of the Earth, fathered children with Gaia, his wife. However, he forbade the children from leaving Gaia's womb. Dissatisfied and enraged by Uranus's cruelty, Gaia defied him and allowed their children to emerge. Terrified of their father, the children hid, except for Cronus, who was unafraid to confront Uranus. In a violent act, Cronus castrated Uranus, an act that led to the creation of Aphrodite. The blood of Uranus also gave rise to the Gigantes, Melian, and Erinyes."

Labrum paused, his gaze sweeping across the room.

"Cronus, for his part, vanished from Earth for a time, only to return and take his sister, Rhea, as his wife. Together, they reshaped the Earth, covering it with trees, grass, and animals. Cronus created humans and ruled over them as their king, with

Rhea as their queen. Yet Cronus's rule was marked by cruelty. He created monsters, terrorized humanity, and, in a horrifying display, consumed his first five children to prevent them from usurping his power.

"Rhea, unwilling to lose her sixth child, tricked Cronus by wrapping a stone in swaddling clothes and presenting it as the baby. She hid the real child, Zeus, on the island of Crete. Zeus grew in secret, and when he reached adulthood, he sought revenge against his father. Disguising himself as a peasant, Zeus offered Cronus a drink laced with metis. The concoction caused Cronus to vomit, disgorging Zeus's siblings. United, the Olympians waged war against the Titans."

Labrum's voice grew grave as he continued. "For ten years, the Olympians battled the Titans. Zeus emerged victorious, claiming kingship over the Olympians, while Cronus and the Titans were banished to Tartarus for eternity—a place of torment and imprisonment. Though Zeus and the Olympians brought order for a time, the damage wrought by Uranus and Cronus left lasting scars on Earth and its people."

Labrum finished his recounting and opened the floor for discussion.

"What plans does Morpheus have to address these issues?" Wega asked.

"We are here to hear your views and suggestions," Labrum responded.

The gods exchanged uncertain glances before Rasalhague spoke. “I’ve spent all night thinking about this, and I have no solutions.”

The others echoed the same sentiment—none had clear answers.

Morpheus leaned forward, frustration evident in his voice. “You are wise, powerful beings. Why is it so difficult to find a solution with your collective knowledge?”

Achernar spoke hesitantly. “We’re dealing with the first god of Earth and his son. What if we make the wrong choice? The consequences could ripple through time and space.”

Labrum raised his hand to calm the room. “Let’s break this down,” he said. “The immediate problem is humanity’s push to explore space. If left unchecked, this will lead to a repeat of history—like the colonization of the Americas. Land was stolen, native peoples were massacred, and greed fueled endless suffering. Now imagine this scenario playing out on a universal scale: countless planets, peoples, and resources at stake. The greed, hatred, and selfishness that plague humanity must be eradicated before it infects the rest of the Universe.”

He paused, letting the gravity of his words settle over the room. “The Earth’s soil is tainted with the blood of Uranus and Cronus—an evil that has seeped into humanity for generations. The High Council has tasked us with preserving the peace and stability of the Universe, which has endured for centuries. Morpheus’s research confirms that the legacy of Uranus and Cronus threatens not just Earth but the cosmic order itself.

Correcting these problems is our responsibility. We must act, even if the actions we take are difficult."

The room fell silent as the gods grappled with the weight of Labrum's declaration. Their course of action could alter not just the future of Earth but the fate of the Universe.

The discussion among the gods took a decisive turn as Denab stood up and voiced her conviction.

"I believe in the plan to destroy evil before it spreads like poison through the Earth and its people," Denab said firmly. "If stopping two evil gods can save the people of Earth and preserve the peace of the Universe, then we must act."

The other goddesses nodded in agreement, echoing Denab's sentiment. They expressed their shared fear that if action wasn't taken, their own people might suffer attacks from humans venturing beyond their planet.

One of the male gods spoke up, acknowledging the women's concerns. "The ladies are right. We can't allow our planets to fall victim to human raids."

Labrum, ever the mediator, addressed the group. "This must be a united decision. Whether it ends in negotiation or conflict with Uranus and Cronus, all of us will be involved until the resolution is achieved."

Sadal Suud raised an important question. "What happens if we change the course of humanity and the Earth forever?"

Labrum's reply was stark. "If we don't act now, the only alternative may be to exterminate the human race entirely. There's no room for hesitation."

He then turned to the gods. "I ask each of you to decide—do we proceed with Morpheus's plan, or do we take the drastic step of eradicating humanity? Cast your votes now."

The gods voted one by one, their decisions forming a unanimous consensus.

"Yes," said Wega and Denebola.

"Yes," echoed Rasalhague and Zaniah.

Achernar and Capella added their agreement, followed by Sirius and Terebellum.

"Yes," Kochab and Rastaban confirmed.

Even Zeus, with his long history and wisdom, sided with Morpheus's plan.

Sadal Suud's voice rang clear. "Yes."

Finally, Labrum and Denab cast their votes.

"The decision is unanimous," Labrum declared. "As the gods of the Universe, we stand united behind Morpheus's plan. Now, with this weighty decision made, it is time to celebrate another matter of great importance—a wedding!"

The room lightened with excitement as Denab suggested, "Let's hold the wedding in the Hologram Hall. We can use images of Achilles as the background to honor our heritage."

The preparations began in earnest. The goddesses busied themselves with crafting an exquisite wedding dress for Sadal Suud and decorating the Dining Chamber for a feast. Meanwhile, the gods celebrated with drinks, laughter, and camaraderie.

Denab approached Sadal Suud with a warm smile. "Congratulations, Sadal Suud. You will make a beautiful bride."

The other goddesses joined in, showering her with well-wishes. "Congratulations, Sadal Suud!"

Among the men, Morpheus received similar congratulations. Achernar, his soon-to-be father-in-law, clapped him on the shoulder. "Morpheus, you are marrying my daughter, Sadal Suud. I couldn't be prouder."

Labrum, ever the proud father, added, "Congratulations, my son. You've made me proud as both a leader and a father."

When the day of the wedding arrived, the gods donned ceremonial garments of breathtaking beauty, each piece unique and extravagant. Morpheus, awestruck by the elegance of the tradition, could hardly believe his eyes when he saw the women's attire.

But his breath truly caught when Sadal Suud entered the hall. Her wedding dress was a masterpiece, and she radiated a beauty that transcended the mortal and divine. As Achernar escorted his daughter down the aisle, lifting her veil to kiss her forehead before stepping aside, Morpheus felt a surge of gratitude and love.

Labrum stood at the head of the assembly and began the ceremony with warm greetings for all in attendance. Achernar gave his daughter's hand to Morpheus, Denab served as the maid of honor, and Wega stood proudly as the best man.

The atmosphere was filled with joy, unity, and hope as Morpheus and Sadal Suud prepared to unite their lives—a powerful symbol of harmony amidst the immense challenges ahead.

"The ceremonial words will be spoken in the ancient language of Achilles," Labrum announced to the gathered gods and goddesses. "Wega will translate the vows into English for Morpheus so their meaning is clear. These words are sacred, symbolizing the eternal bond between two souls destined to share their lives together."

Labrum recited the vows in the melodic Achillesian tongue, Wega translated, each phrase resonating with love, commitment, and unity. When the vows were complete, Labrum instructed Morpheus and Sadal Suud to repeat the sacred words.

With unwavering voices, they pledged their devotion to each other, sealing their union with a tender kiss that symbolized the beginning of their shared journey.

The hall erupted into cheers and applause as family and friends offered heartfelt congratulations. They then gathered for a grand feast. The dining tables were laden with exquisite wedding fare, and the air was filled with laughter, joy, and the sound of recorded Achillesian music, played beautifully by Rasalhague.

Dances followed—first, the groom and bride shared a romantic dance, then the groom and his mother, and the bride with her father. Soon, everyone joined in, creating a lively and joyous atmosphere that reflected the unity and happiness of the occasion.

The celebration continued for hours, filled with stories, songs, and toasts to the newlyweds. At last, Morpheus and Sadal Suud rose from their seats.

"We're retiring to our chambers," Morpheus said, his hand gently resting on Sadal Suud's.

"Goodnight, everyone," Sadal Suud added with a radiant smile.

The couple departed amidst a chorus of well-wishes and cheers.

When they reached their chambers, their love for one another enveloped them. They undressed each other slowly, savoring every moment. Their love-making was passionate and tender, a culmination of their deep connection. Finally, they fell asleep in each other's arms, content and at peace.

The next morning, they woke up still holding each other.

"Good morning," Sadal Suud whispered, her eyes sparkling.

"Good morning, my love," Morpheus replied, his voice filled with warmth.

Morpheus began caressing Sadal Suud, their affection reigniting the passion from the night before. They shared their love once more, their bond growing deeper with each moment.

Afterward, they showered together, and as the warm water cascaded over them, their love-making began anew, playful yet filled with profound devotion. When they finally emerged from the shower, refreshed and glowing, they dressed and prepared for the day.

The intercom buzzed, and Labrum's voice came through. "Morpheus, Sadal Suud, please report to the Meeting Chamber."

When they arrived, Labrum and Denab greeted them with knowing smiles.

"How was your night?" Labrum asked, his tone teasing.

"It was very special," Sadal Suud answered, a blush warming her cheeks.

"And this morning," Morpheus added, his grin wide.

Laughter filled the room, the happiness of the newlyweds spreading to all present.

"That's good to hear," Labrum said. "Now, let's go over the ideas and plans for our quest."

Morpheus stood and addressed the group. "Here's the plan: I will travel back in time, first to meet with Uranus and then with Cronus. My goal is to assess their perspectives and try to communicate the consequences of their actions, both for the future of Earth and the Universe. I'll gauge their intentions and determine the extent of the threat they pose. Based on what I discover, I will decide the best course of action, whether to negotiate, neutralize the threat, or—if there is no other choice—destroy them both."

Achernar furrowed his brow. "Destroy them? How do you plan to accomplish that?"

"I don't have a definitive answer to that yet," Morpheus admitted. "But once I've observed their behavior and assessed the situation, I will figure out the necessary steps. For now, let's focus on the investigation."

Labrum turned to the others. "Are we all in agreement with Morpheus's plan?"

A chorus of "Yes, Morpheus" filled the room.

Wega leaned forward, her voice measured. "Morpheus, do you fully understand what you're dealing with? Uranus and Gaia are not just any beings; they are the origin of life on this planet and the progenitors of their children."

"I'm well aware of their role in the creation of Earth," Morpheus replied.

Rasalhague interjected, "If Uranus and Cronus were evil, as you say, they still played a crucial role in starting the human race. If they hadn't, who would have taken their place? And what would Earth's fate have been without them?"

Labrum raised a hand to quiet the room. "We've already agreed to proceed with the plan. The question now is how Morpheus will approach the situation and what contingencies we must prepare."

"Yes," Rasalhague said, "But there are important considerations to address before we move forward."

Morpheus nodded. "I understand your concerns, and I assure you, nothing will be done impulsively. I will investigate thoroughly and report back with detailed findings. We can then strategize based on what I uncover."

The room fell silent for a moment before Labrum spoke again. "Does everyone agree with this course of action?"

Once more, the gods affirmed their support. With unity in the room, the meeting concluded, and Morpheus prepared himself for the challenging journey ahead.

CHAPTER 16

Meeting Uranus

Morpheus and Zeus prepared to journey back to the origins of the human race, to the time of Uranus and Cronus.

Morpheus turned to his father and mother, saying his goodbyes.

"Be careful, both of you," Denab cautioned.

"If you must resolve the problems you face, then do so," Labrum added firmly. "Remember, we'll be there when you call on us."

Morpheus then approached Sadal Suud. He kissed her gently.
"You'd better come back to me," she said, her voice a mix of love and concern.

Morpheus smiled, his eyes gleaming with confidence. "I am the God of Dreams, the New Life for Planet Earth, and the fulfillment of the Universe's prophecy. What could possibly happen to me?"
Sadal Suud smiled faintly, though her concern lingered. "I'll see you when you return."

Morpheus said his farewells to the rest of his family, and Zeus followed suit. Together, they stepped into the time machine, ready for their monumental journey into Earth's past.

As the machine roared to life and time began to unravel around them, Morpheus and Zeus watched history unfold before their eyes. They witnessed the wars of modern America, the American Revolution, and the bloody conflicts in Europe. They saw the rise and fall of the Roman Empire, the struggles across Africa, and the glory of Egypt's golden age. Their path swept across Asia's vast landscapes, where Genghis Khan's conquests left a trail of fire and empire. They moved further back, glimpsing the primitive lives of the Neanderthals, and finally, they arrived at the time of the dinosaurs.

Here, they paused briefly, taking in the haunting aftermath of the asteroid's destruction. The once-vibrant planet—lush with green jungles, vast landscapes, and sprawling swamps—had been obliterated. Beaches lay scorched, littered with the lifeless bodies of sea dinosaurs and fish cooked by the searing heat of the impact.

Moving forward again, Morpheus and Zeus finally reached the era of Uranus. They observed in awe as a strange spaceship descended to Earth, delivering Uranus and his wife, Gaia. The two gods stepped onto the shattered, barren planet. Morpheus and Zeus exchanged a glance, both wondering who piloted the mysterious vessel and what role its occupants played in this unfolding saga.

Uranus gazed over the ruined Earth with a ruler's eye, seeing it as a domain to command. But first, he knew he must make the environment livable for himself and Gaia. As Uranus exerted his power to control the Earth's foundations and seed its surface, Gaia turned her attention to the skies, crafting an atmosphere and summoning rains to heal the land. Together, their combined powers transformed the planet, bringing life back to its once-sterile plains.

The Earth flourished once more—lush, green, and beautiful. But while Gaia's intentions were rooted in creation and harmony, Uranus saw a different purpose. He began to envision subjects to rule and dominate, while Gaia dreamed of children to populate and nurture the Earth.

Morpheus and Zeus carefully observed the two gods and quickly realized they were opposites. Gaia's vision held compassion and promise, while Uranus's ambition hinted at cruelty and a desire for power that could lead to enslavement. The delicate balance of creation had begun—but already, the seeds of conflict were sown.

Morpheus turned to Zeus and said, "The problems began right from the very beginning."

Together, they searched for the time when Gaia was pregnant and witnessed the grotesque creatures Uranus had created. The sight was almost unbelievable—hideous beasts, vicious and terrifying. At the same time, Gaia nurtured her own creations, children destined to seed the Earth's populations. But when Uranus discovered Gaia's children, his fear and cruelty surfaced. He forced Gaia to keep the children inside her womb, threatening to kill them if she dared to bring them into the world.

Gaia was heartbroken, grieving for the children she could not birth and for the Earth, which she had hoped to populate with life. Determined to end this injustice, Gaia devised a plan: she would ask her unborn children to rise against their father.

Meanwhile, Uranus continued his chaotic rule. He created monstrous beings like the Cyclopes, Giants, and the Hecatoncheires, each more terrifying than the last. His reign became a time of strife, driven by his oppressive leadership and the anguish he caused his wife. Finally, Gaia turned to her son Cronus, urging him to avenge his siblings and free them from their father's cruelty.

Cronus escaped from Gaia's womb, armed with a sickle crafted by his mother. In an act of defiance, he castrated Uranus and hurled the severed testicles into the ocean. From the white foam that rose upon the sea, a woman emerged—Aphrodite, the goddess of love. But Uranus's blood, spilling onto the Earth, gave rise to new beings: the Gigantes, the Meliae, and the Erinyes, fierce and vengeful spirits born of his pain.

Uranus's life ended with the act, and Gaia was finally free of his tyranny. She turned to Cronus and declared, "Cronus, you are now the King of Earth, and these people—your brothers and sisters—are yours to lead."

Cronus took his sister Rhea as his wife and led the Titans into an era of prosperity. Yet power, as it so often does, corrupted him. He soon repeated his father's mistakes. Cronus imprisoned the Gigantes, Meliae, and Erinyes deep within Tartarus, guarded by the monstrous Dragon Campe.

Morpheus and Zeus paused, freezing time to reflect on what they had witnessed.

"The cycle of suffering has passed from one generation to the next," Zeus said solemnly.

Morpheus nodded. "Uranus's blood poisoned the land, giving rise to beasts and nymphs. From the very beginning, chaos was sewn into the fabric of life, and as centuries passed, civilizations only grew worse."

"What do we do?" Morpheus asked. "Do we stop Uranus's blood from tainting the Earth, or do we try something else?"

Zeus shook his head. "I don't know. That's a question for your father."

Morpheus sighed. "Everything we see is being recorded—our journey, the gods we've spoken to, and the truths we've uncovered. For now, let's keep watching and see what unfolds with Cronus."

"Agreed," Zeus replied.

In time, Cronus and Rhea had six children. But Gaia warned Rhea of a prophecy: one of her children would overthrow Cronus, just as Cronus had done to Uranus. Fearing this fate, Cronus became consumed with paranoia. When Rhea attempted to give birth on the island of Crete, Cronus stopped her. Desperate to prevent the prophecy, he devoured each child as they were born.

One by one, Cronus swallowed his children—until Rhea, determined to save at least one, tricked him. She wrapped a stone in swaddling clothes and gave it to Cronus in place of her last child, Zeus. Satisfied, Cronus swallowed the stone, unaware of the deception.

Hidden in the wilderness of Crete, Zeus was raised in secret by his mother, Rhea, his grandmother, Gaia, and Aphrodite. Together, Gaia and Rhea plotted Cronus's downfall.

When Zeus came of age, he disguised himself as a cupbearer and approached Cronus. With the help of Metis, he prepared a potent emetic drink. Cronus, unsuspecting, drank the concoction and was soon overcome with sickness. One by one, he regurgitated his swallowed children, starting with the stone and followed by Zeus's siblings.

Finally united, Zeus and his brothers and sisters fled and prepared for war. The first Olympian gods were born, and their rebellion against Cronus and the Titans began.

The Titanomachy—the great war between the Titans and Olympians—raged for ten years. Cronus and the Titans were formidable, but Zeus proved to be both wise and cunning. He freed the Cyclopes, Giants, and Hecatoncheires from Tartarus, rallying them to his side. The Cyclopes forged powerful weapons for Zeus, including his iconic thunderbolts.

Zeus devised a strategy: while the Cyclopes, Giants, and Hecatoncheires created chaos as a diversion, he unleashed a devastating storm of thunderbolts upon the Titans. One by one, the Titans fell before the wrath of Zeus and his allies.

When the war ended, Zeus banished the defeated Titans to Tartarus, condemning them to eternal imprisonment and torment. Victorious, Zeus and the Olympians ascended to Mount Olympus, where they built the first great temple of the gods.

From the ruins of Titan's rule, a new age had begun—one led by the gods of Olympus, with Zeus as their king. Yet, as Morpheus and Zeus watched the unfolding events, they both knew that the struggles of power, ambition, and chaos would persist, echoing through time.

Morpheus and Zeus observed and recorded the origins of the gods, tracing the violence and chaos that had been passed down through the ages.

"This is why the world remains unfavorable for humanity and unprepared for space travel," Morpheus said solemnly. Zeus nodded in agreement.

"There are two significant sources of evil plaguing the Earth," Morpheus continued. "First, the blood of Uranus, which poisoned the land. Second, and more concerning, Cronus still dwells beneath the Earth's crust, spreading havoc to this day."

"Do you think Cronus is still alive?" Zeus asked, his brow furrowed.

Morpheus's expression was grave. "There are two answers to that question. Whether dead or alive, Cronus continues to poison the land and the people. The other possibility lies in the stories of the devil and his demons—symbols of evil infecting the world. In both cases, the outcome is the same: suffering for humanity and the Earth."

Zeus exhaled sharply. "What now?"

"Let's return to the ship and deliver our report," Morpheus said. "Is everything secured on the time machine?"

Zeus checked the controls and nodded. "Yes, everything is in order."

"Then let's go," Morpheus said.

The two gods traveled through the flow of time and returned to the *UNIV ORION* ship. When they entered, they were greeted warmly by the crew and family.

"How did it go, Morpheus? Zeus?" Labrum and Denab asked.

Morpheus gave a small smile. "It went… as expected."

"Okay," Zeus added simply.

Before anyone else could speak, Sadal Suud ran to Morpheus and threw her arms around him, kissing him deeply. "I missed you, and I love you," she whispered.

"You're just in time for dinner," Labrum said cheerfully. "Come, let's eat and celebrate your return. We can talk about the quest tomorrow."

Together, the gods made their way to the Dining Chamber, where a grand feast awaited them. Plates were filled, goblets overflowed, and laughter echoed through the room.

"How did the pursuit of Uranus and Cronus go?" Sadal Suud asked, curiosity flickering in her eyes.

Zeus answered first. “The stories are true—both about their power and their cruelty. Morpheus faces a monumental challenge ahead if he is to save humanity and the Earth.” He paused. “They’re as tall as I am—fifty feet high, with strength beyond imagination.”

“Morpheus is no pushover,” Achernar said confidently.

“That’s enough, Achernar,” Labrum interjected, his voice calm but firm.

Zeus nodded in agreement. “Morpheus will stand tall when the time comes. He’s proven himself to be fearless, even in the face of gods like Uranus and Cronus… and even against me.”

The feast continued, but Morpheus grew quieter, his thoughts elsewhere. When the meal was finished, he stood and addressed Labrum.

“May I be dismissed for the night?” Morpheus asked.

Labrum frowned slightly. “Is something wrong, Morpheus?”

“No,” Morpheus replied. “I’m just thinking of other ways to approach these problems.”

“Do you want to discuss the quest now?” Labrum offered.

“No. Not tonight. I need to rest,” Morpheus said. “If you’d like to see the recordings, I’ll explain them with Zeus tomorrow.”

Labrum nodded. “Very well. Goodnight, Morpheus.”

"Goodnight," Morpheus said as he began walking to his chamber.

"Wait for me, Morpheus!" Sadal Suud said. "I'm coming too."

In the quiet of their chamber, Sadal Suud turned to him. "Are you all right?" she asked gently.

"Yes, I'm fine," Morpheus said, lying down beside her. "I'm just exhausted from the time travel and everything we witnessed."

"That's okay, my love," Sadal Suud replied, touching his face tenderly. "I understand."

Morpheus kissed her softly. "Goodnight."

"Goodnight," she whispered, lying close to him.

As Morpheus drifted into sleep, Sadal Suud placed her hand lightly on his chest. Through their connection, she could see fragments of his memories—his time travels, the horrors of Uranus and Cronus, and the devastation they had caused. She gasped quietly at the scale of their crimes against humanity and their families.

The next morning, Morpheus awoke to the soft glow of light in their chamber. He kissed Sadal Suud gently and said, "Good morning, my love."

"Good morning," she replied, her voice filled with warmth. "How are you feeling today?"

"Better," Morpheus said. He studied her carefully. "I know you were in my dreams and saw my memories."

Sadal Suud looked apologetic. "I'm sorry, Morpheus. I couldn't help it. We're all worried about you and this journey."

"Do you understand the problems we're facing?" Morpheus asked seriously.

"Yes," Sadal Suud said. "We all do. The challenges ahead are immense."

"Did you speak to my father about this?" Morpheus asked.

"No," she replied softly. "I fell asleep with you, holding you all night."

Morpheus sighed. "It's time to see my father and the others. We need to figure out what comes next."

Sadal Suud nodded, taking his hand. "We'll face this together."

And with that, Morpheus prepared himself to meet with the gods once more. The weight of history, both past and present, rested heavily on his shoulders—but he was ready to stand tall.

CHAPTER 17

Trip Problems

Morpheus and Sadal Suud entered the Dining Chamber, where the gods were already seated, exchanging greetings.

"Good morning," Morpheus and Sadal Suud said as they bowed respectfully.

Labrum turned to Morpheus with a smile. "How did you sleep, Morpheus?"

"Very well, with my wife by my side," Morpheus replied, his voice calm but resolute.

"That's good to hear," Labrum said. "Tell us, what did you and Zeus uncover during the recordings?"

Morpheus straightened, his tone taking on a gravity befitting the occasion. "Zeus and I have traced the origins of the corruption that poisons Earth and humanity. It begins with Uranus and Cronus. First, Cronus castrated Uranus. From his blood, terrible creatures were born, and from his severed flesh, Aphrodite emerged—a rare blessing amidst the chaos."

He continued, his voice echoing through the hall, "Uranus was no king, nor was he a god of virtue. He was pure evil. His actions tainted the land, sea, and skies across generations. Cronus inherited that poison, perpetuating the cycle of cruelty. Both feared the prophecy that their children would rise against them. Uranus imprisoned his children in the womb, while Cronus devoured his offspring—save for Zeus, whom Rhea protected."

At this, Zeus nodded solemnly.

"The wives of these tyrants grieved for their children, devising plans to save them. They succeeded, but what followed was a war lasting ten years—a battle between Titans and Olympians. In the end, Zeus led the gods to victory, banishing Cronus to Tartarus, where he remains tortured for eternity. But the scars of their evil remain. Their blood seeped into the Earth and seas, corrupting everything it touched—including humankind."

Labrum turned to Zeus. "Zeus, how do you feel about Morpheus's explanation?"

Zeus stood, his voice filled with the weight of experience. "Morpheus speaks the truth. I fought Cronus and the Titans. I witnessed the war, the suffering, and the ultimate victory. The recordings confirm this. The poison of Uranus and Cronus has lived through the ages, tainting Earth's people and its very fabric."

"And in Tartarus," Morpheus added, "Their wickedness festers still. It's no wonder hell itself lies within that realm."

The gods murmured among themselves as the weight of the revelations settled over them.

Labrum addressed the group. "Morpheus and Zeus have conducted a thorough investigation. Let us now watch the recordings."

The chamber darkened as the recordings played. Scenes of unimaginable cruelty unfolded—children suffering, land and sea ravaged, and the cruelty of Uranus and Cronus brought to life. By the end, silence reigned. The gods sat in stunned disbelief.

Denab broke the silence, her voice trembling. "The only beauty to emerge from Uranus's horrors was Aphrodite."

Labrum nodded. "It seems Morpheus and Zeus have revealed the full truth. The tale of Uranus and Cronus is one of unchecked power, chaos, and suffering."

Wega spoke up. "These ancient gods were untamed—forces of raw, violent power. They cared for nothing, not even their own children. How can we possibly match them?"

Achernar added, "They are giants, fifty feet tall, with strength beyond imagining. Even with all our power, can we truly stop them?"

Morpheus stepped forward, his voice rising like a tide. "Do you doubt me? I represent Earth and its people. I am the God of Dreams, the harbinger of new life for our world. My wife, Sadal Suud, is the goddess of new beginnings. Together, we are your prophecy—a chance for the Universe to begin anew. Do you believe it, or do you still question me?"

The gods shifted uneasily. Labrum and Denab exchanged glances, quietly observing Morpheus's growing frustration.

"Why do you doubt this quest?" Morpheus demanded. "You questioned me before Zeus and I investigated Uranus and Cronus. And now, despite the truth before your very eyes, you doubt me again. Why?"

Wega hesitated before answering. "Our people—the Achillesians—have not fought in millennia. We are uncertain if you alone can stand against such ancient power."

"If you doubt me," Morpheus said, his voice cold, "then I will step down. You can deal with the wars and suffering spreading through the Universe."

"No!" the gods cried in unison. "The Council of Achilles will never forgive us if we abandon our duty."

Labrum stood, clapping slowly. "You lead with diplomacy, not violence, Morpheus. That is a god worthy of respect—worthy of this Universe and the people of Earth."

Denab joined him, and soon, the other gods nodded in agreement.

"Still, if you wish to test my strength," Morpheus said, his voice firm, "I will not be offended."

Labrum's three brothers grinned. "Yes, Morpheus. Prove your power."

"And who will decide the test?" Morpheus asked.

"You may choose," the brothers said smugly.

Morpheus smiled. "Then I shall raise the continent of Atlantis."

The brothers exchanged glances, their arrogance faltering. "A clever trick, Morpheus."

"Is it a trick—or my strength?" Morpheus challenged. "Do you need proof, or do you remember the comet I moved to save our ship?"

The brothers raised their hands in surrender. "No, Morpheus. We understand your strength, and we apologize for doubting you."

Labrum laughed, and Denab chuckled softly. "Outwitted," Denab said, shaking her head.

Finally, Labrum addressed the assembly. "Are we done with this foolishness?"

"Yes," the gods chorused.

Morpheus's expression darkened once more. "Correcting one problem may create others. If we stop Uranus and Cronus, what happens to the future that follows? What consequences will ripple through time?"

The chamber fell silent again, the gods pondering the weight of his question.

“What do you mean, Morpheus?” Wega asked.

“Everything has a domino effect, a ripple through time when you change the course of things,” Morpheus explained. “We understand our history now, with Uranus and Cronus, but if we stop them—how will we know what history follows? Remember, everything has a place in time. Disturb the course, and what happens then? What if Uranus doesn’t die? What if Cronus doesn’t fall?”

“The human race would be doomed, forced into extinction by the High Council of Achilles,” Labrum replied solemnly.

Kochab and Rastaban added in unison, “Once the present timeline is altered, the future will shift—perhaps creating a parallel world. We cannot predict the consequences.”

“That is exactly what we are trying to prevent,” Morpheus said, his voice filled with determination. “We aim to purge the evil left in the wake of Uranus and Cronus.”

“No matter the outcome,” Labrum said, his tone resolute, “we are accountable to the Council and the Universe. Unfortunately, humanity is too dangerous to venture into space. With their greed, power struggles, and violence, we have no choice but to intervene. Humans never learn from their mistakes. We must eradicate the root of the problem now and hope to save what remains.”

Labrum turned his gaze to Morpheus. “It’s good you are considering all possibilities, but ultimately, we have no choice. Perhaps, in the grand scheme of things, you may be the new ruler of a world reborn—a world free from corruption. All remnants of the past will be erased from Earth's history."

"It might be better to start over with the Earth," Sirius suggested. "I believe humanity will never change for the better, no matter what you do, Morpheus."

"Some of us feel the same," Terebellum added, his voice quiet but resolute.

Capella spoke with compassion, "We must hold onto hope for humanity. We must try to make life better for them."

"Morpheus, you are the New King of Earth," Labrum said, his voice heavy with authority. "The decision is yours. But remember, you are not alone. You have the counsel of your family and the gods and goddesses. We, as your parents, support your efforts to save humanity, but if you cannot, then the end of humanity is inevitable. As Achillesians, we have a duty to the Universe and to all the races of the planets. We have already ended the wars between the planetary nations and established law and order. But Earth... Earth was tainted by Uranus and Cronus, and their poison has spread through the ages. Now, it is our responsibility to undo the damage."

"My first thought is to keep everyone safe and to preserve Earth," Morpheus said, his voice heavy with resolve. "My second thought was to reason with Uranus and Cronus, but after everything Zeus and I have seen, I no longer believe that's an option."

Achernar spoke, his voice calm yet firm. “We understand your desire to help, to prevent further conflict. But you must face these challenges head-on without burdening yourself with guilt. You must make the decisions that are right for you.”

Achernar’s gaze held steady. “Your mind knows what must be done, but your heart remains torn. You must make decisions, Morpheus, and stand by them—no matter the cost.”

Zaniah added, “We all understand your dreams of a new world, a better world. But if you cannot stop the coming disaster, then the decision will be made for you without choice.”

“We could wait,” Labrum suggested, “And allow Morpheus to take his time. He knows our thoughts, and he understands the potential outcomes. But we have discussed this for hours. Now, it’s time for rest. No more talk of the quest until after dinner.”

The gods gathered in the Dining Chamber for a quiet meal, the tension in the air palpable. Conversations were sparse, each god and goddess deep in thought about the quest ahead and the uncertainty of what might come. Morpheus, too, sat quietly, weighing his desire to save everyone—humanity, Uranus, Cronus—against the crushing realization that sometimes faith and fate play cruel games with decisions.

As they finished dinner, the gods retired early to their Sleeping Chambers, each consumed by their thoughts of how to fix the broken world. Morpheus and Sadal Suud, however, stayed behind, discussing the quest and revisiting Morpheus’ original ideas. Together, they worked through the complexities of their choices.

As the gods slept, a soft glow surrounded their ship, a protective aura that offered reassurance. In the morning, they awoke to begin their day, the quiet stillness of dawn reflecting their inner turmoil.

When Morpheus approached his father at the breakfast table, Labrum raised a hand. "Not yet, my son. We speak after breakfast."

"There was a glow around our spaceship," Labrum said, his voice laced with curiosity. "Does anyone know why?"

"We noticed it, but we don't understand the cause," one of the gods replied, exchanging uncertain glances.

"I know why, Father," Morpheus said, his tone steady and assured. "Sadal Suud and I made the decision to confront all the challenges ahead, whatever the outcomes may be."

Labrum nodded, a knowing look in his eyes. "I suspected as much. This glow is the result of your actions, Morpheus—and Sadal Suud. It's a sign from us all that we are on the right path and making the correct decisions. Individually or together, you both have the power to manifest this light. You are both extraordinary in your strength."

Labrum paused, then asked, "Are all the gods and goddesses united with you, Morpheus?"

"Yes," one of the gods answered, his voice resolute. "We stand together, no matter where this journey takes us."

Morpheus took a deep breath, his resolve strengthening. "We will go back in time together. I will approach Uranus first and speak with him. If he continues to defy the natural order, I will end his life. Then, I will release his children and see if they carry any honor. If not, they, too, will face the same fate. All of you will remain ready to assist, lending your powers and, if necessary, your strength in the physical realm."

Labrum spoke first, his voice filled with unwavering support. "I agree."

"Agree," Denab affirmed.

"Agree," Wega echoed.

"Agree," Denebola added.

"Agree," Rasalhague affirmed.

"Agree," Zaniah echoed, her voice steady.

"Agree," Achernar said, a firm tone to his words.

"Agree," Capella agreed, her gaze steady.

"Agree," Sirius followed, his voice unwavering.

"Agree," Terebellum said, voice resolute.

"Agree," Kochab added.

“Agree,” Rastaban echoed.

“Agree,” Sadal Suud affirmed, her eyes locked with Morpheus, her support clear.

CHAPTER 18

Understanding or Battle

The crew began preparing for the quest, each member readying themselves and the two-time machine shuttles. In the first shuttle were Labrum, Denab, Morpheus, Sadal Suud, Kochab, and Rastaban. In the second shuttle were Wega, Denebola, Rasalhague, Zaniah, Achernar, Capella, Sirius, and Terebellum. Supplies were carefully divided between the two shuttles, including food, clothing, tents, and a cloaking device to protect both the time machines and their camp.

Once the shuttles were fully stocked, Labrum spoke, his voice firm. "We need to secure the spaceship *UNIV ORION* and set the computers to monitor the ship's status."

Turning to the group, Labrum added, "One last feast before we venture into Earth's past. Tonight, we'll review the plans and strategy for the quest."

As the crew gathered around the table, Morpheus began reviewing the plans with the family. As they ate, the atmosphere was a mixture of tension and camaraderie.

"I'll begin with Uranus," Morpheus explained. "I will speak with him first. Depending on how he responds, I'll signal for everyone to join the fight. Otherwise, stay alert for any other complications. Once I release his children, the next challenge will begin. We'll have to see how things unfold with Cronus and his offspring."

The meal was a hearty one, filled with laughter and good food. After dinner, the crew relaxed, talking and enjoying each other's company, trying to ease the weight of the task ahead. As the evening drew to a close, Labrum rose, his voice commanding yet gentle. "Let's rest for the night and prepare for the quest. We rise early tomorrow to begin."

Everyone exchanged their "Good nights" and retreated to their sleeping chambers.

In their private chamber, Morpheus and Sadal Suud embraced, their lips meeting in a tender kiss. Slowly, they undressed each other, their movements gentle and filled with love. Their connection deepened, and eventually, they fell asleep in each other's arms, the quiet of the night enveloping them.

The next morning, they prepared for the journey ahead. The gods and goddesses gathered in the Time Machine Shuttle Chamber, checking the time placement coordinates one final time.

Labrum addressed the group, starting with the first shuttle. "Is shuttle one ready?"

Denab nodded, answering firmly, "Yes."

Labrum then turned to shuttle two. "And Shuttle Two?"

Wega responded with a simple "Yes."

MORPHEUS

The time machine shuttles launched, taking roughly a day to reach the time of Uranus and Cronus. Upon arrival, they set up camp near the beginning of Uranus's era. Wega immediately activated the cloaking device and the protection grid around the shuttles and their camp, ensuring their safety from any unwanted attention. Each god and goddess took their designated role in setting up the camp, working efficiently as a team.

Once everything was in place, Labrum turned to Morpheus. "Are you ready to visit Uranus?"

Morpheus nodded. "Yes, Father."

Labrum gave the others final instructions. "Stay alert for any complications, but keep your distance. Watch over Morpheus and remain out of sight unless needed."

With that, Morpheus set off toward Uranus. As he approached, Uranus noticed him and asked, "Who are you?"

"My name is Morpheus, and I'm a friend of the god Uranus," Morpheus replied calmly.

Uranus raised an eyebrow. "Are you sure about that?"

Morpheus stood firm. "Yes. I am your friend."

Just then, Gaia approached and asked, "Who are you?"

"I'm Morpheus, and I'm a friend to the goddess Gaia," Morpheus said, offering a respectful nod.

"Where do you come from?" Gaia asked, curiosity in her voice.

"I come from planet Earth," Morpheus answered.

"This planet is barren," Uranus said, his voice tinged with pride. "I created this land for my wife and me to give birth to life. How do you survive in such a barren world?"

Morpheus smiled, a hint of resilience in his eyes. "There are creatures to eat, and the rains provide me with water."

Uranus considered this for a moment. "You are a creative person, Morpheus."

"It's all about survival in a harsh world," Morpheus replied.

Gaia's expression softened. "Would you like some food and water?"

"Yes, thank you," Morpheus said. He turned his attention back to Uranus. "So, you created this land?"

Uranus nodded proudly. "Yes, I did."

Gaia smiled warmly. "If you'd like, you can rest here, free of worry."

Morpheus looked at her with gratitude. "That would be nice, Gaia. Thank you."

MORPHEUS

The following day, Uranus woke Morpheus and asked, "Would you like something to eat?"

"Yes, Uranus," Morpheus replied.

"I have tasks to attend to," Uranus said. "Can you help Gaia while I'm away?"

"Of course," Morpheus agreed.

As Uranus departed, Morpheus turned to Gaia, only to find her in tears. "What's the matter, Gaia?" he asked, his voice filled with concern.

"I have children in my womb," she said, her voice trembling, "But Uranus won't let them be born."

"Is there anything I can do to help?" Morpheus asked, his heart aching for her.

"Can you speak to Uranus? Ask him to let my children be born," Gaia pleaded.

"I will speak to him," Morpheus promised, his resolve firm.

When Uranus returned, Morpheus approached him calmly. "Your wife was crying about the children."

"That's none of your concern," Uranus snapped, his anger flaring. "It's between me and her."

Morpheus met his gaze. “Uranus, do you love your wife, Gaia?”

“She is mine,” Uranus replied curtly. “That is all.”

“You claim her as yours simply because she is a woman,” Morpheus said, his tone sharp.

“Yes,” Uranus replied, his answer cold.

Morpheus stepped closer, his voice soft yet unwavering. “Where I come from, women are the source of life and beauty. They are essential to existence.”

“I won’t have this conversation with you,” Uranus growled, his fury simmering beneath the surface. Over time, his resentment toward Gaia grew, his anger festering at her complaints to Morpheus.

Morpheus, ever patient, tried again. “Uranus, you are the creator of life on this planet. You have the power to build a civilization, a future for all.”

Uranus sneered, dismissing his words. “I don’t care about your ‘information,’” he spat. “And no, I will not comply.”

Morpheus didn’t back down. “I know your children will seek revenge on you, Uranus. But more than that, I know that you and one of your children will be the source of corruption in the future. You started the cycle of hatred that you’ve passed on, and now, I’m here to stop it.”

Uranus's eyes narrowed. "I am a god of this planet. I will do as I please with this world, Morpheus."

"The prophecy of your children avenging you is true," Morpheus said, his voice heavy with the weight of destiny. "But I'm here to prevent the destruction of the future."

"Then it's a war you want!" Uranus roared, his anger uncontrollable.

"No," Morpheus replied calmly. "I want to stop you from hurting your family, from ruining the future. I need you to release your children. Show mercy. Be kind to Gaia and to your family. Be the god this world needs."

Uranus's fury reached its peak. "I am the god of this world! It's my way or no way!"

"Do you have an army to fight?" Morpheus asked, his voice calm yet firm.

"No," Uranus admitted, his pride undiminished.

"So, it's just you, and you want to fight me?" Morpheus asked, his voice barely a whisper.

"Yes," Uranus hissed. "And I will win because I am a god, and you are nothing."

Uranus's body began to swell, growing larger and more imposing. Morpheus's eyes flickered with a quiet intensity. "Are you sure you want this war?"

"Yes," Uranus snarled.

In response, Morpheus began to glow, his form growing larger than Uranus's. The air around them crackled with energy, the tension between them palpable.

"I am the god of this planet and the new life it shall bear," Morpheus declared, his voice steady but filled with authority. "You will either comply with my will, or you will be gone."

In response, Uranus lunged at Morpheus in a violent attack. But with a swift motion, Morpheus seized Uranus, lifting him effortlessly. "It's over for you, Uranus," he said with finality.

Morpheus looked down at his foe, his tone cold but measured. "You created a world, a civilization, without fulfilling your purpose. You sowed chaos and strife, and now, you must answer for it. I charge you with treason against humanity. Your punishment is just."

Morpheus continued, his eyes unwavering. "In your death, you have also created Aphrodite, a beautiful woman born from the very act that sealed your fate."

Without hesitation, Morpheus walked toward the sea, cutting off Uranus's testicles and letting them fall into the water. Then, with a motion of finality, he hurled Uranus toward the Sun, watching as his body was consumed by flames.

From the foam of the sea, Aphrodite emerged, born of Uranus's blood. Gaia, watching the events unfold, turned to Morpheus. "Are we safe from Uranus now?"

"Yes," Morpheus replied. "Uranus is gone. Your children are free now, Gaia. Let them be born."

Gaia's voice softened with gratitude. "Thank you, Morpheus."

Gaia's twelve children, the youngest of whom was Cronus, gathered around. The children thanked Morpheus, but Cronus, ever defiant, was silent.

Morpheus addressed them all. "I ask you now—will you follow the laws of this world? Will you live in peace?"

Cronus, still brimming with defiance, stepped forward. "Why should we follow any laws?"

Gaia placed a hand on Cronus's shoulder. "This man has saved you and your siblings, Cronus."

Morpheus nodded. "As a god of this world, I want all of you to live a peaceful life—without bloodshed, hatred, or harm to others."

Gaia, understanding the weight of Morpheus's words, said, "I will follow your laws for the sake of my children and for myself."

The other eleven children agreed, their voices unified in assent.

But Cronus's pride burned bright. "I will follow the laws of my father, Uranus. I am the king now."

Morpheus's gaze hardened as he looked at Gaia. "I'll be watching, Gaia. If Cronus strays from the path, I will stop him before it's too late."

Gaia, sensing the looming danger, asked, "Can we walk and talk, Morpheus?"

"Yes," he replied. Together, they walked into the woods, their steps quiet on the earth.

Gaia, her voice gentle but filled with something more, asked, "Are you truly a god, Morpheus?"

"I am," he replied simply.

Gaia, drawn to Morpheus, looked at him with longing, attempting to seduce him. But Morpheus, sensing her intentions, spoke firmly. "I am with another, Gaia. She is my soulmate, the love of my heart."

Gaia persisted. "A god can have more than one love, can't he?"

Morpheus shook his head. "In your world, perhaps. But not here, not on Earth."

Gaia's gaze softened. "We come from a world that was destroyed. Uranus and I were cast here, forced to begin anew."

"I know of your history," Morpheus said, his tone sympathetic. "That is why I saved your children. But if Cronus does not heed my laws, I will return to destroy him. There are things beyond explanation. Some events must unfold on their own. I am only here to stop evil."

Gaia, undeterred, tried once more to seduce him. But Morpheus, standing firm, stopped her. "Enough, Gaia. We are done here."

With those final words, Morpheus said his goodbyes. "Take care of your children, Gaia. But know this—if Cronus challenges the balance of this Earth, he will lose."

And with that, Morpheus left, knowing that the future of this world and its gods hung precariously in the balance.

Morpheus returned to camp with his family and crew, and as he approached, Labrum and Denab hurried over to greet him. Sadal Suud, full of joy, ran toward him, leaping into his arms and showering him with kisses. Denab, smiling warmly, kissed Morpheus on the cheek. "I'm glad you're safe," she said.

The other gods gathered around one by one, each offering their greetings. The air was filled with relief and camaraderie. Labrum, his tone turning serious, said, "Let's sit and talk about Uranus."

Morpheus glanced at Sadal Suud and asked, "Were you watching?"

Sadal Suud's eyes sparkled with mischief. "Yes, I was. And when Gaia tried to tempt you, claiming 'Gods have many women,' and you firmly said, 'I am with a woman, my soulmate, and the love of my heart,' I couldn't have been prouder." She smiled mischievously. "You're in for it tonight, Morpheus."

The other gods laughed in unison, their teasing lightening the mood. "You're in trouble, Morpheus," they joked.

"You made your wife very happy by refusing Gaia's advances," Denab added.

Labrum chuckled before gesturing for attention. "Can we return to the matter at hand? Morpheus, tell us what happened with Uranus and fill in the blanks."

Morpheus took a deep breath and began, his voice steady. "Uranus wasn't a wise god. He was selfish, like a spoiled child with no real understanding of his role. Gaia, on the other hand, was far more intelligent and more compassionate. She cared deeply for her children. When they were finally freed from her womb, they thanked me, but Cronus—he still harbored rage. I warned him. I told him if he broke my laws as a god, I would return and destroy him, just as I did with his father."

Labrum leaned in, his gaze sharp. "And what do you think of Cronus?"

Morpheus hesitated, his thoughts clouded. "I'm not sure yet, Father. I'll handle him as I did Uranus—attempt to reason with him first. If he refuses to listen, I'll take the same actions. But I'm careful with how much I alter the timeline. I don't want to disturb the natural course of life any more than necessary."

Labrum nodded thoughtfully. “Everything played out as it did before, except for the blood of Uranus.”

Morpheus agreed. “Yes. It’s as it was meant to be.”

“If Cronus breaks the laws,” Labrum said, “You’ll act as before, but things will inevitably go awry.”

“Yes, Father,” Morpheus replied, then shifted his gaze to Denab. “Is there any food? I’m starving.”

Denab smiled. “Yes, we were just about to eat ourselves.”

Wega, always pragmatic, asked, “What do we do now, Morpheus?”

“We wait and see what Cronus does,” Morpheus answered, his tone thoughtful but resigned.

Just as he finished speaking, an alarm blared from the ship’s remote controls, cutting through the conversation. Labrum and Wega exchanged quick glances before heading toward the time machine to investigate the disturbance.

CHAPTER 19

Spaceship Troubles

Labrum gathered the crew and addressed them with urgency. "We need to return to the ship and resolve these issues," he said. "We'll split the team. Time Machine Shuttle One will take us back, and Time Machine Shuttle Two will remain here. Morpheus, Sadal Suud, Sirius, and Terebellum will stay behind with all the supplies. The rest of us will head back to the ship to investigate."

Turning to Morpheus, Labrum added, "If we need you, you and the others must leave immediately. Don't wait for the shuttle—travel individually through time. It's faster. But until then, monitor Cronus and his family. If something happens here, finish the job with Cronus, but if we call for you, drop everything and come back."

Labrum, along with nine crew members, departed in Time Machine Shuttle One. The journey back to the ship took a week—time travel via shuttle was far slower than individual time jumps, which only required a day to cross the same temporal distance. Once the crew arrived, Labrum contacted Morpheus.

"We're here at the ship," Labrum reported. "I'll notify you once we know more about the problem."

Meanwhile, Morpheus and his small team—Sadal Suud, Sirius, and Terebellum—remained vigilant, observing Cronus and his family. During their watch, Morpheus took the opportunity to check on Aphrodite, who resided on the island of Cyprus.

Aphrodite, the goddess of love and beauty, wandered the island carefree, basking in her own radiance. When Morpheus visited her for the first time, her eyes lit up with interest.

"Who are you, Morpheus?" she asked, her voice silky and curious.

"I am not here for romance, Aphrodite," Morpheus replied calmly. "My heart already belongs to another."

Intrigued, Aphrodite leaned closer. "Tell me about her."

Morpheus spoke of Sadal Suud, his soulmate, the goddess he cherished above all else. "She is beautiful and kind, the most important being in my life."

Though Aphrodite's expression remained composed, a fire burned inside her, and Morpheus's loyalty only made her more determined to win him over. Still, Morpheus stood firm.

"If you cannot behave with dignity and grace, you can stay here alone," he said sharply. "Goodbye, Aphrodite. I'll return only to help you when needed."

With that, Morpheus left Aphrodite behind and traveled to check on Gaia.

Gaia greeted him warmly when he arrived. "Hello, Morpheus."

"Hello, Gaia. How are things on Earth?"

"Peaceful for now," she said.

"And how are King Cronus and your other children?"

"They are well," Gaia replied, though there was a flicker of something unspoken in her tone. As their conversation continued, Gaia once again attempted to seduce Morpheus. Her eyes lingered, and her words grew soft and suggestive.

"I'm sorry, Gaia, but this can't happen," Morpheus said firmly.

Gaia tilted her head, perplexed. "Why do you resist, Morpheus? This is who we are. The gods of this era live without restraint or rules. We embrace our nature."

"That is precisely the problem," Morpheus said. "I come from a time where love is sacred—where loyalty to one woman is an unshakable bond. The chaos you live in is born from a lack of laws, restraint, and discipline."

Gaia's expression darkened, but Morpheus continued. "I am not here to indulge in temptation. My purpose is to help you and the others—to guide you toward a better future. I have a wife, Sadal Suud, and she is enough for me."

Gaia sighed, sensing Morpheus's resolve. "Perhaps your way is better," she murmured, though her words carried no conviction.

"I hope you will see it one day," Morpheus replied.

"I'm sorry, Morpheus," Gaia said softly. "You saved my children, and I should be grateful."

"That's all right," Morpheus replied. "As long as you understand now." He paused briefly, then asked, "Has King Cronus found a wife yet?"

"Yes, he has. His sister, Rhea," Gaia answered. Her expression grew somber. "Cronus has also heard a prophecy—that his children will one day overthrow his kingship."

Morpheus's expression darkened at this revelation. Gaia noticed his reaction and tilted her head, curiosity flickering in her eyes. "Why does this trouble you, Morpheus?"

"I can't share that with you, Gaia," Morpheus said firmly. "There are things I know that must remain unsaid. My purpose here is to protect both gods and people, but I cannot interfere in the natural course of life—unless there's a direct threat. Order must be maintained above all else."

Gaia frowned. "But what does that mean, Morpheus? What purpose do we all serve?"

Morpheus's tone softened as he explained. "You, Gaia, are the goddess of the Earth, and Uranus was the god of the Sky. Both of you were created with a purpose—to nurture and sustain this world. My role is different. I am here to guide and ensure wrongful acts do not threaten the balance of life, whether they come from gods or humankind. I exist to protect the future—your future and theirs."

Gaia nodded slowly, the weight of his words settling over her. "I understand, Morpheus. I will follow your laws and maintain order."

"That's good to hear," Morpheus said. "But I will also need your children to do the same. Order must not fall apart because of chaos or disobedience."

"I'll do my best to guide them," Gaia promised.

Morpheus offered a faint smile of reassurance. "Goodbye for now, Gaia."

With that, he left Gaia, resolute in his mission. As he returned to his team, he couldn't help but think of the challenges ahead—of Cronus, of Aphrodite, and a world teetering between chaos and order.

Morpheus called the ship to speak with Labrum. "What's happening with the ship?" he asked.

"We're still investigating the issue," Labrum replied. "The sensors were triggered, but we haven't pinpointed the cause yet."

"Do you need me or the other crew members back?" Morpheus asked.

"Not for now," Labrum said. "How are things on Earth?"

"We're holding steady," Morpheus assured him. "Do you need to speak to any of the others?"

"No," Labrum said.

"Understood. I'll stay in touch, Father," Morpheus said.

Labrum nodded. "We'll keep you updated."

Morpheus ended the call and turned back to the others at the campsite. Sirius leaned forward. "How are things with the Titans?"

"We may have a problem with Cronus after all," Morpheus admitted.

"That's not good," Terebellum said gravely. "The cycle of resentment has been passed down through the generation."

Sadal Suud's expression turned anxious. "Morpheus, you must stop Cronus before it's too late."

Morpheus nodded thoughtfully. "Cronus's hatred stems from his time trapped in Gaia's womb. That anger hasn't faded. This is why we're here—to prevent him from devouring Rhea's children before the prophecy unfolds. I spoke with Labrum, but they still haven't resolved the ship's issues. Right now, we're playing a waiting game—both with Cronus and the ship."

Just then, Labrum's voice crackled through the communicator. "Morpheus, bring the crew back to the ship immediately."

Morpheus turned to the others. “Clean up the campsite and load everything into the time machine shuttle. Leave the cloaking device on.”

Once everything was packed, they prepared to time travel individually. Morpheus carefully marked the exact moment they were leaving Earth’s past to ensure a precise return. Traveling individually took a day—faster than using the shuttle.

When they returned to the ship, the crew assembled on the bridge, where Labrum was waiting for them.

Morpheus approached him. “What’s going on?”

“There’s another spaceship in the area,” Labrum said.

Morpheus frowned. “Is it one of ours?”

“No,” Labrum replied firmly. “If it were, the sensors would have identified it immediately.”

“Have they tried to contact us?” Morpheus asked.

Labrum shook his head. “No.”

“Have *we* reached out to them?”

“No,” Labrum said again.

Morpheus paused. “So, what do we do now?”

“We’re waiting for a response from them,” Labrum explained.

Morpheus stepped closer, his gaze sharp. “Can I try something to determine their intentions?”

Labrum turned to him. “What do you have in mind?”

“I can transport myself and be invisible and listen to their talk and intentions,” Morpheus explained.

“Then do it, Son,” Labrum said. “Fast.”

Morpheus prepared himself and transported onto the other spaceship, carrying an open communicator so his crew could monitor everything. Labrum’s steady voice guided him as he entered.

Once aboard, Morpheus immediately noticed that the beings on this ship were unlike any he had seen before. Their appearance was strikingly different. Curious, he consulted his portable computer, but no information about them existed in the Universe’s known records. These people were a mystery.

Listening to their conversations through the communicator, Morpheus learned a troubling truth: they were from an outer galaxy, far on the edge of the Universe, from a planet called Tarvos. The inhabitants, known as Travosians, were an aggressive and dangerous race. It was the Travosians who had brought Uranus and Gaia to Earth. They had sown seeds of hatred, greed, and the lust for power—corrupting both the gods and humanity.

“They intend to continue their chaos,” Morpheus whispered into the communicator. “They didn’t expect another ship to guard Earth. Worse still, they've realized that Uranus failed to poison the planet. Now, their hopes rest on Cronus, through Tartarus, to finish what Uranus couldn't."

Morpheus returned to the *UNIV ORION* and immediately called for a council meeting with the gods and goddesses.

"Will the ship alert us if the Travosians make a move?" Morpheus asked.

"Yes," Labrum confirmed.

The crew gathered around as Labrum explained the situation. "These people are the true poison behind this world. They didn't expect us to interfere."

"We upset their plans with Uranus's death," Morpheus added. "They're monitoring Earth and Cronus. Their technology is primitive compared to ours, but they're persistent—and they're dangerous. Cronus is now their last chance to poison humanity's future."

Achernar leaned forward. "We need to defend Earth."

"Morpheus pinpointed it," Wega agreed. "Uranus and Cronus were their pawns."

Rasalhague spoke with caution. "We need more information before we act. What about Cronus?"

"He's waiting for us, as well as the time machine shuttle," Morpheus said. "For now, we have the advantage of time. I'll board their ship again and confront them directly while you communicate from here."

Labrum considered the plan. "Let's try contacting them first. If we understand their intentions, we can respond appropriately."

Labrum initiated the communication, and after a moment, a voice crackled over the speakers. "This is General Mundilfari of the planet Tarvos. We brought Uranus and Gaia to Earth. Tell me—what happened to Uranus?"

Labrum replied evenly. "Why are you here? Is this about Uranus, or is there something more?"

"We are here for Uranus and Gaia," General Mundilfari stated.

"Cronus killed Uranus long ago," Labrum revealed.

"Cronus?" Mundilfari repeated, his voice edged with disbelief.

"Yes, General," Labrum confirmed.

Mundilfari's tone hardened. "What is your purpose here, Labrum?"

"We are the protectors of the Universe," Labrum answered firmly. "You come from a coalition of planets that defied the Universe Council. Are you here to wage war on Earth?"

"No," Mundilfari replied. "We seek only knowledge—what happened to Uranus, Gaia, and their family."

"We have records from that time," Labrum said. "I'll provide you with copies, but once you have them, you must leave this solar system and return to Tarvos."

"What planet are you from?" Mundilfari demanded.

"I'm not at liberty to say," Labrum countered. "We don't know your true intentions."

"We have no hostile intentions," the general insisted.

"That's not good enough for me," Labrum replied curtly. "Do you want the records or not?"

"Yes," Mundilfari answered. "Send them over."

With that, the communication ended.

The *UNIV ORION* council reconvened immediately on the bridge. Capella sent an urgent transmission to Achilles to report the Tarvosians' presence. The response was swift.

The King of Achilles's voice boomed over the line. "Tarvosians! They are a scourge. They've come to destroy Earth and all connected to it. I'll dispatch reinforcements to aid you in their destruction. My ships will arrive in two weeks. Hold your position until then."

At the meeting, Morpheus spoke calmly but firmly. "We don't need to worry about them."

Wega raised an eyebrow, smirking. “And why not? Are you going to *crush* them yourself, Morpheus?”

Morpheus’s expression darkened. “Yes, Wega.”

The room fell silent as Morpheus’s words sank in.

Suddenly, Capella burst in, breathless. “The King of Achilles has ordered us to destroy them now.”

Labrum turned to Morpheus. “Are you serious about this?”

“We don’t need to fear them,” Morpheus replied. “No matter how vindictive they are.”

Labrum’s voice tightened. “The King has spoken. Reinforcements are on the way. We’ve been ordered to destroy the Tarvosians.”

Morpheus’s gaze was unwavering. “We *still* need to know their true intentions.”

CHAPTER 20

Battle with Tarvosians

Morpheus thought about his next move carefully before reaching out to Labrum. "Let's come up with a plan," Morpheus said, his voice calm but resolute.

"What plan, Morpheus?" Labrum asked.

"Our other spaceships will take two weeks to arrive," Morpheus explained. "That gives us time to understand the Tarvosians' intentions and strike if necessary before reinforcements get here. I'll turn invisible, board their ship, and observe. We'll hear and see everything through the communicator."

Everyone nodded in agreement. For now, it was the best course of action.

"Be careful, Morpheus," Labrum added.

Invisible, Morpheus transported himself onto the Tarvosians' ship. Moving silently, he made his way to their bridge, his communicator relaying everything back to the crew. From the shadows, he listened, observing the alien crew and their primitive systems.

“Their technology is basic,” Morpheus whispered into the communicator. “But we don’t yet know their combat capabilities.”

Labrum’s voice crackled back. “Leave a second communicator on the bridge and search for weapons. We need to know if they’re a threat.”

“Understood, Father,” Morpheus replied.

Moving through the ship, Morpheus found their weapons cache. Though their systems were primitive, their firearms were anything but—they were highly advanced, far beyond what one might expect from their crude technology. Morpheus’s concern deepened when he overheard key information:

“They’re waiting for reinforcements,” Morpheus said, his tone grim. “They have a fleet coming.”

Labrum’s voice grew urgent. “Morpheus, get back here now! The King of Achilles was right—this race will destroy everything if we give them the chance. Earth will be their prize.”

Morpheus reappeared aboard the *UNIV ORION*. Labrum addressed the crew. “We now know their intentions—and we must act. They’re not just angry about Uranus; they’re planning to corrupt Earth’s people and use them as allies to overtake the Universe. If they can’t, they’ll kill humanity instead.”

Morpheus frowned, deep in thought. “They’ve got the firepower to harm us, even in space. And worse—two fleets arriving simultaneously could mean total annihilation.”

"I thought the Universe Council of Planets resolved these conflicts?" Morpheus asked aloud.

Labrum sighed. "Not all planets wanted peace. The Tarvosians agreed to remain on their own world because, at the time, their technology wasn't advanced enough to pose a threat. Clearly, that's changed."

Morpheus nodded. "We're facing the same problem we've been trying to prevent on Earth: advanced weapons, corruption, and greed. First, I'll take out their communications. Then, we'll deal with their reinforcements."

"Can we calculate when their ships will arrive?" Morpheus asked.

Denab quickly responded, "Yes, we can predict their entry into our orbit."

Labrum turned to his son. "Morpheus, how are you so certain about all this? Your powers seem to adapt perfectly to each crisis."

Morpheus shrugged slightly. "I don't know, Father. When the problems come, it's as though the answers are just… there. Like my powers are designed for the challenges we face."

Morpheus considered this, then asked, "What weapons do we have?"

“Ship-mounted lasers and hand-held weapons for ground battles,” Labrum replied. “They’re strong enough to destroy planets or hold off an invasion.”

“Alert our ships for a battle,” Morpheus said, determination hardening his voice. “I’ll be in space when their fleet enters orbit. Denab, can we open communications with both their ships and ours?”

“Why?” Labrum asked, narrowing his gaze.

“I want to give the Tarvosians one chance to understand the reality they face—*me*,” Morpheus said.

Labrum shook his head. “We already know their intentions. They’re the evil you’ve been searching for. They brought Uranus and Cronus to Earth.”

Morpheus’s voice softened but carried weight. “And yet, they were supposed to remain on their planet. You and Mother put me on Earth to learn about humans and understand their struggles and ways. I did that. Now you tell me I’m the god of this world, with my wife. I will fulfill that role. I will protect the humans, the Achillesians, and the Universe.”

“We will follow your lead, from one king to another,” Labrum said.

“Have I ever let you down?” Morpheus asked.

“No,” Labrum replied firmly. The rest of the crew echoed in unison, “No.”

"Denab, open communications with the Tarvosians," Morpheus instructed.

Labrum added sternly, "Do not reveal who we are."

Morpheus nodded. "I understand, Father."

After some effort, Denab established contact. "General Mundilfari, Morpheus requests to speak with you."

"I will speak with him," the General replied.

"Good day, General Mundilfari," Morpheus began, his tone steady and commanding. "I know why you are here."

"What nonsense are you talking about, Morpheus?" the General snapped.

"Allow me to introduce myself properly," Morpheus said. "I am the god of a new life for Earth. I know of the Peace Treaty of the Universe—a treaty you rejected—and I know your true intentions here."

The General scoffed. "You know nothing."

"On the contrary," Morpheus continued calmly. "I've been on your ship. I placed recording devices and listened to everything you said, every move you made. I know about your weapons and your reinforcements heading this way. Your fleet is under our surveillance, and our ships are already en route to confront you. If you proceed with this war, you will lose before it begins."

General Mundilfari hesitated. “How can I believe such bold claims?”

“To prove it,” Morpheus said smoothly, “I’ll show you what I can do. Your Lieutenant just checked the weapons, didn’t he?”

The General frowned. “How could you know that?”

“I’m closer than you think, General. Perhaps I’m sitting beside you now,” Morpheus replied.

“Impossible!” the General snapped.

“To prove my point, I’ll hit you in the head.”

A loud *smack* echoed over the communicator.

“Who hit me?” General Mundilfari shouted, startled.

“I did,” Morpheus said. “Now, listen carefully. You will contact your reinforcements and order them to return home. You will leave this solar system immediately.”

General Mundilfari seethed. “You leave me no choice, Morpheus. I’ll withdraw... for now.”

“One more thing, General,” Morpheus added, his voice carrying an edge. “If you wish to travel through this Universe in peace, you will sign the Peace Treaty with my people and me. But heed this warning: if you break your word, your planet will be my prize, and I will ensure an end to your kind.”

"How can I contact you to sign the Peace Treaty?" General Mundilfari asked.

"Return to your leaders and inform them of the Peace Treaty," Morpheus replied. "When you are ready, call my name, and I will appear."

The General hesitated but finally agreed. "And our weapons?"

"I will disengage your weapons once the Peace Treaty is signed," Morpheus said.

General Mundilfari relayed orders to his fleet. One by one, the Tarvosians' ships turned and began their retreat. Their scanner confirmed the ships were leaving orbit, and the crew on the *UNIV ORION* breathed a collective sigh of relief.

Labrum turned to the crew. "Prepare to receive the leaders of the other ships. This situation is far from over."

Morpheus left to prepare, and Sadal Suud joined him. As she adjusted her dress, she whispered softly, "I love you, Morpheus."

Morpheus smiled, walked over, and kissed her. "I love you, too, honey."

Moments later, the leaders of the Achillesian ships were transported aboard the *UNIV ORION* for a meeting. Labrum greeted them formally and gestured for everyone to take their seats.

Once settled, Labrum began. “We have much to discuss. Morpheus infiltrated the Tarvosians’ ship, uncovered their plans, and planted devices to monitor them. The Tarvosians’ mission was to invade Earth, destroy its people, and spread corruption throughout the Universe—Uranus and Cronus were just the beginning.

“However,” Labrum continued, “Morpheus confronted General Mundilfari directly. He made it clear that any act of aggression would lead to their destruction. The Tarvosians agreed to sign the *Peace Treaty of the Universe* and withdrew their fleet. For now, they are returning to their home planet, Tarvos.”

A murmur spread through the leaders. Captain Howse finally spoke. “Morpheus, you’ve saved countless lives. The Tarvosians were a threat to us all.”

“And you managed this without a single shot fired,” Captain Shrowd added. “You are a true Achillesian, Morpheus. You’ve earned the respect of our people and our Universe.”

Labrum nodded. “In honor of Morpheus’s heroic deeds, we will celebrate tonight. He stopped a war and gave us hope for peace.”

The captains returned to their ships to prepare for the celebration. Word of Morpheus’s actions spread quickly across the Achillesian fleet, his name spoken with reverence and awe.

Meanwhile, Labrum contacted the King of Achilles to share the news. “Morpheus has secured a promise from the Tarvosians to sign the Peace Treaty,” Labrum said.

The King's voice boomed through the communicator. "This is excellent news! And what of Uranus and Cronus? Has the threat been neutralized?"

"Uranus has been resolved," Labrum confirmed. "But Cronus remains. Morpheus will deal with it in time."

Satisfied, the King replied, "Let me know when the Peace Treaty is signed. Achilles will celebrate this victory for the ages."

That evening, aboard the *UNIV ORION*, preparations for the celebration were underway. Morpheus and Sadal Suud returned to their chamber to prepare.

"You are the prophecy to our people," Sadal Suud said softly, her eyes full of love. "And I love you, Morpheus."

"I love you too, Sadal Suud," Morpheus replied, drawing her close. "Let's shower together before the celebration."

Their embrace deepened, and they made love under the warm cascade of water. Later, they dressed in ceremonial attire, elegant and regal for the occasion.

By nightfall, the Achillesian leaders and their crews—over one hundred guests—arrived aboard the *UNIV ORION*. The halls of the ship buzzed with laughter, music, and the clinking of glasses as the Achillesians celebrated their victory. Morpheus's name was on everyone's lips, and his deeds were already becoming legends.

Together, they honored Morpheus not just as a hero but as a symbol of hope for peace in the Universe

CHAPTER 21

Signing the Peace Treaty

All enjoyed the celebration, and thankfully, there were no casualties among the Tarvosians.

"Can I speak with King Saturn and the High Council of Achilles?" Morpheus asked Labrum.

Labrum's expression turned curious. "Why, Morpheus?"

"I need to visit the Tarvosians' planet to present the Peace Treaty and secure their signatures," Morpheus explained. "But before that, I require information from King Saturn about these people—their capabilities and the risks if they betray us."

Labrum nodded. "We'll arrange this before the other ships depart. You'll have the answers you need."

Without delay, Labrum contacted Achilles' planet and requested an audience with King Saturn and the High Council. The communication came through as a live video feed on a large monitor. Present at the meeting were King Saturn, the Council members, Labrum, Morpheus, the captains of the allied ships, and Morpheus's family and crew.

"These Tarvosians are deceitful in many ways," King Saturn said, his voice heavy with caution. "They may present one face but act with treachery."

The King and Council recommended that Morpheus take three spaceships as escorts during the signing of the treaty.

"You could be walking into a trap," King Saturn warned. "If that happens, no one will be able to assist you in time. I've heard of your strength and powers, Morpheus, but even you may find this challenge overwhelming."

The Council and the ship captains nodded in agreement.

Morpheus acknowledged their concerns. "I don't know the full extent of the Tarvosians' powers or their strength," he admitted. "But my priority is ensuring your people aren't harmed in any conflict that might arise."

The King turned to Labrum. "Have you witnessed Morpheus's abilities firsthand?"

"Yes, Your Majesty," Labrum replied. "As have the family and crew aboard this ship. Morpheus is formidable in ways I can scarcely describe."

King Saturn leaned forward, his tone curious but cautious. "Is there any way to test his powers further?"

"No, King Saturn," Labrum said firmly.

Morpheus interjected, "We can station our ships at the outskirts of their territory, prepared for battle if necessary. That way, I can proceed while ensuring the fleet remains ready to intervene."

The King and Council exchanged glances, eventually agreeing with the plan. The captains of the other ships also voiced their support.

Afterward, Labrum called a meeting with the captains, lieutenants, and Morpheus's family and crew. The discussion was broadcast across the ship's intercom for all personnel to hear.

"We will remain on the perimeter, ready for combat, while Morpheus conducts the treaty negotiations on the Tarvosians' planet," Labrum announced. "Morpheus will wear a communicator, enabling us to monitor everything in real-time—visuals, audio, and any potential threats. However, we must also consider the extent of Morpheus's powers. If he engages in combat, there's a possibility he could destroy the entire planet. We must prepare for the fallout, including debris that could endanger our ships."

Captain Shrowd raised an eyebrow. "Destroy a planet? That's impossible."

Captain Howse shook his head. "No one could achieve that, Labrum."

Labrum's gaze hardened. "Have you forgotten how Morpheus moved a comet from within our ship and obliterated it?"

Both captains looked incredulous. "We weren't there for that," they admitted.

"Well, everyone on this ship witnessed it," Labrum said sharply.

"I saw him hurl Uranus into the Sun," Sirius added, his voice tinged with awe.

"And did you see how Morpheus turned invisible to infiltrate the Tarvosians' ship?" Wega chimed in.

Morpheus raised a hand to calm the rising voices. "If things go wrong and you're forced to retreat, prioritize the safety of your crews and people. I'll handle the rest."

A tense silence followed as his words sank in. Everyone understood the gravity of the situation—and the potential consequences of Morpheus's unparalleled power.

Captain Howse turned to Morpheus, his tone cautious. "Can you be destructive if the situation calls for it?"

Morpheus met his gaze steadily. "I don't know the limits of what I can do. But when problems arise, I'll respond with the intensity necessary." He straightened. "Let's begin our journey to their planet. We'll discover the truth behind their words soon enough."

Labrum addressed the assembled captains. "Return to your ships and follow our lead. We'll keep you updated with any developments." Turning to his navigator, he added, "Denab, chart a course to the Tarvosians' planet and share the coordinates with the fleet."

"How long will it take to get there?" Morpheus asked.

"With our current speed, about a week," Denab replied.

Morpheus nodded, his expression resolute. “We need to remain vigilant during the entire journey. Keep a constant watch.”

The captains exchanged glances and agreed unanimously.

Morpheus continued, “If we encounter trouble upon arrival, we’ll use time travel as a last resort to extract ourselves. We can’t afford to be caught off guard. Stay connected—we’ll keep the intercoms open across all ships so we’re aware of each other’s situations at all times.”

As the Achillesian fleet approached the Tarvosians’ solar system, Morpheus addressed the group once more. “Remember, their spaceships are equipped with advanced weapons systems. It’s likely their planet has similar capabilities. Be cautious with our positioning—we don’t know the range of their planetary defenses or if they have support from neighboring systems.”

The fleet halted at the edge of the Tarvosians’ system, maintaining a safe distance. Morpheus’s voice came over the intercom. “Hold position and monitor for any Tarvosian ships. I’ll go ahead, invisible, to scout their planet, and I’ll also plant communicator devices to record their conversations. Report any unusual activity immediately.”

With that, Morpheus activated his invisibility and left the ship, a faint shimmer marking his departure before fading entirely. He approached the Tarvosians’ planet, noting a massive spaceship in orbit. Contemplating whether to investigate the ship, he decided to board. Once inside, Morpheus discovered the communicator recording devices were missing. While there, he overheard a conversation that confirmed his worst fears—the Tarvosians were planning an invasion of Earth and Achilles, with the ultimate goal of conquering the Universe.

Descending to the planet's surface, Morpheus sought out General Mundilfari. He found the General in a meeting with high-ranking officers, discussing their plans to dominate Earth, Achilles, and beyond.

Morpheus checked in with his fleet. "Status report," he said over the communicator.

Labrum's voice came through clearly. "No enemy ships have been detected so far. All systems are normal."

Morpheus relayed the details of the Tarvosians' invasion plan. Labrum's response was swift and firm. "There's no alternative, Morpheus. You need to eliminate them before they can execute their attack."

The other captains voiced their agreement. Morpheus stood in silence for a moment, weighing the gravity of the decision. Finally, he spoke. "Understood. I'll handle it. You focus on battling any ships that leave the planet, and I'll deal with the people and the planet itself."

He paused, considering the broader situation. "We should also scan the nearby planets and surrounding areas for additional Tarvosian ships," Morpheus added, relaying the plan to the captains.

When Morpheus arrived at General Mundilfari's meeting, he remained invisible, standing silently beside the General. His voice echoed in the hall, low and commanding. "Do you remember me, General Mundilfari? I am Morpheus, god of new life for planet Earth."

The General froze, his body trembling. His fear was palpable, and the other meeting attendees noticed his unease.

"General, are you all right?" asked Pyxis, King of Tarvos, his tone suspicious.

The General's voice quivered as he answered, "God Morpheus is here beside me. He's invisible."

King Pyxis frowned. "Expose yourself, God Morpheus."

Morpheus revealed himself, towering above the Meeting Chamber, his presence awe-inspiring and imposing. Gasps echoed through the chamber. King Pyxis recovered quickly and barked an order. "Kill him!"

Morpheus's voice boomed. "Are you sure about that? I have the advantage. Has the General told you my terms for sparing your lives?"

"I don't know what you told him," King Pyxis replied.

Morpheus stepped closer, his massive form casting a shadow over the chamber. "Think carefully, King. I'm here alone, yet I hold the upper hand over your planet and your people. The question is: do you want to live, or do you want to die? I could treat you as you've treated the planets you've conquered. But as a god, I offer you a choice—life or death. The power to decide lies with you."

Pyxis hesitated. "What are your terms, God Morpheus?"

"For starters, make the General pay for his lies," Morpheus said firmly. The King nodded in agreement, adding, "If he lied."

"I want a Peace Treaty with you and your people," Morpheus continued. "You will be free to travel the Universe peacefully, but if you cause any further harm or conflict, you will be eradicated."

King Pyxis nodded reluctantly. "Agreed." He turned to his guards. "Take General Mundilfari into custody. I will deal with him later." Then, to Morpheus, he asked, "Do you have the Peace Treaty?"

"I do," Morpheus replied.

But as Morpheus handed over the treaty, Pyxis whispered to one of his guards, instructing him to attack Morpheus. The captains, who were listening via communicator, overheard the betrayal and prepared for battle. Morpheus, fully aware of the King's intent, played along.

As Pyxis signed the treaty, Morpheus's body began to glow. His sensors alerted him to the guards' movements. Pyxis shouted, "Kill him!"

Morpheus reacted instantly. He grew in size, his glowing form radiating intense heat. Flames erupted around him as he seized both Pyxis and Mundilfari in his massive hands. "Now you will witness my fury," Morpheus thundered. "Your kingdom will burn, and you will burn with it."

The chamber erupted in chaos. People fled, but Morpheus raised a glowing hand, incinerating the fleeing crowds, buildings, and everything in his path. The General and King screamed as they were consumed in his fiery grasp. His burning gaze reduced the planet itself to a smoldering cinder.

From afar, aboard the fleet's ships, Sadal Suud felt Morpheus's fury through their connection. The crew watched in stunned silence as Morpheus obliterated the planet. Captains Howse and Shrowd, appalled by the destruction, transferred to Labrum's ship to confront him.

"This was too much!" Captain Howse exclaimed. "Morpheus destroyed an entire planet and its people."

Captain Shrowd agreed. "This isn't what we signed up for."

Labrum's tone was measured as he responded. "We followed King Saturn's orders. Morpheus gave the King of Tarvos every chance to sign the treaty peacefully. You heard the recordings yourself. The betrayal left him no choice."

The captains exchanged uneasy glances. Denab, meanwhile, stayed close to Sadal Suud, helping her cope with the overwhelming emotions from her bond with Morpheus.

After releasing his fury and calming himself, Morpheus reboarded *UNIV ORION.* As he stepped onto the bridge, the room fell silent. Everyone turned to face him.

"What's wrong?" Morpheus asked, his voice calm.

Labrum spoke up. "The captains weren't happy with how you handled the situation."

Morpheus frowned. "You've heard the recordings?"

"Yes," Labrum confirmed.

"Then, if I've broken any laws, take me to King Saturn and the High Council of Achilles," Morpheus said.

The two captains hesitated, but Zeus interjected. "If you bring Morpheus before the King and Council, and they find his actions justified, it'll reflect poorly on you both."

Labrum nodded. "Especially since the Tarvosians were already marked for destruction by the King and Council. The recordings clearly show Morpheus attempted to negotiate peace."

The captains relented. "We understand. We're sorry, Morpheus."

Labrum addressed the group. "Achillesians ended wars long ago, but the universe is changing. Morpheus acted to protect us all."

CHAPTER 22

King & Counsel

Labrum and the two captains received a summons from Achilles, requesting their presence for a report on the Tarvosian mission.

"Have either of you submitted grievances to the King or Council members?" Labrum asked the captains.

"No, Labrum," they replied in unison.

"Perhaps the king or council simply wants an update on the situation with the Tarvosians," Morpheus suggested.

"You might be right," Labrum agreed. He then made an announcement over the intercom to all three ships: "Attention, crew. We are heading to Achilles for a debriefing regarding the Tarvosians mission."

Morpheus addressed Labrum directly. "Did all three ships record my transmissions and the results of the destruction?"

"Yes," Labrum confirmed.

"And we were acting under orders from the King of Achilles, correct?"

"Absolutely," Labrum said firmly.

“Then we’ve done nothing wrong,” Morpheus said.

Labrum nodded, turning to his crew. “Let’s enjoy the journey back to Achilles. We’ll deal with the King and Council when the time comes.” Then, with a note of pride in his voice, he added, “Morpheus did the right thing by destroying the Tarvosians. I’m proud of my son.”

Achernar raised his voice enthusiastically. “Three cheers for Morpheus!”

The crew joined in, cheering loudly for Morpheus’s actions.

Later, Morpheus approached Labrum. “May I be excused to retire to my chamber?”

Labrum studied him with concern. “Morpheus, are you all right?”

“I’m just tired from the battle with the Tarvosians,” Morpheus replied.

“Do you want to visit the Medical Chamber?”

“No, Father. I’ll be fine,” Morpheus assured him.

Labrum turned to Sadal Suud. “Stay with him and make sure he’s okay.”

“I will,” Sadal Suud promised.

When Morpheus reached his chamber, he looked at Sadal Suud and said, "I'm going to lie down and rest."

Sadal Suud smiled softly. "I'll stay beside you, Honey."

As they both drifted into sleep, something unusual began to happen. Their bodies started to glow faintly, the light pulsing gently at first, then growing stronger. The glow intensified, spreading outward and filling the chamber. It wasn't long before the light began to radiate through the ship, capturing the attention of everyone onboard.

Alarmed, Labrum and Denab rushed toward Morpheus's chamber, followed closely by the rest of the family. When they opened the door, they were stunned by the sight. Morpheus and Sadal Suud lay in bed, surrounded by an intense, almost blinding glow.

Labrum and Denab called out, "Morpheus! Sadal Suud!"

At the sound of his name, Morpheus stirred. He leapt from the bed, instinctively ready to attack. His fiery eyes scanned the room, but then Labrum called again, his voice calm but firm. "Morpheus. It's me."

Morpheus blinked and seemed to come to his senses. "Father? What's happening?" He glanced around the chamber, noticing the glow enveloping everything. Alarmed, he turned to Sadal Suud and tried to wake her. When she awoke, she, too, was disoriented, rising to defend herself against an unseen threat.

“Sadal Suud!” Morpheus said urgently. “It’s me! It’s okay!”

Gradually, Sadal Suud calmed, her eyes refocusing on him. “What’s going on?” she asked, her voice trembling.

“I don’t know,” Morpheus admitted, his tone heavy with concern.

“You were glowing, and it was consuming the ship,” Denab said, her tone edging with concern and curiosity.

“Did anyone get hurt?” Morpheus asked quickly, his eyes scanning those gathered.

“No,” Labrum reassured him. “But we need to perform a full medical evaluation on you and your wife to understand what’s happening.”

Turning to Sirius and Terebellum, Labrum issued a directive. “Conduct a complete physical on Morpheus and Sadal Suud. This glowing phenomenon has now occurred three times—once before the battle and twice since. I want answers.”

Sirius and Terebellum worked diligently, running every conceivable test on Morpheus and Sadal Suud. Physically, both were in peak condition. Shifting their focus, they conducted psychological assessments. The results were striking: Morpheus and Sadal Suud displayed exceptional mental resilience and independence. But it was their combined energy that truly stood out. Together, their bond amplified their powers exponentially, creating a force unlike anything the universe had ever seen.

When the tests were complete, Sirius and Terebellum presented their findings to Labrum and Denab in the ship's conference room.

"They're both in excellent physical health," Sirius began. "Individually, they're already extraordinarily powerful. But together—when they channel their love for one another—their combined energy surpasses anything measurable in the known universe."

Labrum leaned forward, his brow furrowed. "Does this make them a threat to us? Or to the universe itself?"

Terebellum shook her head. "Quite the opposite. They're an extraordinary asset to the universe. Time and again, they've demonstrated their commitment to protecting others. Their glow is a reflection of their love—not just for each other but also for the people they defend."

Sirius added, "However, there's one thing to remember. Morpheus has a deep aversion to lies, deceit, and betrayal. His sense of justice is unwavering, and his wife shares his devotion to truth. This could lead to moments of intense action, as we've seen."

Labrum relaxed slightly, nodding as he absorbed the explanation. "So their glow represents the growth of their love and their dedication to those they protect."

"Precisely," Terebellum said with a small smile.

Labrum stood, his posture firm and authoritative. “Then we have nothing to fear. They are a blessing to the universe—and to us.”

As the three spaceships approached the planet Achilles, their sensors picked up an unusual event—a massive comet hurtling toward the planet. Alarmed, Labrum and Denab immediately summoned Morpheus and Sadal Suud to the bridge. The crew, sensing the urgency, quickly gathered there as well.

“What’s happening?” Morpheus asked as he entered.

“A comet is on a collision course with Achilles,” Labrum explained, his tone heavy with concern.

Without hesitation, Morpheus sprang into action. His body began to glow, an intense light emanating from him. Beside him, Sadal Suud started glowing as well, their combined energy illuminating the entire bridge.

Morpheus extended his glowing hands toward the approaching comet. The ship itself seemed to respond, glowing brighter as if empowered by their presence. On the other two ships, the crews watched in awe as the comet, once an unstoppable force, froze in its trajectory just outside the planet’s atmosphere.

With immense control, Morpheus manipulated the comet, holding it suspended in space. Then, in a remarkable display of power, he crushed it with his energy, reducing the massive celestial body to harmless space dust.

The communication channels lit up as Captain Shrowd and Captain Howse called Labrum's ship.

"What just happened?" Captain Shrowd asked, his voice tinged with disbelief.

"Morpheus and Sadal Suud stopped the comet and saved Achilles," Labrum replied calmly.

"And the glowing? What was that?" Captain Howse pressed.

"That was Morpheus and Sadal Suud. Their energy consumes the ship when they channel their full power," Labrum explained.

Captain Shrowd's tone turned contemplative. "Wasn't that the same glow we saw during the battle with the Tarvosians?"

"Yes, it was," Labrum confirmed.

Captain Howse hesitated before adding, "They possess incredible power. It's awe-inspiring, but it could also become a problem in the future."

Labrum nodded. "That's exactly why we've returned—to address these matters with the King and the Council."

The three ships docked in orbit around Achilles, and their crews prepared to descend to the planet. This time, they were greeted by King Saturn himself, accompanied by the High Council Members.

The three captains stepped forward first, bowing respectfully before the King and exchanging formal greetings with the Council.

Then King Saturn's gaze shifted. "Bring Morpheus and Sadal Suud forward," he commanded.

Morpheus and Sadal Suud approached with a calm yet commanding presence. As they bowed slightly in respect, the King nodded in acknowledgment.

"We thank you for your service," the King began. "For now, I want all three crews to rest and recover. Tomorrow, we will commence the inquiries into the battle with the Tarvosians and the remarkable powers of Morpheus and Sadal Suud."

The crews dispersed, their minds heavily anticipating the coming day.

King Saturn sent letters to the entire crew of *UNIV ORION* and the officers of the other ships, requesting their presence the following morning at the Council Chamber. In the meantime, the crews enjoyed a feast to celebrate their return from war, spending time with their families and friends. The next morning, everyone gathered at the Council Chamber to present their findings to the King and the Council Members.

Labrum presented the recordings, from the planning stages to the battle itself. Captain Howse and Captain Shrowd corroborated the recordings with their own incident reports. Each captain submitted their full accounts of the events, along with any relevant evidence.

King Saturn and the council members carefully reviewed all the information and scheduled a follow-up meeting two days later.

When the time came, the entire crew of *UNIV ORION* and the officers from the other two ships were called back to the Council Chamber.

"What is the issue?" King Saturn asked, his voice commanding.

The captains spoke in unison. "Our crews and officers disagree with how Morpheus handled certain matters during the mission."

King Saturn turned his gaze toward the two captains. "You were present when I gave the order to destroy the Tarvosians."

"Yes, King Saturn," they replied.

The King's eyes narrowed. "Is there any further complaint against the crew of *UNIV ORION* or Morpheus and Sadal Suud?"

Captain Howse and Captain Shrowd exchanged a glance before responding. "Did you see how Morpheus destroyed the Tarvosians?"

The King's expression remained steady. "You do not fully understand the aggressiveness of the Tarvosians. The crew of *UNIV ORION* followed my orders precisely. Morpheus and Sadal Suud acted as they should, and I stand by their actions. You two are dismissed from this inquiry."

With a subtle nod, Labrum stepped forward. “We followed your orders, Your Majesty. However, we have learned much about Morpheus and Sadal Suud. Their bond is extraordinary—both physically and mentally. Their love is more powerful than anything we’ve encountered, and they will protect the Universe and its people without hesitation.”

King Saturn leaned forward, intrigued. “Are you suggesting they could ever turn against us or the Universe?”

“No, Your Majesty,” Labrum replied firmly. “I believe the recordings will show the truth of their actions and the challenges they face together.”

Zeus, a member of the Council, spoke up. “I’ve seen how Morpheus dealt with me. He didn’t let my attempts to provoke him escalate. He defused the situation with wisdom, and he did the same when dealing with Uranus. But Uranus refused to listen, and in the end, Morpheus allowed him to make his own choices—except when Uranus’s blood would have poisoned the Earth.”

King Saturn turned his attention to Zeus. “I want to see Morpheus and Sadal Suud in action for myself. Set up a scenario where I can observe their abilities firsthand.”

Labrum and Zeus exchanged a glance. “We advise against this, Your Majesty,” Labrum cautioned. “Morpheus and Sadal Suud despise betrayal. Provoking them could lead to unintended consequences.”

Zeus added, "Perhaps you could visit Earth in a different ship. Observe how Morpheus handles the situation with Cronus, and form your own judgment."

The King considered the suggestion. "I will come to Earth and see for myself. I'll observe Morpheus and Sadal Suud in their element."

"Understood, Your Majesty," Labrum said. "We are scheduled to depart for Earth in one week. You may accompany us then, if you wish."

Zeus added, "We hope you'll observe quietly, without interference."

The King nodded. "I agree. I will come as a silent observer."

As the conversation concluded, King Saturn dismissed the meeting. "Enjoy your week. I will join you on Earth and observe Morpheus, Sadal Suud, and your crew."

The next day, Morpheus and Sadal Suud set off on their own adventure on Achilles. Sadal Suud knew of a secluded, beautiful spot—a beach with crystal-clear waters, where they could escape and share their love in peace. Unfortunately, unbeknownst to them, King Saturn had sent spies to watch their every move.

On the beach, as Morpheus and Sadal Suud made love, their glowing energies intensified. The plants around them began to bloom with unnatural vigor, and the nearby fish swarmed in increased numbers, drawn to the energy they radiated. The King's spies, observing from a distance, recorded every detail of the glowing powers they witnessed.

CHAPTER 23

The Return to the Earth

Labrum and the crew, along with Morpheus and his family, made final preparations to leave for Earth. Unknown to Morpheus, King Saturn followed in a separate ship, cloaked and hidden just out of scanner range.

As Labrum's spaceship began its journey, he called a meeting with the crew, his family, and Zeus.

"We need to be vigilant and cautious of any external threats," Labrum said.

"What kind of threats?" Morpheus asked, his tone measured.

"I can't provide specifics," Labrum admitted. "But you and Sadal Suud must be particularly careful. There are forces at play beyond what we can foresee."

Morpheus nodded thoughtfully. "Then we should carry recording devices at all times. It will protect us and ensure the truth is documented."

Labrum agreed, ordering everyone to equip themselves with personal recording devices immediately.

As the spaceship reached Earth's moon, Labrum held the ship in a stationary orbit behind it, hidden from view. The crew prepared to travel through Earth's past to track down Cronus. Meanwhile, King Saturn's ship, still cloaked, lingered just outside Labrum's scanner range, awaiting its own moment to act.

"Morpheus, do you recall the exact time and date you left Cronus?" Labrum asked.

"9205851," Morpheus replied.

Labrum checked the time machine shuttle's logs. "Good. The shuttle still has that time locked in. We're ready to proceed."

Two time-machine shuttles were prepared for the journey to locate Cronus and assess the consequences of his actions. Before departure, Morpheus turned to Zeus. "Are you comfortable with this part of the mission?"

Zeus hesitated briefly but then nodded. "Yes. I've battled Cronus before, and I know what to expect."

Morpheus's gaze narrowed. "If anything goes wrong, Zeus, you must retreat without hesitation. Promise me."

Zeus sighed but agreed. "I will."

The shuttles traveled through time, arriving at their designated destination. The crews set up a small base camp and prepared a meal to unwind. However, King Saturn's ship overshot their time coordinates, forcing him and his crew to search for Morpheus across time. When the King located their camp,

MORPHEUS

Morpheus and his crew were already resting after a peaceful dinner. King Saturn and his crew established their own camp nearby, remaining undetected. The next morning, the King ordered his men to observe Morpheus and his crew closely, maintaining their cover as spies.

At dawn, Morpheus turned to Sadal Suud. "Would you like to take a walk with me and check on Cronus and his family?"

Sadal Suud smiled warmly. "Yes, I'd like that."

Before leaving, the two informed Labrum of their plan.

"Be cautious with Cronus," Labrum warned. "And don't forget to use your recording devices."

Morpheus placed a reassuring hand on his father's shoulder. "Understood, Father."

Hand in hand, Morpheus and Sadal Suud began their journey toward Cronus's campsite, ready to confront whatever awaited them in this critical chapter of their mission.

As Morpheus and Sadal Suud approached Cronus's camp, they quickly sensed something was amiss. The chaos around them was undeniable. Determined to get to the bottom of things, they set out to find Gaia. Upon locating her, Morpheus asked, "How are you, Gaia?"

"Hello, Morpheus, Sadal Suud," Gaia greeted them. "Cronus has the children, and Rhea and I were trying to devise a plan to rescue them."

“Is Zeus still on the island?” Morpheus inquired.

“Yes,” Gaia replied.

“Cronus hasn’t... eaten the children, has he?” Morpheus asked, concern in his voice.

“No,” Gaia reassured him.

“That’s a relief,” Morpheus said, visibly relieved. “At least we’ve avoided that disaster.” Gaia nodded in agreement.

“I’m leaving Sadal Suud with you,” Morpheus announced, “While I go after Cronus.”

“Understood, Morpheus,” Gaia replied.

Morpheus turned to Sadal Suud. “Watch over Gaia and yourself, and remember what my father said.”

Sadal Suud nodded. “I will.”

Unbeknownst to them, King Saturn had dispatched spies to monitor Morpheus and Sadal Suud. As Morpheus set off to find Cronus, the spies split up, some following him and others keeping watch on the women.

When Morpheus finally found Cronus, he called out, “Cronus, how are you?”

In a sudden burst of rage, Cronus picked up a massive rock and hurled it at Morpheus.

"What are you doing, Cronus? It's me—Morpheus!" Morpheus exclaimed, dodging the rock. "I'm the one who freed you and your siblings from Uranus!"

Cronus froze, his anger dissipating as he recognized Morpheus.

"Morpheus!" he said, his voice softening. "I didn't realize it was you. I'm sorry, my friend. I've missed you."

Morpheus raised an eyebrow. "Do you remember throwing a rock at me just now?"

"No," Cronus replied, guilt creeping into his tone. "I'm sorry, Morpheus. I didn't mean to."

"Where are the children?" Morpheus pressed.

"I don't know," Cronus said, his voice tinged with confusion.

"We need to find them," Morpheus said, his mind racing. "I just hope you didn't eat them."

"I didn't," Cronus insisted.

"Are you sure?" Morpheus asked, still skeptical. "Because you didn't even recognize me a few minutes ago."

Cronus looked ashamed. "Let's just find the children."

Meanwhile, the King's spies, observing Morpheus and Cronus's conversation, quickly reported back to King Saturn. "Morpheus has calmed Cronus," they said.

"Then let's test him," Saturn ordered. "Attack Gaia and Sadal Suud, and see how Morpheus reacts."

The spies swiftly attacked the women, and Sadal Suud, alarmed, called out for Morpheus. "Morpheus, help!" she cried.

"Cronus, come with me," Morpheus commanded. "Something has happened to your mother and my wife."

Rushing back to the campsite, Morpheus and Cronus arrived to find men trying to seize the women. Without hesitation, Morpheus unleashed his powers, his hands emitting lightning as he grabbed the attackers.

"Cronus, grab some rope and tie them up!" Morpheus instructed.

As the scene unfolded, Labrum and his crew arrived, rushing to Morpheus's aid.

"These men—where did they come from?" Morpheus demanded.

"Be careful, Morpheus," Labrum cautioned. "Check on the women first."

Morpheus nodded, then turned his attention to Gaia and Sadal Suud. "Are you both all right?"

“They came out of nowhere and tried to take us,” Sadal Suud said, visibly shaken.

“Is anyone hurt?” Morpheus asked, his concern growing.

“No,” Gaia and Sadal Suud replied in unison.

Morpheus turned back to the men he had subdued. “Where are you from?” he asked sternly.

When the men remained silent, Morpheus’s anger flared. He grabbed one of the men by the throat, using his powers to read his mind. The answer he uncovered made his blood boil.

“King Saturn!” Morpheus bellowed, fury in his voice.

The King emerged from behind the rocks, “Yes, Morpheus?”

Morpheus’s eyes narrowed as he faced the King. “What are you doing here, and why would you attack these women?”

King Saturn’s expression remained unshaken. “I wanted to test your powers and see how you handle such situations.”

Morpheus’s disbelief was palpable. “Seriously? What the hell?”

King Saturn stood tall. “I’ve come to challenge you for the Kingdom of Achilles.”

Morpheus’s gaze hardened. “That is not a kingdom for me to claim. My kingdom is Earth—protecting this world and assisting our home planet, Achilles. That's all. I have respect for my elders and the power of authority. I will not challenge you, King Saturn."

Before the King could respond, Labrum stepped forward, his voice laced with authority. "What is this, King Saturn? Stop making these threats before the council members strip you of your kingship. I am one of them, and Zeus holds the power to end your reign. We have recordings of everything that will be sent back to Achilles."

"Enough talk," King Saturn snapped. "Let's fight, Morpheus."

Zeus's voice rang out, steady and resolute. "King Saturn, you will die if you go through with this."

Labrum, his tone both protective and incredulous, added, "Why would you harm my son, who cares for both our worlds?"

King Saturn's eyes burned with conviction. "Morpheus is the prophecy of our people. He is the new ruler— and my replacement as King of Achilles and the Universe. He will bring peace and harmony to all."

"Morpheus is the King of Earth," Labrum countered, his voice unwavering. "He and his wife will bring peace to humanity and our planet."

The King shook his head. "Once Morpheus aids the humans, Achilles will be his next domain to rule."

Labrum's gaze was steely. "If you fight Morpheus, you will be cast out as King by the people of Achilles."

Zeus's words were a final warning. "This fight is one you cannot win, no matter the circumstances."

Morpheus, anger rising, stepped forward, his voice sharp. "King Saturn, you are supposed to be the peacekeeper of the Universe, and yet you are willing to throw away your kingdom for a new King of Achilles?"

King Saturn stood firm. "Yes, Morpheus."

Morpheus's eyes blazed with fury. "Then you are the bringer of destruction to Achilles. Is this how a King destroys everything he's built over eons—his universe, planet, and people?"

King Saturn's resolve hardened. "Yes, I will do whatever it takes to destroy you, Morpheus."

Morpheus exhaled sharply, his decision made. "I have no choice but to fight you, then. But I have some rules for this battle. First, we fight to the death. Second, the fight takes place in the barren lands, far from the green lands. Third, if I win, I appoint Zeus as your successor. And finally, I will take Zeus's place as the rightful ruler."

King Saturn's lip curled in defiance. "That will never happen, Morpheus, or with Zeus. Let's go to the barren lands and settle this."

Labrum, ever the voice of reason, intervened. "We have been recording everything, King Saturn—your actions, your threats. We will use this evidence to justify your downfall to the people of Achilles."

King Saturn and Morpheus stood at the center of the barren wasteland, ready to face each other in battle.

"We must keep our distance from this fight," Labrum said, his voice steady. "This will be the greatest battle ever fought. Everyone, position your recorders and capture every moment."

As King Saturn and Morpheus approached the center of the wasteland, Morpheus tried one last time to reason with his opponent. "We don't have to do this," he said.

King Saturn's response was venomous. "No, we fight to the death. When I win, I will destroy both your families, Morpheus."

Labrum transmitted the unfolding battle live to Achilles for the High Council and the masses. The tension in the air was palpable as the two titans clashed. When Morpheus heard the King's threat, his fury ignited. He hurled lightning bolts at the King, striking his feet. In retaliation, King Saturn threw massive boulders, but his aim was off, and the rocks crashed to the ground.

Morpheus grew larger and retaliated by hurling rocks of his own. King Saturn rose to match him, and their colossal forms collided in a brutal exchange. The ground trembled as Morpheus soared through the air and crashed into the earth. Undeterred, he leapt up and charged King Saturn, throwing him into a distant mountain. The King hit the rocky peak with a thunderous crash, the impact momentarily halting his advance.

As the fight wore on, Morpheus began to reflect. *This isn't a battle of skill,* he thought, *but a primitive brawl.* "King Saturn, we can stop this madness at any time," Morpheus urged.

"No!" the King roared. "You said 'to the death,' and I will see you dead!"

Morpheus sighed. "I've only shown you a fraction of my power. Imagine if I unleashed my full strength. Remember, I once threw Uranus into the Sun. Don't make me do the same to you."

The King sneered. "You should have thrown me into the Sun already if you had the chance."

Summoning his magic, King Saturn created rock warriors who relentlessly attacked Morpheus. With every punch Morpheus landed, the warriors crumbled only to reform, turning the battle into a vicious cycle. The relentless attacks battered Morpheus like a ball tossed between opponents.

"You forget, Morpheus," the King taunted. "When you lose, I will kill both your families."

Fueled by anger, Morpheus used his mental powers to lift King Saturn and hurl him into another mountain. The impact gashed the King's side, blood flowing freely. Distracted by his wound, the rock warriors disintegrated.

"This is your last chance to stop," Morpheus said, his tone firm.

"Never," King Saturn growled. "To the death!"

"Then it's over," Morpheus declared. "You're hurt and need medical attention. Accept defeat, King Saturn."

Morpheus extended a hand to the King, helping him to his feet. But as soon as he stood, King Saturn betrayed the gesture. Grabbing a sharp rock, he stabbed Morpheus in the stomach. Morpheus fell, blood pooling around him. Yet his healing powers activated, expelling the rock and sealing the wound. Rising again, Morpheus's expression was one of deep disappointment. "You betray even kindness," he said, his voice sorrowful.

Growing to an immense size, Morpheus seized King Saturn and spun him around with colossal force, hurling him into the Sun.

Returning to the ground, Morpheus's blood mingled with the King's, and an extraordinary transformation began. The wasteland bloomed with life. Grass, flowers, bushes, and trees spread across the barren land. Labrum watched in awe. "Their blood is seeding the Earth," he said.

Gaia stepped forward. "I will nurture this new life and keep the Earth green and beautiful."

Cronus approached, guiding the children. "They were hiding and playing," he said with a smile.

Morpheus turned to Cronus. “Will you follow the rules of Earth and protect this new life?”

“Yes, Morpheus,” Cronus replied. “But where is the King?”

Morpheus’s gaze was distant. “He died as a king in battle. His sacrifice has given this planet the greenery it needed. In time, humans will come to call this Earth their home.”

CHAPTER 24

Zeus is King

Labrum informed Morpheus that they must return to Achilles for a trial before the High Council Members, during which Zeus would be appointed King of Achilles.

"I need to settle matters here on Earth first," Morpheus replied. "Then we can leave for Achilles, Father."

Labrum nodded. "Very well, Morpheus."

Morpheus then took Sadal Suud to introduce her as the future queen of Earth and himself as its future king. Their first visit was to Aphrodite. Morpheus explained his plans, saying, "I will be King, and Sadal Suud will be Queen. Aphrodite, I need you to adhere to the laws of Earth."

Aphrodite responded calmly, "You may appoint Zeus as King of Achilles when the time comes, but for now, Cronus remains King of Earth, with Rhea as its queen."

Morpheus nodded, satisfied. After uniting the gods of Earth under a shared purpose, he met with Cronus. "Will you follow the laws of Earth?" he asked.

"Yes, Morpheus," Cronus replied.

Morpheus elaborated, "For now, you and Rhea shall reign as King and Queen of Earth. In the future, Zeus and Aphrodite will assume those roles. We Achillesians plan to send people from other planets to populate Earth. Until then, I need you and Rhea to uphold Earth's laws. When the time comes, Zeus and Aphrodite will do the same for its future inhabitants."

Cronus and Rhea agreed to Morpheus's terms.

"I will watch over Earth to oversee its people and gods," Morpheus concluded. Then, he prepared to return to Achilles.

As Morpheus and Sadal Suud finalized their discussions, Labrum and his crew dismantled their campsite. When Morpheus and his wife returned, Labrum asked, "Are you both ready to leave Earth?"

"We are," they replied.

The two crews boarded their respective time machines and departed for the spaceship *UNIV ORION*. Once aboard, preparations began for their week-long journey to Achilles.

Upon arriving, the *UNIV ORION* docked in space, and the crew descended to Achilles's surface in a smaller craft. A messenger greeted them, directing Labrum and his team to the Council Chamber, where they reported to the High Council Members.

"What happened with King Saturn?" one council member inquired.

"Have you received the recordings of the incidents on Earth?" Labrum asked.

"We have," a council member confirmed. "Why did the King leave Achilles to pursue you and your ship to Earth?"

Labrum explained, "The King knew that Morpheus was the fulfillment of the prophecy and the true King of our Universe. He couldn't accept this and feared being replaced. Despite Morpheus, Zeus, and I trying to reason with him, King Saturn refused to listen. Even as council members attempted to counsel him, he ignored our advice. When the King confronted Morpheus, they agreed to a duel to the death. Morpheus tried to stop the fight midway, but Saturn was relentless. During the battle, the King declared that if he won, he would kill both of Morpheus's families. At that point, Morpheus and Sadal Suud acted decisively, and the King was defeated. Morpheus cast him into the Sun."

A council member sighed. "The King's actions violated our laws and caused unnecessary strife. He ignored wise counsel and brought about his downfall."

Another council member asked, "Who will be King now?"

"Per the late king's agreement," Morpheus replied, "Zeus will ascend as King of Achilles. When Earth's matters are resolved, I will take his place."

The council unanimously approved this decision.

"We must hold a ceremony to honor King Saturn's passing and officially welcome Zeus as the new King," one council member declared. “Additionally, we should induct Morpheus as a council member with a formal ceremony.”

Morpheus agreed, emphasizing the importance of honoring King Saturn’s death in battle with the appropriate rites. The council concurred, deciding to notify Achilles’s citizens of the ceremony’s date and time.

The council also explained that they would send all recordings to their population so they would understand why King Saturn died in battle.

The meeting adjourned, and preparations for the ceremonies began.

Labrum and his family cherished their time on their home planet while awaiting the upcoming ceremonies. The council announced to the public three significant events: a memorial for King Saturn, the coronation of Zeus as the new King, and the appointment of Morpheus as a council member. The ceremonies were scheduled for the following day, beginning at first light and continuing throughout the day.

At dawn, the citizens of Achilles gathered in their ceremonial attire, with the leaders donning special garments for the occasion. The first ceremony honored King Saturn. The council members led the proceedings as King Saturn’s royal regalia was displayed in a glass shroud. An image of the late King was paraded through the courtyard for all to see before being brought to the Altar of Achilles’ Kingdom.

Labrum approached the podium and, speaking in the Achillesian language, greeted the gathered crowd.

"King Saturn died as a warrior and a King," Labrum began. "He devoted his life to his people, protecting the lands of Achilles and the entire Universe. He safeguarded planets and their inhabitants, fostering unity among diverse nations. King Saturn knew the prophecy of Morpheus would come true and that Morpheus was destined to be more than the King of Achilles—he would be the King of the Universe. With this understanding, King Saturn gave Morpheus his blessing to follow in his footsteps as the new King of Achilles and the Universe."

Labrum continued, "For now, Morpheus will rule Earth and resolve its challenges. Once Earth is at peace, he will succeed Zeus as King of Achilles. These were King Saturn's final words before his passing on Earth."

The ceremony concluded with prayers for King Saturn as his glass shroud was solemnly carried to the Tomb of the Kings. The leaders offered final blessings as the shroud was placed in the tomb, laying King Saturn to rest.

"Now, let us prepare for the coronation of our new King, Zeus," Labrum announced, signaling the end of the memorial.

The royal servants quickly rearranged the courtyard for the next ceremony. Zeus was guided to his throne in the courtyard square, and Labrum began the traditional rites in the Achillesian tongue. Addressing Zeus, Labrum recited the ceremonial acceptance of kingship.

“Zeus, do you accept the terms of your kingship?” Labrum asked.

“I do,” Zeus replied.

“And what are your terms for accepting this kingship?” Labrum continued.

“I accept on the condition that, in time, I will relinquish my rule to Morpheus. I pledge to serve the people of Achilles faithfully until that day,” Zeus declared.

Labrum then asked, “Will you carry out your duties in the best interests of the Achilles people at heart?”

“Yes, I will,” Zeus affirmed.

The people prayed for the prosperity of their new King, and the council unanimously approved his appointment.

“To all Achillesians, I present your new King, Zeus,” Labrum proclaimed. “Let us celebrate this momentous occasion.”

Hours later, the council prepared for the final ceremony, Morpheus’s induction as a council member. As the royal servants escorted Morpheus to the courtyard square, the crowd erupted in chants of “The God of the Universe!” Despite Labrum’s attempts to calm them, the chants grew louder until Morpheus himself intervened.

"Let us proceed with the ceremony," Morpheus said, his voice commanding yet composed. The people quieted, and the proceedings began.

King Zeus led the induction, speaking in the native tongue of Achillesians. "Morpheus has demonstrated unparalleled dedication to Earth, Achilles, and the Universe," Zeus declared. "He is indeed the God of the Universe, a true leader for all."

Zeus continued, "I pledge my life to Morpheus, his family, and the people of Achilles. Let us pray for his success as a god and leader, ensuring a prosperous future for our Universe."

With the final words of the ceremony, Morpheus was formally inducted as a council member. The day concluded with a grand celebration that extended into the night.

Amid the festivities, Morpheus and Sadal Suud slipped away to spend time alone. They discovered a secluded cave by a serene beach, where they talked, swam, and enjoyed each other's company in privacy. Their bond deepened as they celebrated in their own way, away from the crowd.

Meanwhile, Zeus noticed their absence and approached Labrum.

"Where are Morpheus and Sadal Suud?" Zeus asked.

"They're likely spending time together," Labrum replied with a knowing smile.

“I meant what I said, Labrum,” Zeus said earnestly. “I devote my life to you, your family, and especially to Morpheus and Sadal Suud.”

“I know, King Zeus,” Labrum said. “Thank you.”

The celebrations continued, filled with joy, unity, and hope for the future.

CHAPTER 25

Time & Councils

Morpheus and Sadal Suud returned from their private time together. Labrum greeted them with a curious look.

"Where were you two?" Labrum asked.

"We spent some time together, celebrating in our own way," Morpheus replied.

Labrum nodded thoughtfully. "And what are your plans for yourselves now?"

"I'd like to remain here for a while," Morpheus said. "I want to be part of the council and learn more about our civilization and government. Sadal Suud will also begin her role as a leader and learn about her duties within our government."

"That's an excellent idea for both of you," Labrum said. "The crew will stay here on Achilles to support you."

"Can you guide me through the laws and government systems of Achilles?" Morpheus asked.

"Of course," Labrum replied. "But all the council members will assist you, as will King Zeus. You won't be alone in this."

"I know," Morpheus said. "Zeus has always been there for the people and for us."

As if on cue, King Zeus approached them, his regal presence impossible to ignore. "How is everyone today?" he asked.

"We're doing well," Labrum said.

"I noticed you and Sadal Suud leaving the celebration," Zeus said, turning to Morpheus.

"Yes," Morpheus admitted. "We found a quiet beach and spent some time alone together."

Zeus smiled. "That's good for both of you. May I speak to you and Sadal Suud privately?"

Morpheus shook his head. "You can speak freely in front of my father. There will be no more secrets from our people or government."

"You're right," Zeus said. "I'm here for you, Morpheus, Sadal Suud, and our people. My loyalty to you and this planet is unwavering."

Morpheus met his gaze. "I know, King Zeus. I can see it in your eyes and feel it in your soul."

"What are your plans?" Zeus asked.

“My father just asked me the same,” Morpheus said. “I plan to stay here for some time to learn about our culture, laws, and government.”

“That sounds wise,” Zeus said. “In that case, let’s begin tomorrow with a council meeting.”

The following morning, the council convened in the High Council Chamber. The council was comprised of thirteen members: King Zeus, Labrum, Oberon, Creed, Caliban, Prospero, Triton, Galatea, Pluto, Makemake, Chaldene, Deimos, and the newest addition, Morpheus.

As they gathered around the large circular table, King Zeus stood to address the assembly.

“Today, we officially welcome Morpheus as the newest council member,” Zeus announced. “We also have Queen Sadal Suud, who will be learning about Earth and our governments as part of her duties. Morpheus will serve as the third in command, replacing my position. All other roles remain unchanged. I ask all council members to guide Morpheus and Sadal Suud in understanding our laws, government, and the history of the Universe.”

Zeus turned to Morpheus. “You will also gain knowledge of the Universe, its planets, their cultures, and much more.”

“My parents, Labrum and Denab, have already taught me much,” Morpheus said. “And Sadal Suud has shared her insights about our world.”

"That's good," Zeus said. "But there is always more to learn."

The discussion shifted to the origins of the Universe. Zeus began, "Let us start with the ancient gods and religions of the Universe. The creator of the Universe was known as Vishnu. He initiated the Big Bang with his colossal hands, forming galaxies, planets, and life itself. Over time, Vishnu entrusted another god, Abraham, to create humanity on Earth.

"Abraham, also called God Abraham, fashioned the first humans, Adam and Eve, and placed them in the Garden of Eden. However, their disobedience introduced evil, symbolized by the serpent Nahas. This marked the beginning of humanity's struggles with morality and sin. God Abraham was the origin of the Hebrew religion on Earth, and his story intertwines with the history of other civilizations and deities across the Universe."

Zeus continued, delving into the stories of Gaia and Uranus and the rise and fall of civilizations such as Atlantis, the Maya Empire, and others. He explained the cosmic threats of black holes and the destructive wars between advanced civilizations, highlighting the role of Achillesians in brokering peace.

"We must ensure that Earth humans understand the stakes when they venture into space," Zeus said. "War or crime among humans in space would provoke conflict with the Universe and risk their extinction. This is why we watch over Earth from behind its moon and protect it from external threats."

Labrum then spoke, adding, "The Universe is vast and complex, spanning billions of eons. Understanding its history, dimensions, and parallel realities is a monumental task. After lunch, we will discuss the Ten Dimensions of the Universe and the adjacent parallel realities."

As the Council Members exited the building, Labrum turned to Morpheus. "How are you handling all this information?"

"I'm doing okay," Morpheus replied, his voice steady despite the weight of the day's revelations.

Labrum smiled. "Let's take a break and have lunch with our family."

The group gathered for a meal, sharing quiet moments of camaraderie and reflection before returning to the Council Chamber.

After lunch, the Council Members resumed their meeting in the Council Chamber. Labrum stood before the group and began to explain the ten dimensions of the Universe.

"The first dimension is simple: a straight line that represents length," Labrum began. "The second dimension adds height. With two lines—length and height—we can visualize a plane. The third dimension incorporates width or depth. Combine these three, and you have a cube, giving us volume and spatial orientation in the Universe. This is expressed mathematically as Length × Height × Width."

He paused, making sure the concepts landed. "These three dimensions create the physical space we understand, but the fourth dimension introduces time. By adding time to spatial dimensions, you can travel through both space and time."

Labrum glanced at Morpheus. "We covered this on the spaceship, including demonstrations of time travel."

Morpheus nodded. "Yes, I remember. It was enlightening."

Labrum continued, "The fifth dimension acts like a looking glass, offering a broader view of travel, distance, and the vastness of the Universe. This dimension allowed us to navigate back in time to Earth and Uranus.

"The sixth dimension is a plane of possibilities, encompassing past and future timelines across planets and the Universe. The seventh dimension expands on this, introducing endless possibilities since the inception of time itself. The eighth dimension weaves together the histories of times and places across infinite Universes, offering an understanding of countless realities and parallel Universes.

"The ninth dimension shifts focus to varying laws of physics and the fundamental rules governing these infinite possibilities. Finally, the tenth dimension transcends even these boundaries, presenting scenarios so complex and unimaginable that they defy comprehension.

"And this," Labrum said, turning toward Morpheus, "is where you come into the picture. As the King of the Universe, your powers span all ten dimensions. They manifest as you need them, making you the embodiment of hope and justice for all beings. Your abilities are far beyond what any lower being could comprehend. You were chosen not just for your power but for your empathy, open mind, and unwavering commitment to justice. These qualities make you the righteous ruler of the Universe."

King Zeus added, "Your powers will endure as long as you remain faithful, honest, and just to all beings in the Universe."

Labrum shifted the discussion. "Now, let's talk about the Parallel Universe and its dangers. Our Universe was originally named Vishnu, after the first King of the Universe, before later being named Orion, as we know it now. The Parallel Universe, however, is called Caligula, named after the infamous Roman emperor.

"These Universes are similar but fundamentally opposed. Occasionally, the Caligula Universe breaches our own, causing chaos. A prime example is the Tarvosians civilization, in which you had to destroy, Morpheus. The Tarvosians lived near the border between our Universes and fled their own due to internal wars and conflict. Unfortunately, they brought their chaos with them, disrupting peace in our Universe. Despite the multiple chances you gave them to coexist peacefully, they chose a path of destruction, forcing you to make the difficult decision to end their civilization."

King Zeus interjected, his tone grave. "Our greatest concern is that the Caligula Universe may attempt a full-scale invasion to take over our Universe."

Labrum elaborated, “It’s similar to colonists fleeing tyranny in their homeland, such as the settlers who left England for the Americas to escape the rule of the English King. Once there, they turned against the Indigenous Nations, stealing land, committing atrocities, and justifying it as survival. These historical parallels on Earth reflect why we cannot allow humans unrestricted access to space.”

King Zeus continued, “Earth’s history shows how humans often act out of fear and self-interest. The Revolutionary War is a classic example of colonists rebelling against England, followed by their oppression of Native Americans. Such cycles of conflict and conquest demonstrate why humans are not yet ready to interact with the wider Universe. Their inability to resolve internal conflicts peacefully poses a threat to the balance of the cosmos.”

Labrum concluded, “These are lessons from both our history and Earth’s. As leaders, it is our responsibility to protect our Universe from the chaos that has destroyed so many civilizations. That is why we tread carefully with humanity.”

The weight of the discussion lingered as the Council Members prepared to delve even deeper into the mysteries of existence and their shared responsibilities.

CHAPTER 26

Good and Evil

Morpheus deepened his understanding of the Achillesians' heritage and the intertwined histories and prophecies of the two Universes. He explored the nature of good and evil that shaped all beings across these realms. When he first came to his family from Achilles, Morpheus already knew of Earthlings' moral struggles and their ancient gods of virtue and malevolence. He believed that by removing the stain of Uranus's first blood and preventing Cronus from being buried on Earth, he could weaken the grip of evil that plagued humanity.

Morpheus discovered that Uranus and Gaia originated from the Caligula Universe. This revelation provided crucial insights into their origins and the source of Uranus's unyielding malice. Morpheus contemplated traveling back in time to observe humanity's descent into corruption, seeking to understand the roots of their wickedness. He also considered venturing into the Caligula Universe to uncover the other side of the story and unravel the truth about how evil spreads its influence.

A meeting convened at the Council Chamber, where the gods gathered to discuss the escalating concerns. As the attendees exchanged greetings, the air was charged with anticipation.

Morpheus addressed the assembly. "May I speak first and ask some questions?"

"Of course," King Zeus replied.

Morpheus began, "What is the true nature of good and evil? How do these forces manipulate the minds of people and the balance between our two Universes?"

Zeus responded, "It stems from the mind's perception and how individuals treat one another. Intentions can corrupt just as much as actions."

Morpheus pressed, "If someone harbors malevolent intentions, does that define evil? And what about those who seek revenge after enduring repeated cruelty?"

"Both are aspects of it," Zeus admitted.

Morpheus then shared his concerns. "I understand the chaos among Earth's people and suspect that evil originated with Uranus, Cronus, and Lucifer. Now, I learn of a counterpart Universe—the Caligula Universe—from which Uranus and Gaia emerged. If their malice took root there and infiltrated our realm, we must act to prevent its spread."

He paused before continuing. "In my dreams, I saw a tragedy destined for our Universe."

A murmur of unease rippled through the council. Morpheus revealed that his wife, Sadal Suud, had experienced similar visions foretelling doom. The council, aware of an ancient prophecy predicting a cataclysmic war between the Universes, grew visibly troubled.

Morpheus proclaimed, “I am the God of the Universe. Why do you fear this?”

Zeus responded gravely, “We have known of the prophecy, Morpheus. It foretells that you will fight and win, but at the cost of your life—and your wife’s.”

Sadal Suud, listening from the side, stood resolute. “That will not come to pass. Morpheus and I, our family, and our ship, *UNIV ORION*, will ensure it.”

“The prophecy speaks louder than your defiance,” Zeus countered.

Sadal Suud challenged further. “Will the planets align with us? Will others join this fight?”

Labrum, a senior council member, intervened. “With your powers, you could annihilate the enemy, but the destruction could engulf our Universe. Their cruelty will replicate here, leaving devastation in its wake.”

Morpheus declared, “Sadal Suud and I will journey to the Caligula Universe to uncover their intentions and seek the truth.”

Zeus warned, “If you go, they will try to kill you both.”

“We won’t provoke a war unless necessary,” Morpheus assured. “But if conflict is inevitable, it must not spill into our Universe. Meanwhile, Earth remains vulnerable—dispatch ships to guard it.”

The council agreed, albeit with trepidation. Sadal Suud pledged her unwavering support. “You are the King of the Universe, and I am your queen. Together, we will face this challenge.”

Preparations began for their mission. Morpheus directed his forces, ensuring communicators were active across all ships and planets. As they approached the secretive entrance to the Caligula Universe, they witnessed an alarming sight: ships from the Caligula Universe crossing into their realm.

Morpheus immediately transmitted a warning. “Alert all ships—prepare for an incursion!”

Labrum confirmed Earth’s defenses. “We’re surrounding the planet, ready for their attack.”

Sadal Suud identified five enemy ships breaching the boundary. “They’re headed for Earth,” she warned.

The couple acted decisively. Morpheus forced a massive enemy ship back through the gate while Sadal Suud disabled its engines, causing a catastrophic explosion that sealed the entrance between Universes. Ensuring no other portals remained, they scanned the boundary before returning to Earth to defend its people.

Morpheus and Sadal Suud defied the constraints of time and space, appearing instantly in Earth’s orbit aboard the *UNIV ORION*. They made their way to the bridge, searching for Labrum.

"How did you both get here so quickly?" Labrum asked, astonished.

"I'll explain later," Morpheus replied. "Labrum, where are the enemy spaceships?"

"They haven't arrived yet," Denab interjected.

"Can we locate them using the scanners?" Sadal Suud asked.

Denab shook her head. "Not yet. They're cloaked or out of range."

"Turn on the intercom," Morpheus commanded.

Once the system was live, Morpheus addressed the entire fleet and planetary networks. "Attention, everyone. The gateway to the Caligula Universe has been sealed, but five enemy ships managed to cross into our realm. Two are headed toward Earth, two toward Achilles, and one remains stationary, likely to support either assault. Be vigilant. Report any unusual movements or contacts immediately to the *UNIV ORION*."

Turning to Sadal Suud, Morpheus said, "I'm going out into space." Without hesitation, Sadal Suud followed.

"Why?" Labrum called after them.

"We'll search for the ships ourselves," Morpheus replied.

In the vastness of space, Morpheus and Sadal Suud held hands, channeling their combined powers. Their energies rippled across the Universe, seeking the hidden ships. In moments, they located all five. As their consciousness touched the vessels, they discerned the Tarvosians commanders' thoughts—fueled by revenge and a singular mission to destroy Achilles and Earth.

The Tarvosians' plans soon reached the Caligula Universe, alerting their allies. Driven by vengeance, they aimed to conquer the Vishnu Universe entirely. Sensing the threat, Morpheus and Sadal Suud projected their image into all five enemy ships, their presence emanating authority and power. At the same time, their message was broadcast to both Universes.

Morpheus addressed the Tarvosians commanders. "Cease your attack, or face the consequences. I offer you a single chance to live in peace, as I did with Pyxis, the King of the Tarvos planet in my Universe."

One commander sneered. "You killed our King and General Mundilfari, my brother. We will have our revenge, starting with you and your queen!"

Morpheus's voice remained calm but resolute. "You cling to vengeance, a path that leads only to destruction. Your armies are cut off; the gateway between our Universes is sealed. Your weapons are useless, and your shields won't save you."

"Impossible!" a general spat. "No being has such power."

"Test it," Morpheus challenged. "Try using your transporters or weapons. See what happens."

Skepticism gave way to panic as the generals confirmed their transporters were disabled. Morpheus warned them again. "If you attempt to fire your weapons, you'll only destroy yourselves."

"What do you want, Morpheus?" another commander demanded.

"I will offer you mercy," Morpheus replied. "I'll transport your ships to the far edge of your Universe, away from this conflict. But remember, this is your only chance to avoid annihilation."

The lead general hesitated, then reluctantly agreed. "Will our shields come down?"

"Not until you're back in your Universe," Morpheus said. "Understand this: my wife and I are now protectors of both Universes. You will not challenge us again."

The generals exchanged uneasy glances but ultimately complied. Morpheus and Sadal Suud used their powers to transport the Tarvosians' ships back to the Caligula Universe, ensuring their safe return.

Once the ships were back, Morpheus reached out to the lead general. "Is everything intact?"

The general responded, his tone subdued. "Yes, all ships are accounted for. Morpheus… Why did you spare us?"

Morpheus answered, “Because my wife and I protect life, not destroy it. Now, we will extend that protection to your Universe. This is your chance to bring peace to your people.”

“That may be difficult,” the general admitted. “Our Universe is consumed by strife.”

“Then stop the fighting,” Morpheus said. “Explain to your people what happened here. Tell them about our powers. We are unstoppable by any weapon you possess. Cooperate, and you’ll prosper. Resist, and your Universe will face the same fate as your father’s reign. You have been warned.”

“When will you come to our Universe?” the general asked cautiously.

“I have other matters to address first,” Morpheus replied. “But I’ll be watching. Work toward peace in my absence.”

The general sighed, defeated. “Goodbye, Morpheus.”

“Goodbye,” Morpheus said. “And remember, your choices shape your future.”

CHAPTER 27

Return to Earth

Morpheus and Sadal Suud returned aboard the *UNIV ORION,* greeted warmly by Labrum and Denab.

"Both of you truly are the greatest in the Universe," Labrum declared with admiration.

"You've stopped two Universes from descending into war," Denab added.

Labrum, curious, asked, "How did you manage to transport all those ships simultaneously?"

As the rest of the crew gathered around, their faces beaming with joy for their King and Queen, Morpheus explained, "We used our powers to isolate each ship within a force field bubble. Then, we projected them back into their Universe."

Achernar, wide-eyed, asked, "Were you both glowing while you did it?"

"Yes," Sadal Suud replied with a soft smile.

"Morpheus," Labrum interjected, "Do you believe the Tarvosians will agree to a peace treaty for their Universe?"

"No," Morpheus replied firmly.

“Then why would you go there?” Labrum pressed.

“We need to understand their plans,” Morpheus said. “Future conflicts could arise, and knowledge is our best defense.”

Labrum nodded thoughtfully. “Let’s celebrate and head back to Achilles.”

“Not yet,” Morpheus said. “We must first understand why the Tarvosians were targeting Earth.”

“I see your point,” Labrum conceded.

“The crew can return to Achilles after we’ve visited Earth,” Morpheus stated.

Denab asked, “Why are we going down to Earth?”

“I promised Gaia and Cronus I’d return to check on them,” Morpheus said. “And I want to visit my Earth family to see how they’re handling the problems of the twenty-first century.”

“If you’ve halted the root of their problems, everything should improve naturally,” Denab observed.

“That’s precisely why I’m going,” Morpheus replied. “I need to uncover the truth about good and evil and ensure Earth is on the right path.”

Turning to the crew, Morpheus said, “We’ve lived in a mostly peaceful Universe, except for Earth. Humanity has yet to venture into space, but when that time comes, they must do so as peaceful beings.”

"As King and Queen, it's our responsibility to safeguard not only our Universe but also the Caligula Universe," Morpheus continued.

"You're absolutely right," Denab affirmed.

"Let's visit Gaia and Cronus to see how they're doing," Morpheus said.

The crew prepared to travel through time, arriving at a period when Gaia and Cronus thrived. From orbit, they noticed the Earth looked more vibrant than ever. Descending to the surface, they approached Gaia's village.

"Greetings, Gaia," Morpheus said warmly. "How is life on Earth?"

"Life is pleasant and bountiful," Gaia replied.

"Where are Cronus and Rhea?" Morpheus asked.

"They're living together in their own home," Gaia said with a smile.

"And Zeus and Aphrodite? How are they faring?"

"They're doing well, too," Gaia answered.

Morpheus glanced around. "I see you've transformed the Earth into a beautiful landscape."

"Yes, it's one large garden filled with animals," Gaia said proudly.

“That’s wonderful,” Morpheus said. “My family and I will stay for a while. Feel free to visit us whenever you’d like.”

“I will, Morpheus,” Gaia replied.

Morpheus then addressed his family. “Walk around and ensure everything is as it seems. Look for any falsehoods or deceitful situations.”

The family agreed and dispersed. Turning to Sadal Suud, Morpheus said, “Come with me. We’ll see more from the sky.”

As they flew over the Earth, something unusual caught their attention in the distance. Investigating further, they descended to find a massive, red-skinned figure with horns—a sight both rare and alarming.

Walking closer, Morpheus’s thoughts turned to descriptions of the devil. Sadal Suud, reading his mind, understood his unease.

Morpheus and Sadal Suud approached the towering figure, who radiated an intimidating aura. Yet, their resolve remained unshaken as they greeted him.

“How are you doing?” Morpheus asked calmly.

The man turned around, his crimson form gleaming in the eerie light. “I’m fine. And who might I be speaking to?”

“I am Morpheus, King of this planet, and this is my queen, Sadal Suud. And who are you, sir?”

The figure's lips twisted into a smirk. "I am Saint Lucifer, King of the Underworld."

Morpheus immediately sent a telepathic warning to his family, alerting them to the presence of the Devil himself. They understood the message and quickly came to their King and Queen's aid, their expressions resolute.

Morpheus continued the conversation while telepathically explaining Lucifer's nature to his family. "Why are you here, Saint Lucifer?" he asked.

"I needed a place to live," Lucifer said with a cold, menacing tone. "I saw this planet and decided it would be mine. I'm taking over the Earth and enslaving its people forever."

"That will never happen," Morpheus replied firmly. "A new order reigns here."

Lucifer raised a skeptical brow. "And that would be you and your queen?"

"Don't underestimate me," Morpheus said. "I know all about you—your evil deeds, manipulation, and quest for destruction. Your reign of terror ends here."

Lucifer laughed, his voice a guttural rumble. "And what makes you think you can stop me? Look at my size, my strength! And I haven't even begun to show you my powers."

Morpheus stood unwavering. "You seek to destroy and enslave, but I fight for life, for freedom, and for the souls you would damn. Your rebellion against God Abraham cast you from heaven, and now you aim to corrupt Earth."

"How do you know about my fall?" Lucifer demanded, narrowing his fiery eyes.

"That's my secret, Lucifer," Morpheus said sharply. Then, turning to Sadal Suud, he spoke telepathically: *Get behind the rocks with the others. This is going to escalate.*

Lucifer sneered. "What did you do with Uranus and Cronus? They were the foundation of my kingdom, yet they're not in hell."

"I saved their souls," Morpheus declared. "Just as God Abraham saved heaven from your chaos, I've safeguarded them from your grasp."

At that moment, the landscape began transforming—fire and brimstone replaced the serene earth beneath their feet. Morpheus turned to his family. "Get far away from here. A battle is coming."

Lucifer lunged at Morpheus, but the King of two Universes evaded the attack effortlessly. Enraged, Lucifer hurled a massive boulder, which missed its mark. Morpheus began to taunt the Devil.

"Is that the best you can do?" Morpheus jeered. "Where are your so-called powers?"

Lucifer, consumed by rage, charged again. Morpheus dodged with ease, mocking him further. “You’re just a bully, Lucifer, with no real strength to back it up.”

Lucifer roared, “To the death, then!”

Morpheus smiled grimly. “As you wish.”

The battle escalated, with Lucifer attempting to crush Morpheus, but his strength had no effect. Morpheus, now towering above the Earth, threw Lucifer off and declared, “Your time is over, Lucifer. You were given a second chance, and you wasted it.”

Lucifer, sensing his defeat, begged for mercy. “Forgive me, Morpheus,” he pleaded. “I can change.”

“No,” Morpheus said, his voice like thunder. “You have been cast out of heaven and now Earth. Your fate lies in the Sun, where you’ll meet your fiery end.”

With a final surge of his immense power, Morpheus hurled Lucifer into the blazing Sun. The Earth trembled, and the battle was over.

As the family approached, Labrum asked, “Are you all right, Morpheus?”

“I’m fine,” Morpheus said.

“We saw Lucifer throw you around like a rag doll!” Labrum exclaimed.

"He had strength but no true power," Morpheus replied. "His only magic was feeding on fear."

Labrum pondered aloud, "Was he really just a man here on Earth?"

"Yes," Morpheus confirmed. "A man corrupted by his own evil."

The family returned to Gaia's village, where they found its people visibly shaken.

"What happened here, Gaia?" Morpheus asked.

"The red beast influenced us," Gaia admitted. "He used our own fears to control our minds."

Morpheus reassured her. "Lucifer is gone. He will never return."

After ensuring the village was safe, Morpheus addressed his family. "We must visit 2024 next," he announced.

"Why, Morpheus?" Labrum asked.

"To see my Earth family and determine how to handle humanity's problems," Morpheus explained.

Denab cautioned him. "Sharing the truth about us and Achilles might harm them. Consider this carefully before deciding."

Morpheus nodded. “You’re right, Mother. I’ll think it through.”

With that, the family prepared for their next journey, determined to bring balance and hope to Earth’s uncertain future.

CHAPTER 28

Visit to the Caligula Universe

Morpheus and his crew arrived at their spaceship, *UNIV ORION*, just as a distress call from Achilles came through, summoning them home. Labrum attempted to re-establish contact with Achilles but received no response. Turning to the crew, he ordered, "Secure all systems for departure. Prepare for immediate travel."

Labrum and Denab reviewed the ship's controls, ensuring everything was operational for the voyage. "Everyone, check in once you're ready," Labrum commanded. The crew confirmed their readiness one by one.

"How long will it take us to reach Achilles?" Morpheus asked.

"Approximately two days," Labrum replied.

Morpheus exchanged a glance with Sadal Suud. "We'll leave ahead of you and get there faster," he decided.

"Good plan," Labrum said with a nod.

Morpheus turned to his wife. "Are you ready?"

"Always," Sadal Suud replied with a faint smile.

Together, they departed, knowing their individual speed could halve the journey time.

When they arrived on Achilles, the scene before them was chaotic. Smoke billowed from damaged buildings, fires raged uncontrollably, and people scrambled to extinguish the flames. The city was in turmoil.

Morpheus and Sadal Suud headed straight for the palace to find King Zeus and the council. Upon arrival, they found them gathered in a tense discussion.

"What happened here?" Morpheus demanded.

King Zeus's expression was grim. "The Tarvosians attacked. They destroyed two of our patrolling spaceships at the edge of the Universes and disabled our communication systems."

Anger flared in Morpheus and Sadal Suud, but King Zeus held up a hand. "Calm yourselves. We need clear heads right now. Is your father on his way?"

"Yes," Morpheus replied, his mind already racing. "If the communication systems are down, they're likely planning to return and finish the job. I'll alert our ships and crew telepathically."

Sadal Suud closed her eyes, scanning the planet with her telepathic abilities for any trace of the Tarvosians. "No signs of them yet," she reported.

"Let's search Achilles ourselves," Morpheus suggested.

The two took to the skies, sweeping over the landscape, their keen senses scanning for any sign of the enemy. After covering the planet, they extended their search to the surrounding space. It wasn't until the *UNIV ORION* arrived that Morpheus received a telepathic inquiry from Labrum.

"What's happening on Achilles?" Labrum asked.

"The Tarvosians attacked," Morpheus informed him. "Be cautious as you approach, and have the crew ready for anything. Also, try to establish contact with our other ships. Achilles' communication systems are down."

Once the *UNIV ORION* landed, Labrum and Denab joined Morpheus and Sadal Suud at the palace.

"This damage is catastrophic," Labrum remarked, surveying the wreckage.

"Two of our patrol ships were destroyed," Morpheus explained. "The Tarvosians may still be nearby, hiding and waiting for reinforcements."

Labrum nodded grimly. "We'll need to search every corner of Achilles—and beyond."

After coordinating efforts with Wega aboard the *UNIV ORION*, Labrum ensured other ships were dispatched to the edge of the Universe to locate survivors and scout for enemy ships.

Meanwhile, Morpheus and Sadal Suud expanded their search into neighboring space. They soon discovered three Tarvosians' vessels lying in wait behind a dead planet.

"They're planning an ambush," Morpheus said, his eyes narrowing.

He immediately telepathed Labrum, relaying their location: "We've found three enemy ships. I'm sending coordinates now."

"We're en route," Labrum replied. "Our other ships are guarding Achilles."

Morpheus and Sadal Suud activated their invisibility cloaks and infiltrated the lead Tarvosians' ship. Hidden within the shadows, they overheard the general's plans to annihilate the Achillesians and expand their control over the Vishnu Universe.

Morpheus telepathically reached out to Sadal Suud, saying, "We must eliminate them quickly and discreetly before *UNIV ORION* arrives."

With resolute determination, Morpheus and Sadal Suud exited their ship, harnessing their combined powers to obliterate the enemy vessels in a blinding instant. When Labrum arrived, all that remained of the hostile fleet was a smattering of debris scattered across the void.

Spotting Morpheus and Sadal Suud amidst the wreckage, Labrum opened a channel to them as they boarded *UNIV ORION*. Inside, the family and crew gathered to assess the situation.

“What happened, Morpheus?” Labrum asked, concern etched on his face.

“We intercepted and destroyed the ships,” Morpheus replied firmly.

“Did you manage to warn their planet or allies of the consequences?” Labrum pressed.

“Sadal Suud and I infiltrated their lead ship to uncover their plans,” Morpheus explained. “The Tarvosians aim to annihilate and conquer our universe, Vishnu. Now, I intend to visit their Caligula Universe and ensure they can’t follow through with their schemes. But first, we must locate the entry point they’re using to invade our realm.”

Labrum frowned, his voice calm yet firm. “I understand your anger, Morpheus, but don’t let it cloud your judgment. We must act with fairness, even in dire situations like this. Justice must guide our actions, not fury.”

Morpheus’s tone was resolute. “Father, they’ve been given countless chances for peace. Each time, they lied, deceived, and continued their aggression. We’ve reached the end of diplomacy.”

Sadal Suud spoke softly, her voice tinged with sorrow. “I could feel Morpheus’s anguish when he destroyed the Tarvosians. It’s not an easy burden to bear for either of us. You all know that Morpheus values life above all else.”

Labrum nodded. "You've done everything to avoid destruction, Morpheus. But we need to be thorough to ensure their threat is truly neutralized."

Denab interjected. "What are your next steps, Morpheus?"

"We need to find the entrance they've been using to breach our universe," Morpheus said. "We'll begin at the old gateway I destroyed. It's the most likely starting point."

Labrum adjusted the ship's controls. "Setting a course for the gateway."

As UNIV ORION approached the remnants of the gateway between the two universes, the crew witnessed an unsettling sight—the Tarvosians had already begun reconstructing the passage.

"Labrum, is our monitoring ship still watching over Earth?" Morpheus asked.

"It is," Labrum confirmed.

Morpheus turned to Denab. "Check in with them for any signs of Tarvosians activity."

Denab relayed the message, only to receive an urgent response: the monitoring ship was under attack.

"Labrum, hold the gateway. Destroy any ships attempting to pass through," Morpheus commanded.

In an instant, Morpheus and Sadal Suud time-traveled to Earth's orbit, only to find one of their ships besieged by Tarvosians forces. Rage surged through them as they prepared to act. Channeling their power, they transported the Tarvosians' vessel mid-assault back to their own universe. Positioned above their home planet, the ship's weapons unleashed their fury—not on Morpheus's allies, but on the Tarvosians themselves.

Morpheus and Sadal Suud then boarded their Achillesian ship to assess the situation.

"You arrived just in time to turn the tide," the captain said, relief evident in his voice.

The captain confirmed, "We are all set for now."

"Okay, Captain," Morpheus replied. "But remain vigilant for more Tarvosians ships and call for assistance if needed."

Morpheus and Sadal Suud returned to *UNIV ORION*, and Morpheus addressed the crew. "It's time for all of us to travel to the Caligula Universe."

Labrum and Denab nodded in agreement, and the rest of the crew echoed enthusiastically, "Let's go!"

Morpheus outlined the plan. "Sadal Suud and I will position ourselves outside the ship and transport it—and ourselves—together. Once there, we'll remain invisible to all within the Caligula Universe. Our first priority will be investigation: identifying problems and addressing them. Destruction will only ever be a last resort."

The family and crew agreed, aligning with Morpheus's approach.

As they entered the Caligula Universe cloaked in invisibility, the crew was stunned by the chaos unfolding around them—battles raged across the expanse of the Universe.

"We need to secure the boundary between the two Universes first," Morpheus directed. "Once it's stabilized, we'll search for the root causes of the conflict."

Labrum scouted the edges of the Universe and reported back. "The boundaries appear intact. No issues there."

Morpheus nodded. "Sadal Suud and I will investigate the Tarvosians' planet directly. We'll keep our communicators and body cams active at all times."

While Morpheus and Sadal Suud embarked on their mission, Labrum meticulously documented the unfolding conflict, identifying the Tarvosians as the aggressors while the others struggled to defend themselves. He relayed this critical information back to Morpheus.

"Labrum, deploy protective shields around the victims and defenders," Morpheus instructed.

Labrum attempted to activate the shields, but the relentless firepower was overwhelming. Calling for reinforcements, he reached out. "Morpheus, we need your powers to encapsulate everyone in a protective bubble."

Morpheus and Sadal Suud combined their abilities, enveloping the battlefield in transparent, impenetrable bubbles that halted the fighting.

Meanwhile, on the Tarvosians' home planet, Morpheus and Sadal Suud observed and listened to their leaders' conversations. The Tarvosians' King Volans, visibly agitated, questioned his advisors.

"How are our ships firing on our own planet?" King Volans demanded.

One advisor hesitated before speaking. "This god, Morpheus, intervened. He warned he would bring law and order to this Universe and his own, Vishnu. He redirected our ships' firepower back to us."

King Volans' frustration grew. "Who is this Morpheus? What does he want with our Universe?"

At that moment, Morpheus appeared before the King. "I am Morpheus," he declared. "And it was you who started this war."

King Volans raised a hand to silence his men. "What is this about, Morpheus?" he asked cautiously.

"I know your lies and deceptions," Morpheus replied. "Your people were granted refuge near the Universe's border by the Achillesians. But your greed and violence escalated into this chaos."

Morpheus paused, then asked, “Do you remember Uranus, Gaia, and St. Lucifer?”

King Volans’ eyes narrowed. “Yes, we have ties to them, including the fallen angel, Lucifer.”

“You, King, are the harbinger of chaos,” Morpheus said coldly. “If you knew I intervened with your ships, why do you persist in attacking others?”

“This is my Universe,” King Volans declared defiantly. “I will do as I please.”

Morpheus stepped closer. “You’re nothing but a bully, lording over chaos. But I offer you one chance: peace or the complete annihilation of your people and culture.”

King Volans sneered. “Kill this god, Morpheus. I’ve had enough of him.”

Morpheus met his gaze. “Your wish is my command.”

Suddenly, one of the King’s men began to dissolve, then another, and another, until King Volans stood alone.

“Now, King,” Morpheus said, his voice echoing with finality. “Whom will you rule? Your people are scattered to the winds of time. You continued to persist, so this fate will now befall upon you and every Tarvosian across this Universe.”

Leaving King Volans in silence before he himself disintegrated, Morpheus and Sadal Suud returned to *UNIV ORION*, their mission clear and their resolve unshaken.

CHAPTER 29

Law and Order

When Morpheus and Sadal Suud returned to *UNIV ORION*, the crew gathered with eager questions.

"What happened to the Tarvosians?" one of them asked.

"You have the recordings from the body cams and communicators," Morpheus said calmly.

"You made the right decision by destroying them," Labrum said. "I heard you give the King a choice: peace or annihilation. He chose destruction for his people."

"How did you destroy them all?" Denab asked, her curiosity evident.

"When the King ordered his men to kill us," Sadal Suud explained, "Morpheus responded, 'Your wish is granted.' Their own words sealed their fate, and they were dissolved by the sands of time."

Labrum shifted the conversation. "Now, we need to help the survivors of this war and establish a government that ensures law and order in this Universe."

Morpheus nodded in agreement. Together, they began the monumental task of creating a constitution for the Caligula Universe. While Morpheus and Labrum drafted the framework, the other crew members traveled to the various civilizations to explain the events surrounding the Tarvosians' downfall. They also introduced Morpheus and Sadal Suud as the new King and queen tasked with maintaining peace and justice.

The Achillesians listened to countless stories of how the Tarvosians had ruled through terror, ruining countless civilizations and planets. In response, they promised a new beginning and peace for all.

"We are working on a constitution for the Caligula Universe," they announced.

Two weeks later, the constitution was complete. Copies were prepared for every civilization, and arrangements were made for a grand signing ceremony on a neutral, uninhabited planet.

On the day of the ceremony, spaceships from across the Universe gathered in orbit, and representatives assembled on the planet's surface. Morpheus and Sadal Suud stepped onto the podium to address the crowd.

"I am King Morpheus, and this is Queen Sadal Suud," he began. "We preside over the Universes of Vishnu and Caligula with a single purpose: to establish peace, law, and order. Today, we present this constitution, a pact to end war and foster harmony among civilizations."

Morpheus's tone grew serious. "Understand this: any breach of this treaty will result in the end of your civilization. We are here because you all expressed a desire for peace, and we expect you to honor those words. I will return periodically to ensure the promise of peace is upheld."

Representatives from every civilization signed the agreement over the following days. When the final signatures were collected, the *UNIV ORION* crew distributed copies to all civilizations, ensuring every planet had a record of the historic treaty.

With their mission complete, the crew set a course for home. As they approached the boundary of the Vishnu Universe, Morpheus and Sadal Suud used their powers to transport *UNIV ORION* safely. Once back in their own Universe, Labrum navigated the ship to Achilles, where they were greeted with cheers and celebrations.

King Zeus and the Council welcomed the crew warmly. "Excellent work preserving the peace of the Universes," Zeus commended.

"We had to destroy a civilization to achieve peace," Morpheus said, his voice heavy with regret.

"I understand," Zeus replied. "They made their choice when they rejected your offer."

After a moment of silence, Morpheus asked, "May I have some time alone?"

"Of course," Zeus said with understanding.

As Morpheus walked away from the celebration, Sadal Suud followed him. "Where are you going, Morpheus?" she asked softly.

"To our special place," he replied. "Will you join me?"

"Always," Sadal Suud said, taking his hand.

Meanwhile, Labrum and King Zeus spoke privately.

"Morpheus carries the weight of defending law and order," Labrum said. "It's taking a toll on him. When he's betrayed, his fury is unmatched, and the burden of his decisions weighs heavily on him and Sadal Suud. Their hearts bear the scars of every battle, and these wounds will never fully heal."

Zeus nodded solemnly. "I've seen it too. We need to ensure Morpheus is supported. Let's talk to him when he's ready."

"I agree," Labrum said.

The two leaders exchanged a look of mutual concern, united in their resolve to support Morpheus as he bore the responsibility of shaping peace across two Universes.

Meanwhile, Morpheus and Sadal Suud retreated to their secret place—a tranquil cave by the beach where they often found solace.

"Morpheus, what's wrong?" Sadal Suud asked, concern in her voice. "Let's relax and enjoy ourselves together."

"I'm sorry, my love," Morpheus replied, gazing out at the waves. "I just need some time to think. But I want to enjoy the sun with you."

"Will you share what's on your mind when you're ready?" she asked gently.

"Yes, Sadal Suud. There will never be secrets between us," Morpheus said. "Just give me a little time, and I'll tell you everything."

"Alright," Sadal Suud said with a smile. "Let's go for a swim."

Morpheus slipped out of his clothes and dove into the clear waters, followed closely by Sadal Suud. They swam together, diving for fish and laughing as they playfully splashed each other. When they grew tired, Morpheus built a fire while Sadal Suud prepared their catch. As she cooked, Morpheus's thoughts drifted back to the Tarvosians and the parallels he saw with Earth.

They stayed at the cave for a week, a much-needed respite. By the end of their time there, Morpheus finally shared his inner turmoil.

"I've been thinking about the Tarvosians," he began. "Their evil consumed them—it mattered more to them than any chance at goodness or peace. I wonder if humanity is any different. Immorality and corruption seem to win every time."

"That's not true, Morpheus," Sadal Suud said, taking his hand. "You are living proof that goodness can prevail. You uphold the laws and protect the people of two Universes. That is no small feat."

"But I had to destroy the Tarvosians," he said, his voice heavy.

"Sometimes, doing what is necessary isn't easy or pleasant," she replied. "But you made the hard choices to ensure a better future for countless others."

Reassured by her words, Morpheus and Sadal Suud returned to the city and sought out King Zeus and Labrum, requesting a meeting with the Council.

When the Council convened, Morpheus spoke of his doubts. "I feel conflicted about destroying the Tarvosians. They were consumed by evil, and yet… it's hard to reconcile that decision. It also reminds me of humanity—how they destroy each other and everything they don't understand, often driven by greed."

"What are you suggesting?" King Zeus asked, leaning forward.

"I'm saying the orders from King Saturn and the previous Council were right about humanity," Morpheus admitted.

"These orders predate you," Zeus said. "Now you are the King of the Universe—a role we didn't have before. While we advise you, the ultimate decisions are yours. So far, you've done an extraordinary job. The people of both Universes admire you and Sadal Suud for your wisdom and strength."

“I lived on Earth as a child,” Morpheus said, “And while there are good people, there are also criminals and corruption. The balance is delicate.”

“You’ve answered your own question,” Labrum interjected.

“What do you mean, Father?” Morpheus asked.

“If you need to correct humanity, then protect the good and remove the criminals,” Labrum said. “Establish clear laws and strict consequences. This is part of the reason you were sent to Earth—to understand and address its complexities.”

King Zeus added, “You’ve gained knowledge and experience through time. Use it wisely.”

“You’ve also mastered time travel and the dimensions,” Denab said. “Remember how you defeated St. Lucifer and saved Cronus? You eradicated evil and preserved good. You’ve already proven that this approach works—it worked with the Tarvosians, and it can work with Earth.”

Morpheus nodded slowly. “Then we need to monitor Earth. We’ll assess humanity’s progress and see if my actions have made a difference. If not, we’ll intervene.”

One by one, the Council members voiced their agreement.

Before the meeting ended, Denab raised another issue. “Morpheus, introducing us to your Earth family could be complicated. For them, learning the truth about you might be overwhelming—or even tragic."

"We'll think carefully about that," Morpheus replied.

King Zeus shifted the tone. "For now, let's celebrate the *UNIV ORION* crew. They saved two Universes and upheld the laws of peace. Morpheus, Sadal Suud, you must attend—and no disappearing to your secret beach!"

Laughter erupted around the room, breaking the tension. The celebration lasted for a week, a fitting tribute to the crew's heroic efforts and the promise of a brighter future across the Universes.

CHAPTER 30

Morpheus Returns to Earth

Morpheus and Sadal Suud often spoke of returning to Earth, especially to visit Morpheus's Earth family.

"We're still searching for the roots of good and evil on Earth," Morpheus said one evening.

The two pondered deeply: why, how, and when had evil entered human lives? Their minds wandered to the Tarvosians, St. Lucifer, and the gods Uranus and Cronus. Morpheus also reminded Sadal Suud of the Sun's transformations across solar systems, tracing humanity's ancient origins.

After the weeklong celebration honoring their successes, Morpheus and Sadal Suud approached Labrum.

"When will we leave for Earth?" Morpheus asked.

"We can prepare now if you're ready," Labrum replied.

Denab joined them. "Morpheus, do you intend to introduce us to your Earth family?"

"Yes," Morpheus said confidently. "I want to tell them everything and introduce them to my wife, Sadal Suud."

"You might hurt them with the truth," Denab cautioned.

“I’ve always been honest with my Earth family,” Morpheus said firmly. “I won’t start lying to them now.”

Labrum added, “Earth’s governments have long feared telling their people the truth, worried about the chaos it might bring.”

“One day, humanity will have to accept they’re not alone in the Universe,” Morpheus said. “And that day might come sooner than they think. If humans don’t learn the truth now, they may cause harm to other civilizations when they venture into space. It’s better to prepare them before that happens.”

Labrum nodded. “You’re right, Morpheus. Let’s ready the crew and supplies for our mission.”

As preparations began, Morpheus asked Labrum, “Is there still a ship monitoring Earth?”

“Yes,” Labrum said, his tone cautious. “Why do you ask?”

“I have a feeling something is wrong,” Morpheus replied.

“We’ll find out soon enough,” Labrum assured him.

The crew and family bid their farewells to the people of Achilles and boarded the *UNIV ORION*. Supplies were loaded, systems checked, and coordinates set for Earth. The journey, at an average speed, took about a week.

As the ship approached Earth’s orbit, they discovered debris floating in space—a shattered vessel.

“Labrum, what happened here?” Morpheus asked, his voice tense.

“I don’t know,” Labrum admitted.

“Was there a distress call from the ship?”

“No, none at all,” Labrum replied.

“I’m going back in time to see what happened,” Morpheus said.

“I’m coming with you,” Sadal Suud insisted.

“Be cautious,” Morpheus told her. “We’ll stay in constant communication.”

Labrum interjected, “Wait and assess the situation further before taking action. Let’s not rush.”

Morpheus nodded but proposed a plan. “Sadal Suud and I will search the orbit in one direction while you, Father, take the opposite route.”

Labrum agreed. Morpheus and Sadal Suud left the ship, gliding effortlessly into space.

“Scan for radiation and any unusual compounds,” Morpheus instructed.

Denab’s voice came through the communicator. “We’re detecting high radiation levels and traces of plutonium.”

"A nuclear weapon," Morpheus concluded grimly.

As they continued their search, Morpheus found a large metal fragment with recognizable symbols. "These are from Earth—the United States," he said. "It's clear a nuclear weapon hit this ship."

Morpheus relayed the information to Labrum. "We're going back in time to learn more. Stay cautious and keep behind the moon."

"Understood," Labrum replied.

Morpheus and Sadal Suud traveled back a day before the ship's destruction. They watched as the events unfolded—a missile launched from Earth toward the unsuspecting ship. The crew onboard had no warning.

Returning to the *UNIV ORION*, Morpheus reported their findings. "We're heading to Earth to uncover the reasons behind this attack," he said, determination hardening his voice.

When Morpheus and Sadal Suud arrived on Earth, they used their ability to remain invisible to walk undetected through even the most top-secret facilities.

Their first stop was the White House in Washington, D.C., where they searched for information about the use of nuclear weapons in space. After finding no relevant data there, Morpheus suggested they head to the Pentagon.

As they approached the Pentagon, Sadal Suud asked, "What exactly is this building used for?"

"This is the Military Defense Office," Morpheus explained.

Inside, they combed through classified files until they uncovered documents detailing a nuclear strike in space. The papers revealed that scientists using the Hubble Telescope had detected multiple unidentified spaceships in Earth's orbit. This information was relayed to the Pentagon, which then authorized the launch of a nuclear weapon. Tragically, the military had misinterpreted the situation; by the time they acted, the battle they had observed was over, and the strike had inadvertently destroyed the ship protecting Earth.

Morpheus sighed heavily and turned to Sadal Suud. "The scientists observed a battle between the Tarvosian ships, but by the time the military got involved, they had destroyed one of their own guardians. This is a grave mistake—a tragic misunderstanding."

"We need to stay near the Pentagon for a few days to learn more about this situation," Morpheus said. "This act could be perceived as a declaration of war by the United States—and possibly other nations—against extraterrestrial civilizations."

"What do you mean by that?" Sadal Suud asked, her expression tense.

"In space, this might appear to be an unprovoked attack. The U.S. military acted out of fear and ignorance," Morpheus explained. "They couldn't distinguish between friend and foe because they still see all extraterrestrial life as alien threats. Their governments lie to the people, insisting humanity is alone in the Universe, even though they know otherwise."

"This is another reason why we must visit my Earth family," Morpheus said. "They deserve to know the truth, even if the government won't admit it."

Sadal Suud nodded in agreement. "I understand why the Tarvosians troubled you so much, Morpheus. Humanity is no different. They and the Tarvosians share a common ancestry and the same destructive tendencies."

"Yes," Morpheus said solemnly.

Meanwhile, aboard the *UNIV ORION*, Labrum and the crew monitored the data Morpheus and Sadal Suud uncovered. They listened intently as the couple learned more from the Pentagon's top generals. The files confirmed long-standing rumors about extraterrestrial incidents, including the 1947 UFO crash in Roswell, New Mexico.

"The government created a program called Project Blue Book to investigate UFO sightings," Sadal Suud noted. "It started in 1952, ended in 1969, but was quietly revived in the 21st century. The Roswell incident and others like it prompted renewed interest."

Morpheus thought of Area 51 and said, "We're going there next, Sadal Suud."

"Why Area 51?" she asked.

"That's where they took the Roswell spaceship, the aliens—what they call the Grays—and other recovered materials. We might find critical information about the government's hidden projects."

Sadal Suud agreed. Over the communicator, Labrum added, "Find everything you can, Morpheus. We need to understand how deeply human governments are involved in reverse-engineering alien technology."

At Area 51, Morpheus and Sadal Suud once again used their invisibility to move undetected. Inside the facility, they saw old photos, reports, and remnants of alien spaceships. They discovered that humanity had copied technology from the Roswell crash, leading to significant advancements in computing and other fields.

Morpheus also uncovered records spanning humanity's history, including references to Atlantis, the Mayans, the early Egyptians, Jesus Christ and the Romans, the Giants of Earth, the Greek gods, and Nostradamus. These secrets were stored in archives across the globe—in government vaults, church repositories, and even private collections. Many secrets were hidden within the Catholic Church in the Vatican City.

"The world's governments have spent centuries suppressing the truth about human origins," Morpheus said. "They fear what would happen if the people knew."

"And the people have suffered for it," Sadal Suud replied. "The lies, the betrayal—it's no wonder they rise up against their leaders."

Morpheus turned to her. "This suppression has left humanity divided, disconnected from their true history and purpose. But we now know where the records are kept. The time for truth is coming."

When Morpheus and Sadal Suud returned to the *UNIV ORION*, Labrum convened a meeting with the crew. His anger was palpable.

"The depth of human deceit is staggering," Labrum said. "They've hidden the truth about their existence and their actions for too long. This must change."

Morpheus nodded. "It's time to decide what we do next—for Earth and the Universe."

Labrum asked, "Morpheus, did you learn about these problems when you lived on Earth?"

"I knew about some of the issues, and people suspected things, but as I read the documents, the officials had hidden everything from the people," Morpheus said. "Plus, they have Secret Societies that control everything as well. So, Labrum got mad and upset after hearing about these Secret Societies.

"Morpheus, what do you know about the secret societies of Earth?" Labrum asked, his tone heavy with concern.

Morpheus shook his head slightly. “Not much, Father. Their operations are shrouded in secrecy, even from those who seek the truth.”

Labrum frowned. “Then it’s time we expose them. The people of Earth deserve to know the truth about their planet’s past and the forces shaping their future.”

Morpheus raised a hand to pause him. “Wait. We must tread carefully. Before exposing anything, we need to understand the intentions of the human race. Only then can we decide how to act.”

Denab nodded in agreement. “Morpheus is right. Investigate first, then act accordingly. We can’t afford to make hasty decisions.”

Labrum’s frustration was evident. “I can’t believe the scientists, the leaders of government, and their so-called progress are marching humanity toward a death sentence.”

“Why do you think that, Father?” Morpheus asked, his voice calm but probing.

Labrum sighed deeply. “The Tarvos war still haunts me. I saw firsthand how blind ignorance and arrogance led to destruction. And now, I see the same patterns in humans. They are no different from the Tarvosians.”

Morpheus’s gaze sharpened. “There must be a connection—some shared ancestry or deeper link—between Earth and Tarvos, their planets and histories intertwined. Both races exhibit the same ignorance, the same destructive tendencies."

He paused before adding, "King Saturn was right when he proposed destroying humanity to save the greater balance. As the King of Earth and the Universe, I find myself aligning with his vision."

Sadal Suud stepped forward, her voice steady and resolute. "And as Queen of Earth and the Universe, I agree. This cycle of ignorance must end."

Denab interjected thoughtfully, "I share your concerns, but we must find definitive answers first. Action without understanding could lead to greater chaos."

Labrum nodded reluctantly. "You're both right. Our first step is to investigate. We must uncover the truth about these secret societies and their influence, as well as any other hidden truths about Earth."

The crew murmured their agreement.

"We should divide our efforts," Labrum suggested. "Each team will take a different area of focus: the White House, the Pentagon, the secret societies, the Vatican archives, secret laboratories, Antarctica, and any other hidden locations or leads we uncover. We'll document everything and analyze it together afterward."

Morpheus raised a hand. “Before we begin, I’d like to visit my Earth family. They may hold insights into the current state of the planet.”

Denab smiled slightly. “That’s a reasonable request. We can coordinate the visit with our investigations.”

Labrum nodded in agreement. “Their knowledge of Earth’s present problems could provide valuable context.”

Sadal Suud placed a comforting hand on Morpheus’s arm. “Then let’s proceed. We’ll uncover the truths hidden by the powerful and determine the fate of Earth and its people. Together.”

With renewed determination, the crew began preparations for their investigation, their mission more urgent than ever.

CHAPTER 31

Families Reunite

Morpheus and his Achillesian family finally met his Earth family in an emotional reunion. Labrum and his crew had arrived on Earth in 2023, and Morpheus took the opportunity to introduce both sides of his life.

Morpheus knocked on the door of his childhood home and greeted his parents warmly, saying, “Hello, Dad and Mom.” Hearing his voice, his brothers and sister came running down the stairs, overjoyed to see him after so long.

“Where have you been, Morpheus?” his father, Giuseppe, asked, both relieved and puzzled.

“That’s a long story, Dad,” Morpheus replied with a smile. “But first, let me introduce my family.”

Giuseppe and Sophia exchanged confused glances as Morpheus gestured to the group behind him. “Everyone, this is my Earth family. My dad, Giuseppe, my mom, Sophia, and my siblings: Marcus, Maria, and Joseph.”

Turning to his Earth family, he continued, “And this is my Achillesian family from the world of Achilles. This is my father, King Labrum, and my mother, Queen Denab; my uncles Wega, Rasalhague, and Achernar; my aunts Denebola, Zaniah, and

Capella; my cousins Sirius, Terebellum, Kochab, and Rastaban; and my wife, Sadal Suud."

The room fell silent as Morpheus added, "Now, let me explain everything. I belong to two worlds. Earth is where I was born and grew up, and Achilles is where I discovered my heritage. Both my Earth parents and my Achillesian parents shaped who I am. Dad and Mom gave me a loving home and a foundation of learning, while Labrum and Denab taught me my destiny as a King—not just of Earth, but of the universe."

Gasps of surprise echoed as Morpheus explained further. "*UNIV ORION* is a spaceship hidden behind the moon, and my Achillesian parents are its leaders. They've also served as Earth's protectors for generations. I wanted both of my families to meet because we need to work together for the future of this world and beyond. There's much to discuss, but it will take time for all of us to process."

Overwhelmed but trusting Morpheus, Giuseppe, and Sophia nodded. Sophia broke the tension with a practical question: "Who's hungry?"

Labrum smiled. "We all are!"

"Well then," Giuseppe said, "Let's have a great Italian dinner."

The women joined Sophia in the kitchen to prepare the meal while the men headed outside to talk about life on Earth and Achilles. Morpheus and his brothers made a quick trip to the store for drinks. Meanwhile, Sadal Suud set an extended dining table to accommodate everyone.

When the food was ready, Giuseppe called everyone to the table and led a heartfelt prayer. “Let’s thank God for this meal and this reunion.”

After dinner, everyone praised Sophia’s cooking and thanked the Cappuccinos for their hospitality. While the women cleaned up, the men moved to the TV room to discuss serious matters.

“What’s happening in the world, Dad?” Morpheus asked.

Giuseppe sighed heavily. “People are frustrated with the government. It feels like the leaders care only for themselves, while ordinary people bear all the burdens.”

Sophia joined in, adding, “There are so many secrets, and people share videos of suspicious government activities online. It’s creating chaos.”

Morpheus turned to Giuseppe. “Can we stay here for a while? We need to gather information and ensure everyone’s safety.”

Giuseppe hesitated, but Labrum reassured him. “We’re here to protect you and your family. Take these communicators—they’ll help you monitor any government-related conversations. They also have an alert function that transmits your location to us if needed. Just be discreet.”

Trusting Morpheus's judgment, Giuseppe agreed. "Our family is with you, Labrum. Let's face whatever comes together."

Labrum devised a plan to uncover government and global secrets, aiming to save the world from its own flaws and misguided leadership. Each family member and their team received a specific mission. The Cappuccino family was tasked with gathering information by discreetly listening to conversations, recording them, and passing the data to Labrum. Simultaneously, the crew of the *UNIV ORION* turned invisible and infiltrated top-secret locations across the globe.

Labrum and Denab visited the government offices of leading nations to gather intelligence. Morpheus and Sadal Suud investigated NASA's archives and secret vaults. Wega and Denebola focused on extracting information from the Pentagon. Rasalhague and Zaniah explored the Vatican Archives. Achernar and Capella infiltrated various secret societies. Sirius and Terebellum visited the White House, while Kochab and Rastaban investigated Area 51.

Before departing, Labrum instructed, "Gather all the information you can and return in ten days."

The teams successfully collected vital intelligence while the Cappuccino family recorded critical conversations with locals. When everyone reconvened from their assigned destinations, Labrum turned to Giuseppe. "Did everything go smoothly with your family and the recordings?"

"Yes," Giuseppe replied. "No one faced any issues."

Labrum then posed a profound question: “Giuseppe, Sophia, would you consider leaving your lives on Earth to join us?”

Surprised, Giuseppe hesitated. “We’re not sure, Labrum. Why do you ask?”

“You were chosen to be Morpheus’s parents,” Labrum explained. “It feels right for your family to join our race and legacy.”

Sophia interjected, “We’ll need time to think this over.”

Labrum nodded. “Of course. In the meantime, would you like to visit our spaceship in orbit?”

The Cappuccino family agreed, their curiosity piqued. Together, they boarded a shuttle and traveled to the hidden ship behind the moon.

Upon arrival, the Cappuccinos were awestruck by the vastness and sophistication of the ship. “This is incredible,” Sophia whispered.

“We need to input all the gathered information into the ship’s computers,” Labrum said. “Wega and Denebola will show you around, and you can eat or rest as needed.”

While the recordings were being processed, Wega and Denebola guided the Cappuccinos to a dining area and provided a place for them to sleep.

"We'll wake you when the analysis is complete," Wega reassured them.

As the family rested, Morpheus turned to Labrum. "While we wait, I'll visit Gaia and Cronus to check on their realm."

"Good idea," Labrum said.

Morpheus and Sadal Suud traveled through time to meet Gaia and Cronus. When they arrived, the deities greeted them warmly.

"How are things in your world?" Morpheus asked.

"Everything is peaceful," Gaia replied, and Cronus added, "Nothing unusual to report."

"Where is Zeus?" Morpheus asked.

"He's spending time with Aphrodite by the sea," Gaia said.

"Have any Travosians appeared recently?" Sadal Suud inquired.

"No," Gaia replied.

"And St. Lucifer?" Sadal Suud asked.

"Destroyed by Morpheus," Cronus affirmed.

Satisfied, Morpheus said, "Remember, call my name if you ever need help."

Before leaving, Morpheus and Sadal Suud, still invisible, decided to observe Zeus and Aphrodite by the sea. Finding nothing amiss, they revealed themselves and approached the pair.

Zeus rose to greet them. "Morpheus, my old friend! And Sadal Suud, how are you both?"

"We're well," Morpheus replied. "Is everything stable with your family here on Earth?"

"Everything is fine," Zeus assured him.

"Good. Call my name if any problems arise," Morpheus said.

Zeus nodded. "Of course."

Morpheus and Sadal Suud returned to the present and rejoined their families on the ship. They headed to the bridge, where Labrum and Denab were processing the gathered data.

Labrum asked, "How are things in Earth's past?"

"We spoke with Gaia, Cronus, Aphrodite, and Zeus," Morpheus replied. "They assured us everything was fine, and I spoke with each of them individually to confirm."

"That's good news," Labrum said, nodding thoughtfully. Then he turned to Wega. "Please wake the Cappuccino family and have them join us."

Morpheus inquired, "Do we have the information from the computers?"

"Yes," Labrum confirmed.

When the Cappuccino family entered the Meeting Chamber, Labrum gestured toward the seats. "Please sit down. We've processed the recordings through the computer, and we now have detailed insights. I'll explain the key concerns first, and afterward, we'll open the floor for discussion."

Once everyone was settled, Labrum began. "The data from the recordings revealed critical issues. I'll provide the computer's analysis along with my interpretation. The first problem is the destruction of one of our other ships by a nuclear weapon deployed by Earth's governments. We have evidence that humans intentionally tested and used nuclear weapons in space. While the target was a decoy we provided to deter a Tarvosian invasion, their willingness to act with such aggression confirms our worst fears. Humanity is fast becoming the aggressor species of the Universe."

Labrum paused, allowing the gravity of his words to settle. "Morpheus wanted to save humanity, and I understand his hope. However, we cannot allow humans to threaten or destroy other civilizations for their own gain—whether motivated by greed, wealth, fear, or insecurity. History shows that humans are predisposed to savagery, seeking conflict at the expense of countless lives. Despite the efforts of Morpheus, Gaia, and even the ancient gods, humans remain warlike and destructive. This was evident not long ago as we fought battles against Uranus, St. Lucifer, and the Tarvosians.

"Currently, in 2024, the United States, Russia, and China dominate as the most powerful nations. There is a prophecy predicting these three powers will come into conflict, represented by their symbols: the Eagle for the U.S., the Bear for Russia, and the Dragon for China. When this war occurs, it will escalate into a nuclear catastrophe, contaminating and burning the Earth as we know it. This prophecy was foreseen by King Saturn, and it aligns disturbingly well with recent human actions, such as launching nuclear weapons into space."

Labrum leaned forward, his tone somber. "This brings us to the state of humanity on the ground—the people's side of the story. First, trust between governments and citizens is almost nonexistent. Social divisions have grown. Once, America had three social classes: the rich, the middle class, and the poor. Now, only two remain—the rich and the poor—leaving the middle class virtually extinct.

"Governments exploit their people through oppressive taxation and laws designed to benefit the elite while burdening the masses. This interference causes division among citizens, pitting them against each other instead of uniting them. Corruption permeates every level of society. Politicians, driven by greed for power and money, serve themselves, not the people.

"Many struggle to survive paycheck to paycheck, while the government takes a third of their earnings. Criminals often escape justice, and innocent victims bear the brunt of the system's failures. These problems extend to white-collar crimes, violent acts like murder and rape, and the rise of street gangs that terrorize communities. Even families are not spared, with abuse and dysfunction eroding the core of human connections.

"Innocence and safety are nearly extinct on Earth. The top of society festers with corruption, while the bottom collapses into chaos. Countries like North Korea, Iran, and Iraq, though secondary powers, exacerbate the situation with their threats and destabilizing actions. Humanity is teetering on the brink of total disorder."

Labrum's voice grew resolute. "We must act decisively. The first priority is eliminating the criminal element at every level. Without this foundation, there is no hope for peace or justice. While debate has its place, action and solutions are what Earth needs now."

The room fell silent, the weight of Labrum's words settling over the group. Finally, he looked around the table. "Now, let us discuss. Your thoughts are welcome, but remember—we are here for answers, not prolonged debates."

CHAPTER 32

Corruption

"These are the complaints and recordings from the Earthlings," Labrum began. "I want to start by speaking only with the Cappuccino family to hear their thoughts. Giuseppe, I'd like to hear from all your family members."

Giuseppe nodded and spoke with conviction. "I believe I speak for my entire family when I say your reasons and insights are sound. Earth is deeply corrupted in many ways. Unfortunately, there is no authority to report or hold accountable the wrongdoings of its leaders and governments. As Morpheus explained about Uranus and his unchecked free will, today's world mirrors that problem. Governments and even individuals act with impunity, creating laws only to bend them for the benefit of the wealthy and powerful."

Labrum looked around. "Does the rest of the Cappuccino family share Giuseppe's perspective on Earth's corruption?" The family members exchanged glances and nodded in agreement.

Labrum then posed another question. "Given the choice, would you prefer to remain here with us or return to Earth? I want each of you to answer directly. Let's begin with the children."

One by one, Morpheus's Earth siblings expressed their desire to stay with the Achillesians. Following them, Giuseppe and Sophia also chose to remain.

Labrum smiled. "You will soon see what life can be like without wars, greed, and chaos. But before we proceed, I need to know: Will you remain loyal to our family and yourselves?"

The Cappuccino family unanimously pledged their loyalty. Giuseppe then asked, "What are your plans for Earth and its people?"

Labrum held up a hand. "That is a discussion for another time. Right now, I need clarity on where your loyalties lie. With Earth or with us. Understand, we have strict laws against betrayal."

"My family stands with you, the Achillesians," Giuseppe affirmed.

"Good," Labrum replied. Morpheus interjected, his tone serious. "Remember, this is a permanent choice. Once decided, there is no turning back."

"We are committed to the Achillesians," the Cappuccino family declared in unison.

Morpheus offered a word of caution. "Do not break our laws. Offenders will face the consequences."

Giuseppe met his gaze. "We understand, Morpheus, our son."

The meeting was interrupted when Morpheus turned to Labrum. “I’d like to pause here. I want to do some research with the computers before we continue.”

Labrum nodded. “We can break for lunch and start the research. What are you hoping to uncover?”

“We’ll examine Earth’s history as recorded by humanity,” Morpheus explained.

“Why revisit it now?” Labrum asked.

“To ensure the decisions we make are well-informed,” Morpheus said.

“Very well,” Labrum agreed. “Let’s see what you uncover. We can discuss it over our meal.”

As they began their research, Morpheus reflected aloud. “Man has shed blood on Earth since the dawn of time. Before humans, gods and goddesses walked the land. Humanity began with Adam and Eve, followed by their children Cain and Abel. When Cain killed Abel out of jealousy, it marked the first sin of murder. Even God warned Cain to master his sin, yet he succumbed. This pattern of good versus evil has persisted through the ages like a puzzle slowly taking shape.”

He continued, “Earth has seen multiple beginnings of civilizations, both before and after humanity. The Achillesian race was among those who brought humans to Earth. But conflict has always plagued this planet, unlike anywhere else in the universe. It makes me wonder if the issue lies in some fundamental chemical reaction—perhaps tied to the Sun, Earth, or humanity's extraterrestrial origins."

Labrum added somberly, "The evil seeded by human blood has turned Earth into a battleground of Heaven and Hell. Humanity has brought their own version of hell to the surface, fueled by greed, power, and hatred."

Giuseppe looked at his son with a faint smile. "You must have paid attention in religion class and church."

"This isn't just religion, Dad," Morpheus replied. "It's history intertwined with faith. I was partially right about the chemical reaction and about the evil ingrained in human blood. Earth has become the embodiment of Heaven and Hell, created by humanity's own hands."

After finishing lunch, the family gathered in the Computer Chamber, where Morpheus turned to Denab. "Show us Earth's history, from its earliest days to the present," he instructed.

Morpheus addressed the group as Denab prepared the display. "This computer is more than a machine—it's a window through time. It can reveal every event or mistake ever made, whether across the Universe or in a single place, like Earth."

Giuseppe and his family were captivated, their awe growing as the screen projected Earth's tumultuous history. Scene after scene revealed blood-soaked wars, each more devastating than the last. They watched in silence as the computer unveiled the machinations of secret societies and governments working in tandem to shape the world to their vision. Hidden agendas, sinister alliances, and schemes for personal gain were laid bare.

Denab paused the display at Morpheus's request. Turning to his family, Morpheus explained, "This is the story of power—of the rich and powerful building their own kingdoms without the people's knowledge. It's like the communist regimes: promises made for the people while the elite benefit behind closed doors. Lies and deception are the foundation of this system, designed to maintain control and profit. Secret societies and governments have exploited and divided humanity for their convenience, conquering through manipulation. Their tactics trickle down, creating division even within families and communities. Bullies on the streets mirror the bullies in power."

Morpheus's tone grew heavier as he continued. "The world cries out for independence, but instead of unity, it breeds greed, power struggles, and hatred. Everyone competes with their neighbor, their government, and their authorities. Humans, for all their potential, remain primitive in many ways. Even animals show greater kindness to one another than humans do to their own. History, as we see, repeats itself, and the cup of human failings overflows."

He paused, his gaze steady. "It falls to me and Sadal Suud to confront these problems. The situation leaves us with three choices. First, we could save the planet but eliminate humanity entirely. Second, we could remove only those who break the laws we establish for Earth. And finally, we could create a new constitution—not just for one nation, but for the entire world."

"I like the second and third options," Labrum said firmly.

"Me too," Giuseppe agreed.

The others nodded, echoing, "Those are perfect ideas, Morpheus."

Labrum then raised a question. "But how will you make them follow these laws when they've shown no regard for any rules?"

Morpheus's expression hardened. "Humans must come to terms with a universal truth—they are not alone in the Universe. They must understand that gods ruled this world long before them and will continue to do so long after their time. With this realization, we can implement a new constitution with rules, laws, order, and equal justice for all. And to enforce these laws, those who break them will be punished, their very existence turning to dust by their own actions."

Labrum nodded in approval. "That's an excellent plan, Morpheus."

The others agreed in unison, their voices united: "It's a good and just solution."

"How will you present this new Constitution to all the governments?" Giuseppe asked, his tone laced with concern.

"We must first draft the new laws and consolidate them into what we'll call the *Constitution of Earth,*" Morpheus explained. "Once it's ready, Sadal Suud and I will approach the President of the United States to arrange a summit with all the world's leaders."

"You're risking your lives, you and your wife," Giuseppe warned. "They'll shoot you before you even speak."

"Don't worry, Dad. I have everything under control," Morpheus reassured him with calm confidence.

"When do you plan to start this new Constitution?" Labrum asked.

"Now," Morpheus declared firmly.

Labrum interjected with a practical suggestion. "Let's begin tomorrow morning. It's nearly dinner time, and everyone will think more clearly after a good night's rest."

The group nodded in agreement and prepared for dinner. Before eating, Giuseppe offered a heartfelt blessing, asking for guidance and wisdom. The meal was a feast fit for gods and goddesses, full of rich flavors and vibrant dishes that reflected the grandeur of their gathering.

After dinner, Rastaban and Terebellum invited the Cappuccino family to explore the Hologram Hall. The family eagerly accepted, their excitement palpable as they departed.

Once they were alone, Labrum turned to Morpheus. "How do you feel about your Earth family? Do you trust them to adapt and stay loyal to us?"

Morpheus paused thoughtfully before replying. "I believe in my Earth family. They're tired of the lies and corruption that plague their governments and societies. I trust they're telling the truth about wanting a better way."

Labrum nodded. "You were wise to warn them of the consequences of betrayal. They need to understand the gravity of their commitment to this family."

"We'll monitor their choices carefully," Morpheus said. "Time will reveal their true intentions. Testing their loyalty is essential, especially as we implement changes to Earth's governance."

"How will you handle any defiance from them or other humans when the time comes?" Labrum asked.

"With all due respect, Father," Morpheus replied solemnly, "Sadal Suud and I will take full responsibility. We are the King and Queen of Earth and the Universe. If the worst happens, we will not hesitate to enforce the ultimate punishment."

Labrum regarded him with a stern expression. "You must not break the rules and laws of the Universe, Morpheus."

"Father," Morpheus said, meeting Labrum's gaze, "Do you think I would ever do that?"

Denab interjected gently. "No, Morpheus, we trust you. This is merely a reminder of the weight of your decisions."

Morpheus acknowledged their concerns with a nod. "The recordings we gather will serve as evidence of every event on

Earth. It's the only way to protect Sadal Suud and me from any accusations or misunderstandings."

Denab offered an approving smile. "That's a wise precaution, Morpheus."

Soon, the Cappuccino family returned from the Hologram Hall, their faces glowing with excitement. Giuseppe and Sophia recounted how they revisited the moment they first fell in love, while Morpheus's siblings marveled at experiencing life as gods and goddesses, like their brother.

Morpheus stood and addressed his Earth family. "May we take a walk and talk privately?"

"Yes, of course," they all agreed.

He motioned for Sadal Suud to join them. "Come with me, my love."

"I'm coming," she replied warmly, taking his hand.

Once they reached his chambers, Morpheus gestured for everyone to sit. "I have some important questions to ask."

He looked to his family. "Do you mind if Sadal Suud stays for this?"

"She's your wife," Giuseppe said. "Of course, it's fine."

Morpheus began. "How are you all feeling about being here?"

Giuseppe spoke first. “Your mother and I love it here.”

Marcus added, “I like it.”

Maria chimed in, “I do too.”

Joseph, however, was more emphatic. “I don’t want to go back to Earth.”

Morpheus nodded. “You do understand that if any of you break the laws, there will be consequences.”

“We understand,” Giuseppe replied. The others nodded in agreement, their expressions serious.

Morpheus pressed on. “And you know I will be responsible for punishing you, should it come to that?”

“Yes, Morpheus,” they said in unison.

Satisfied, Morpheus relaxed slightly. “Good. That’s all I needed to hear.”

CHAPTER 33

New Constitution

The day after their arrival, Morpheus and Labrum began drafting a new Constitution for Earth. They gathered the gods, goddesses, and humans aboard the ship to collaboratively shape a framework for a better world.

"We could draw inspiration from the Constitution of Achilles, the Caligula Universe, or even our Universe Constitution," Labrum suggested.

"That's a good starting point," Morpheus replied. "We already have three solid examples to work with."

"What about the one from the United States?" Giuseppe interjected.

"We could leave things as they are on Earth," Morpheus said thoughtfully, "or we could strive to create a better, unified Constitution for the world."

"I think improvement is necessary," Giuseppe said. "Our mission here is to protect humanity—from themselves and from the Earth. I didn't realize how dire things had become until now."

Morpheus nodded. "Your input is invaluable because you are family to us. But I know my Earth family isn't fully aware of everything happening—on Earth or across the Universe."

Turning to Rastaban and Terebellum, Morpheus instructed, "Take my Earth family to the Hologram Hall. Show them the real conflicts humanity faces—past, present, and future."

As Rastaban and Terebellum led the Cappuccino family to the Hologram Hall, Morpheus and Labrum returned to their drafting. The holograms depicted humanity's turbulent history, the consequences of their actions, and their potential future among the stars.

Labrum proposed an outline for the Constitution: "We'll start with the Universe, then narrow it down to Earth and its population."

Morpheus agreed, and with that, they penned the new Constitution.

The Constitution for Earth and the Universe

Universe:

1. Humans will not be permitted to enter space or interact with the Universe until they establish lasting peace on Earth in all forms and aspects.
2. Violating this directive will result in humanity's banishment from the Universe.
3. Universe civilizations will not tolerate war, planetary theft, or criminal activity of any kind.
4. Crimes committed by humans in the Universe will result in severe consequences, including capital punishment.

Earthwide Directives:

1. All wars and conflicts must cease. Failure to comply will result in the offending country's banishment or destruction.
2. Governments will be unified under a single agenda for the benefit of humanity and Earth.
3. Officials' salaries and budgets will be halved, redirecting resources to public welfare. Taxes will primarily fall on businesses.
4. Criminal acts—hate crimes, discrimination, theft, murder, rape, and abuse—will not be tolerated. Offenders face immediate banishment from Earth.

Global Standards:

1. All individuals must contribute through work unless incapacitated by illness.
2. Every child will receive an education.
3. Weapons of all kinds will be eradicated. Peace is non-negotiable, and violators hold their fate in their own hands.
4. Errors by governments or individuals will carry the ultimate penalty.

Governance:

1. King Morpheus of Earth and the Universe, alongside Queen Sadal Suud, will oversee and enforce these directives.
2. Orders from the King and Queen must be obeyed, or violators will face banishment.
3. Amendments to the Constitution will be made as necessary for the greater good.

After completing the draft, Labrum remarked, “We’ve done well with this new Constitution.”

Morpheus, however, looked pensive. “You know the humans won’t readily accept this.”

Labrum placed a hand on his shoulder. “That’s true. But remember, Morpheus, you are the King of both Earth and the Universe. Problems on Earth could destabilize your reign in the Universe.”

“I know, Father,” Morpheus replied. “If humans fail to cooperate, we have the authority to banish them from Earth. But I want to give them the same chances I gave the Tarvosians. If they wage war, they will bring about their own downfall.”

“You’re right,” Labrum said. “The Constitution reflects this, and I’m here to guide you—not to oppose you.”

“I understand,” Morpheus said. “I’m drawing on all the knowledge I’ve gained from Earth and Achilles. On Achilles, you were all concerned about the war with the Tarvosians. Humans share many of their flaws—deceit, hatred, and the relentless pursuit of power.”

Labrum sighed. “These problems are not unique, Morpheus. But we must try, even if humanity resists.”

At that moment, Rastaban and Terebellum returned with the Cappuccino family.

"We'll discuss this later," Labrum said as he turned back to his son.

Giuseppe and his family approached Morpheus and Labrum. Giuseppe spoke earnestly, "We didn't realize how terrible life was throughout Earth's history. We only see today's problems—how governments hurt people worldwide."

Labrum nodded. "That's understandable. Much of humanity's suffering stems from the secretive systems of greed and power created by governments. But you don't need to apologize for the mistakes or intentions of others."

"I feel I must," Giuseppe replied. "It's my race—my people."

Labrum regarded him thoughtfully. "Have you seen the future of your world?"

"No," Giuseppe said quietly.

"That's for the best," Labrum said. "The future can be a heavy burden. We've completed the draft of the Constitution. I'd like you and your family to read it and share your opinions."

"Yes, Labrum," Giuseppe said. His family echoed their agreement.

"But before you read it," Labrum added, "How do you feel about being here with us? Would you prefer to return to Earth?"

Giuseppe glanced at his family and smiled. “We’re grateful to be here with Morpheus and his family. We’ve decided to stay with all of you.”

“That’s good to hear,” Labrum said warmly. “Once we resolve Earth’s issues, we’ll work together to help you gain Achillesian knowledge—starting with education. For now, go and review the Constitution.”

As Giuseppe and his family left, Labrum turned to Morpheus. “What’s your plan for introducing yourself to Earth?”

Morpheus thought for a moment. “We’ll take over their broadcast systems and make a global speech. We’ll announce a date for all world leaders to prepare for a virtual meeting. Their initial reactions will reveal their intentions. Afterward, we’ll arrange an in-person summit with the most influential leaders.”

Labrum smiled. “A solid plan, Morpheus.”

Giuseppe soon returned, looking resolved. “Labrum, we’ve read the Constitution, and we all agree with its terms.”

Labrum raised an eyebrow. “Did everyone agree individually?”

“Yes,” Giuseppe affirmed.

“Will the gods rule Earth as we know it?” Giuseppe asked cautiously.

"No, Dad," Morpheus interjected. "We're not here to rule. Our goal is to foster peace on Earth and help humanity prepare for space exploration—without aggression or conflict. We want them to live without the burdens they face now."

Labrum nodded and turned to Kochab and Rastaban. "We need a method to interrupt Earth's broadcast systems and establish a virtual communication network. Can you handle this?"

"It should be straightforward," Kochab replied confidently.

"Good," Labrum said. "We'll also need a monitoring system to observe reactions, especially in government offices."

Labrum considered deploying his family, crew, and the Cappuccino family to Earth to witness the reactions firsthand. When he shared this idea, Morpheus agreed. "Perfect, Father."

"Tomorrow, we'll hold a feast," Labrum announced. "It will be a time to relax while Kochab and Rastaban complete their task."

That evening, everyone gathered for a grand dinner. The atmosphere was filled with joy and camaraderie. Giuseppe, Sophia, and their children were amazed by the celebration.

"Morpheus, is this what good times are like for the Achillesians?" Sophia asked, marveling at the festivities.

"It's even better," Morpheus said with a smile.

Giuseppe nodded. “We made the right decision to stay with your family, Morpheus.”

“We’ll all be on Earth during the first broadcast,” Morpheus explained. “You’ll see humanity’s reactions firsthand. While we won’t receive a warm reception from leaders, we’ll focus on the public’s response. Everyone will wear communicators to record and monitor interactions. If there’s trouble, the system will bring you back to the ship immediately.”

As the night ended, Morpheus addressed his Earth family. “You can visit the Library Chamber, Hologram Hall, or your Sleeping Chamber, but avoid restricted areas on the ship.”

“Understood,” Giuseppe replied.

“If you need Sadal Suud or me, contact Labrum or Denab,” Morpheus continued. “I’ll be spending some time with my wife.”

“That’s perfectly fine,” Sophia assured him.

Later, as Morpheus and Sadal Suud settled into bed, their powers began to strengthen and glow as they fell asleep holding each other. The luminous energy stirred the ship, awakening Giuseppe and Sophia. Concerned, they sought out Labrum and Denab.

“What’s happening?” Giuseppe asked.

“It’s Morpheus and Sadal Suud,” Labrum explained. “Their powers are intensifying while they sleep.”

Denab added, “This is a natural process for them. Would you like some coffee while we wait for the glow to subside?”

“Yes, that would be nice,” Giuseppe said. Sophia agreed.

Together, they went to the Dining Chamber, where they shared coffee and conversation, easing into the quiet night.

CHAPTER 34

Communicating with Earth

The next day, Giuseppe and Sophia approached Morpheus and Sadal Suud. Giuseppe spoke hesitantly, "Can we talk to you both?"

"Of course, Dad and Mom," Morpheus replied warmly. "Is this a private matter, or can we speak openly?"

"Everyone on the ship already knows about your powers," Giuseppe said. "Your mom and I want to hear it directly from you and Sadal Suud."

"Do you think we should include Labrum and Denab in the conversation?" Morpheus asked.

"No," Giuseppe said. "This is just between us."

"Understood," Morpheus said. "Let's go to my chamber for some privacy."

Once inside the chamber, Sophia asked, "What exactly happened to you and Sadal Suud last night?"

Morpheus exchanged a glance with his wife. "We'll show you," he said gently. "But don't worry—nothing will happen to you."

Taking Sadal Suud's hand, Morpheus closed his eyes. The two began to glow, their energies intertwining in a radiant display of light and power. After a moment, the glow subsided.

Giuseppe stared in awe. "Do you always do this when you're together?"

"Yes and no," Morpheus explained. "Our powers come from our love for each other and the prophecy that destined us to care for and protect the Universe and its civilizations. We don't need to be together for the power to manifest, but when we are, our strength becomes unstoppable.

"These powers began when I first arrived on this spaceship and have grown over time. Being with Sadal Suud has amplified them even further. This is why we are the King and Queen of the Universe and also the rulers of Earth."

He paused, then continued, "You would have seen our abilities eventually, but it's important to understand: our powers serve two purposes—defense and protection. Does this explanation help you understand better?"

Sophia nodded. "Yes, it does, Morpheus," she said.

"And are you afraid?" Morpheus asked, his gaze searching their faces.

"No, Morpheus," Sophia said firmly. "We love you just the same, our child."

"Good," Morpheus said. "Remember, though, I am responsible for all five of you. If you ever step out of line, I will have to act."

"You'll never have to worry about us," Giuseppe said. "We're family—always."

Satisfied, Morpheus smiled. "We all need to prepare to contact Earth now."

Kochab and Rastaban soon approached with updates.

"We're ready to intercept Earth's broadcast systems via their satellites," Kochab reported. "The virtual meeting will be broadcast simultaneously across their television networks."

"Excellent work," Morpheus said.

Labrum joined them, adding, "The monitors and communicators are fully operational."

Morpheus turned to everyone. "Does everyone know their assignments for Earth?"

In unison, they responded, "Yes, Morpheus."

"We will pair off," Morpheus announced, his tone firm yet reassuring. "I want one member of my Achilles family paired with one from my Earth family."

"Why is that necessary?" Giuseppe asked, curiosity and concern evident in his voice.

"They will protect you if any problems arise," Morpheus explained. "Here are the teams: Labrum with Giuseppe, Denab with Sophia, Wega with Marcus, Denebola with Maria, Rasalhague with Zaniah and Joseph, Achernar with Capella, and Sirius with Terebellum. These pairs will cover key locations on Earth. Meanwhile, Kochab and Rastaban will remain on the ship with Sadal Suud and me to oversee the operation."

Morpheus outlined the assignments. "Labrum and Giuseppe, you will head to the White House. Denab and Sophia, the Pentagon. Wega and Marcus, Russia. Denebola and Maria, China. The rest of you will go to Boston, New York, and Los Angeles.

"Kochab and Rastaban will manage the remote monitors from the ship, ensuring all input is received and relayed back to us. Earth family members, listen carefully to your partners and follow their guidance—no exceptions. Sadal Suud and I will broadcast a message to Earth through their communication systems, addressing the world directly. Your job is to observe the reactions of the people and leaders."

He paused, his gaze sweeping over the group. "If things go well, we will meet with humanity in person. If not, we'll learn their true intentions as they venture into space and decide on the necessary course of action. Is everyone ready to proceed?"

"Yes, Morpheus," the group responded in unison.

"Then get to your destinations, check in, and we'll begin the broadcast," Morpheus instructed.

Once everyone had reached their locations and confirmed their readiness, Morpheus and Sadal Suud stood before the cameras, their presence commanding and serene. The broadcast began, transmitting to every corner of the Earth.

"You are not alone in the Universe," Morpheus began, his voice steady and resolute. "I repeat, humans are not alone in the Universe. My name is King Morpheus of Earth and the Universe, and this is my wife, Queen Sadal Suud. We come in peace to help save Earth from yourselves.

"We have drafted a new Constitution for all the world's people and wish to discuss it with your leaders. This meeting can be virtual or in person. The choice is yours. However, I urge you to set aside your arguments and conflicts long enough to listen to us.

"We do not lie or deceive, and we strongly advise against any military action. While we abhor war, we will defend ourselves if necessary, and the consequences would be catastrophic for Earth. We will wait for your response, which can be broadcast to us in one week. There is no need for panic. Every time we communicate, the world will witness our words and actions. We come in peace."

Meanwhile, Labrum and Giuseppe observed the chaos unfolding in the White House. Invisible to the human eye, they watched as the President and his advisers erupted in panic. Phones rang incessantly as orders were given to alert the Pentagon and activate all branches of the military.

A general attempted to reason with the President. "These beings claim to come in peace. Starting a war with them could provoke a conflict we cannot win. Instead, we should see what they have to offer."

Similar scenes of fear and militarization played out in Russia and China, where leaders hastily mobilized their forces. Despite the leaders' reactions, the monitors revealed a starkly different sentiment among the public.

In cities like Boston, New York, and Los Angeles, people were hopeful. Crowds gathered, cheering, "The gods have returned to bring justice to Earth!" They celebrated the prospect of an end to government corruption, war, and crime.

Morpheus, back on the ship, was perplexed. "Why are Earth's leaders more afraid than its people?" he asked Kochab, Rastaban, and Sadal Suud.

The three exchanged uncertain glances. "We don't know, Morpheus," Kochab replied.

Morpheus sighed, deep in thought. The stark contrast between the fear of the leaders and the hope of the people hinted at a deeper rift within humanity—one that would need to be addressed before Earth could truly find peace.

Labrum and Giuseppe listened as the generals in the White House debated the situation. One general addressed the President with conviction.
"Mr. President, if these beings wanted to destroy us, they already would have. There's no logic in them bluffing when they could

simply take what they want. We need to meet them in person and assess their intentions directly."

Morpheus, monitoring the situation, summoned all his people back to the ship. "Leave the remote monitors active to record the world's reactions," he instructed. Once everyone had returned, he announced, "Meeting Chamber."

In the chamber, Morpheus directed Denab to analyze the data from the monitors. Turning to Labrum, he asked for his observations.

"The people welcomed the gods' arrival," Labrum reported. "Their reaction was completely different from their governments. The leaders seemed secretive as if they were hiding information—possibly from their own people."

Morpheus nodded thoughtfully. "I saw the same in the recordings. While living on Earth, I often noticed how governments manipulated their people. Scientists, too, have misrepresented history, inventions, and countless other truths."

"That's precisely why we're here," Labrum said. "To correct the problems humans have created over eons."

Morpheus leaned back, his expression somber. "But how do we help those who refuse to change? The ignorance of humans runs deep. They think in limited ways, often resorting to war. The recordings prove their fierceness. And yet, they dream of exploring the unknown reaches of space."

"They won't survive out there," Labrum replied. "Other advanced civilizations would destroy them quickly. If left unchecked, humanity's aggression could bring ruin to the Universe."

Morpheus sighed. "King Saturn was right when he compared humans to the Tarvosians—fierce and unyielding. It's hard to fix such destructive tendencies."

However, Wega interjected, "The people, at least, are on our side. They see us as gods and hope we'll bring justice."

"Yes, but the leaders will fight their own people if it suits their agenda," Morpheus countered. "Corruption pervades every level of society, from governments to individuals. It has to end."

Sadal Suud spoke up, her voice firm. "When we meet with the humans, we'll come with the best intentions. But if they attack, we'll defend ourselves. They need to understand the consequences of their aggression. Their actions will determine their fate, and the whole world will see it unfold."

Morpheus added, "Sadal Suud and I have discussed ways to handle those who attack and those who harm society. We must be decisive."

"I agree," Achernar said.

Denab nodded. "It's the only way to deal with aggressors."

Giuseppe and Sophia exchanged a glance before speaking. “The leaders won’t stop unless they’re confronted and removed permanently,” Giuseppe said.

The group reached a consensus. Sadal Suud summarized, “Those who attack us or perpetuate harm will be banished from Earth.”

Morpheus concluded, “Then it’s settled. We’ll wait for their response. Until then, let’s take this time to relax.”

That evening, the family gathered for a feast. As they sat at the table, Labrum raised his glass. “A toast to Morpheus and Sadal Suud for their leadership and courage in presenting themselves to the human race.”

“To Morpheus and Sadal Suud,” Giuseppe added, “And their mission to bring peace and justice to Earth.”

Morpheus and Sadal Suud stood, raising their glasses in return. “To the crew of the *UNIV ORION,*” Morpheus said, “And to a hopeful future for humanity and Earth.”

After the meal, the family retired to their chambers for the night.

The next morning, Denab received a transmission from Earth. The President of the United States requested an in-person meeting with Morpheus and Sadal Suud. The message stated:

The Achillesians will broadcast the meeting worldwide. There will be no aggression toward Morpheus and Sadal Suud, and we assure peace during the discussions. The meeting will take place on the White House lawn in two days at 9 a.m. End of message.

Denab called the family to the ship's bridge to share the news.

CHAPTER 35

Meeting with Earth Leaders

"We have the meeting confirmed," Labrum announced. "The place, time, and details are set for two days from now. Morpheus, let's review the plan for the event."

"Sadal Suud and I will attend alone," Morpheus said. "Kochab and Rastaban will manage the remote monitors and broadcast the event worldwide. The rest of you will remain on the ground, recording the people's reactions. Teams will stay in their designated locations, and all data will be sent to the ship in real-time."

"What if they attack?" Sirius asked.

"Our body shields will protect us," Morpheus reassured. "We have two days to prepare the remote monitors and ensure the safety of my Earth family. Stay vigilant."

The day of the meeting arrived. The ship stirred with early preparations as Morpheus's family gathered to finalize the plans.

Morpheus addressed the group. "Does everyone understand their role in protecting our Earth family?"

"Yes, Morpheus," they replied in unison.

He turned to Kochab and Rastaban. "Are the remote monitors operational?"

"They're fully functional, Morpheus," Rastaban confirmed with a nod.

"Good. We can't predict how this will unfold, so stay cautious. If things escalate, activate your shields and return to the ship immediately," Morpheus instructed.

Labrum stepped forward. "It's time, Morpheus."

Morpheus and Sadal Suud left the ship, descending gracefully through Earth's atmosphere. Their gliding entry captivated onlookers, who gathered in awe as they landed on the White House lawn.

The President and his generals waited, their faces betraying a mix of apprehension and forced composure. Morpheus and Sadal Suud extended their hands in a gesture of friendship. After a brief pause, the President reciprocated, shaking hands.

"I am Morpheus, and this is my wife, Sadal Suud," Morpheus introduced.

"I am the President of the United States, and these are my generals and advisers," the President replied. "Why have you come to Earth?"

"We are here to help and to save your world from itself," Morpheus said.

"Our world is fine as it is," the President replied, his tone defensive.

"If your world is truly perfect, then explain why wars persist, why famine devastates nations, and why governments fail to cooperate, leaving the people to suffer," Morpheus challenged. "Explain the rampant crimes—murders, thefts, rapes, and corruption, including white-collar crimes committed by those in power."

The President looked visibly shaken by Morpheus's detailed knowledge of Earth's problems.

"Are you a leader or merely a puppet for others?" Morpheus pressed. "I am aware of your secret societies and the hidden power they wield. They are the true rulers of your world, not you."

The President, stunned, said nothing.

One of the generals broke the silence. "What is your true purpose here?"

"Sadal Suud and I have returned because this planet was once ours, many eons ago," Morpheus said. "We are here to educate humanity about their origins and expose the lies that have shaped their history. We aim to correct the falsehoods and set the record straight for all of humankind."

Sadal Suud watched Morpheus closely, sensing his deliberate provocation of the human leaders. She remained quiet, allowing the exchange to play out.

Morpheus shifted his gaze to the President. "Did your government fire a nuclear weapon into space and strike a spaceship?"

"I don't have that information," the President said hesitantly.

Morpheus turned to the generals. "Do any of you know?"

The generals remained silent.

"It was a ship from my planet. Such an act could be considered a declaration of war," Morpheus said firmly. "But we are not here to destroy humanity. We are here to save this world called Earth."

"And how do you propose to save Earth?" the President asked, his tone skeptical.

"There is a *New Constitution for the World*," Morpheus said, "Drafted with clear laws and consequences for those who break them. It ensures fairness, equality, and justice for all."

As he spoke, government leaders worldwide received the document on their computers. The President began reading it aloud. When he finished, he and the generals laughed dismissively.

"What's so amusing?" Morpheus asked, his expression unwavering.

"No one will follow these laws," the President said smugly.

"You're mistaken," Morpheus replied, his voice steady but firm.

"No, *you're* mistaken," the President retorted. "You have no understanding of humanity."

Morpheus's eyes narrowed. "I have lived among your people for centuries. Your scientists know little about past civilizations, and your governments have failed time and again. I am here to offer humanity a better way—a chance to live in harmony and prosperity."

He leaned closer, his voice growing sharper. "Why are you here, Mr. President? To lead or to exploit your people for greed and power? Your systems harm those you are meant to serve. I am here to guide Earth's people to a brighter future, free from corruption and deceit."

Morpheus turned to address everyone present. "Earth is the only planet that does not live in peace. Your people owe their existence to us, and we owe them a world of harmony. The time for corruption has ended. I am here to resolve these problems and ensure a future worth living for all."

The President and the generals erupted into laughter again, their mocking tone clear. It was a deliberate attempt to provoke Morpheus.

"Laugh all you want," Morpheus said, his voice calm but commanding. "I will still do my job here on Earth."

"And what job is that, Morpheus?" the President asked smugly.

Without another word, Morpheus raised his hand, and a transparent glass-like box formed around the President and his generals. The laughter ceased instantly.

"You are now prisoners of the King and Queen of Earth and the Universe," Morpheus declared, his voice echoing with authority. "Who's laughing now?"

Turning away from the stunned men, Morpheus and Sadal Suud addressed the global audience.

"We came in peace to help this world," Morpheus said, his voice firm but resolute. "But the level of corruption is staggering. To end it, those who commit grave crimes will face the ultimate consequence so that the good can prosper and reclaim a world of peace."

He continued, "I am here to guide you and uphold laws that protect humanity. The people will govern their countries, states, cities, and towns—but under a system free from greed and injustice."

Suddenly, the military opened fire on Morpheus and Sadal Suud. The couple activated their body shields, rendering the weapons useless. Morpheus raised his hands, addressing the world once more.

"This is wrong," he said. "We stand here peacefully, yet we are attacked. Why?"

Sadal Suud stepped forward, her eyes flashing with controlled fury. "There is nothing more dangerous than a woman's temper," she said, her voice low but deadly. With a wave of her hand, the soldiers' weapons flew from their grips, crumpling into useless scraps before vanishing into dust.

"We are not aggressors," Morpheus said. "But do not mistake our patience for weakness. I have orders to banish every human on Earth if necessary. Yet, as King of the Universe, I offer one chance—for all of you to live in peace and harmony."

Reports poured in from their family and crew members: Russian, Chinese, and American military forces were mobilizing for war against the Achillesians.

Sadal Suud shook her head. "We tried the peaceful way. Now you will see the fury of the gods."

With a single command, Morpheus banished all weapons on Earth. Every gun, missile, and tool of war disappeared without a trace.

"I will show you the intentions of your corrupt governments and secret societies," Morpheus said, his tone sharp. "There is a war brewing in the East, designed to pull Americans into the conflict. Afterward, nuclear weapons would be unleashed on America and its people. Now that there are no weapons, this plan—and all future wars—will fail. Peace begins today."

Morpheus addressed the crimes of the world. "These are the amendments to the New Constitution:

1. Anyone rebuilding weapons will be banished.
2. Murderers will be banished before the act is carried out.
3. Those who instigate wars will be banished before any conflict begins.
4. White-collar criminals will be banished.
5. All acts of rape, incest, forced sex, or slavery will result in immediate banishment.
6. Thieves of any kind will be banished.
7. Hatred of any form will lead to banishment.
8. Liars will face banishment for spreading falsehoods.
9. Members of secret societies will be automatically banished.

Government officials will have their pay reduced by half and serve only four years, followed by a mandatory four-year hiatus. All officials will remain accountable for their actions while in office and afterward. Law enforcement and government systems will operate under this new Constitution.

No human will suffer again in any way, shape, or form. The gods will oversee Earth at all times. When peace and harmony prevail, we will teach humanity to travel in space and explore the universe. Amendments to the Constitution can only be made by the gods, with public support."

As Morpheus finished, some soldiers attempted to attack Sadal Suud. With a flick of her wrist, she disintegrated them into dust, which the wind carried away.

“I hope this demonstrates the consequences of aggression,” Morpheus said, his tone unyielding.

Sadal Suud turned to the world’s families. “If you love your children, you will not commit crimes, for your actions will leave them as orphans.”

Morpheus added, “From this moment forward, there will be no tobacco, drugs, or alcohol. We will cure all ailments on Earth and eliminate pollution entirely.”

Turning back to the President and generals, Morpheus said, “If you have more heroes, my wife and I will be waiting here on the lawn.”

He released them from the glass enclosure. “I’m waiting,” he said simply.

The President’s voice trembled slightly. “There will be no more attacks on the King and Queen of Earth.”

Morpheus nodded. “Good. But I already know that Russia and China are searching for ways to destroy us. They will fail. Weapons can no longer exist, and anyone attempting to create them will turn to dust.”

Sadal Suud addressed the global audience. “We want you to continue your lives. We will provide new education and pathways for success. Elections will be held worldwide to replace corrupt governments. This process will take one month to implement, and we will monitor its progress.”

Morpheus smiled faintly. "Sleep well tonight, knowing that the world will soon be a better place for everyone. We will leave now and return in the morning for the next thirty days."

With that, Morpheus and Sadal Suud ascended into the sky, their promise of change lingering in the minds of all who watched.

CHAPTER 36

Troubles

The next day, Labrum reviewed a recording and discovered that humans had unearthed hidden weapons in underground bases across America, Russia, and China. Alarmed, he rushed to Morpheus's chamber and woke both Morpheus and Sadal Suud.

"Morpheus, something happened last night on Earth," Labrum said urgently, recounting what he had seen.

Morpheus listened calmly before replying, "We were already aware of these secret bases."

Labrum frowned. "Then why allow them to keep such weapons?"

"We must trust humanity initially," Morpheus explained. "When they fail, it gives me the justification to act decisively."

"But this could be turned against both of you," Labrum warned.

Morpheus nodded thoughtfully. "Sacrifices must be made to demonstrate the necessity of our leadership. The people need to see the consequences of defiance."

Labrum sighed but eventually conceded. "You have a point."

Morpheus stood. "We'll address these problems head-on. Sadal Suud and I warned humanity against crimes and aggression toward the gods who have protected Earth for eons. Now, we will show them the repercussions."

He instructed Sadal Suud to wake the crew. "We must prepare for the day ahead."

Once everyone reported to their stations on the ship's bridge, Morpheus issued his orders. "Take your positions. Record and report any issues."

With their team in place, Morpheus and Sadal Suud descended to Earth.

As they entered the atmosphere, radars from three nations detected their presence. Silent alarms were triggered, and military forces were mobilized to intercept the two figures descending toward the Atlantic Ocean off the coast of Washington, D.C.

"Activate your shield and grow to one mile in height," Morpheus instructed Sadal Suud as they approached the surface.

Moments after they landed in the ocean, fighter jets arrived. On their second pass, the jets launched missiles at the gods. The explosions were fierce but harmless, dissipating against the impenetrable body shields.

Morpheus and Sadal Suud stood firm while monitors on their ship broadcast the attack to televisions, computers, and radios worldwide. Thus, the aggressive actions of the leaders from America, Russia, and China were exposed to a global audience. Pilots reported back to their respective governments, describing the impossibility of harming the gods. Their fear spread quickly through military ranks and leadership circles.

Speaking through the monitors, Morpheus addressed humanity. "Nothing on Earth can harm us. Your leaders have shown their disregard for the people by provoking this attack. Now, the gods will take control to protect the world's population from corrupt governance."

Sadal Suud stepped forward. "We demand adherence to the laws of the people," she said. "When individuals commit crimes, they will turn to dust, punishing themselves. Prisons and jails will no longer be needed. Law and order will reign supreme."

Morpheus continued, "We will start with the governments of America, Russia, and China. We will cleanse their corruption. This cleansing will extend to all governments, businesses, and citizens. Our goal is to restore integrity and justice."

He paused to outline the next steps. "Elections will be held worldwide within one month. Only qualified candidates with proven credibility may run for office. Once elected, they will initiate reforms to ensure accountability and transparency."

After the elections, Morpheus took decisive action. Those involved in the attack on the gods were rounded up and transported to a site in Nevada, where they were turned to dust. The event was broadcast globally, sparking a mix of fear and awe.

The people questioned the gods' methods. "Why would you kill those who attacked you?" they asked.

Morpheus's response was firm. "How would you respond if someone attacked, harmed, or killed your family? These laws are clear—there must be consequences for breaking them. Earth is plagued by individuals who believe they can escape justice. That ends now."

Sadal Suud added, "We came to Earth in peace, but we have been met with violence. Yet, we offer a better life—a world free of corruption, illness, and suffering. Those unwilling to embrace this future will not be part of it."

Morpheus outlined the gods' plans for a healthier planet. "The Earth suffers from the remnants of biological, chemical, and nuclear experiments. Harmful elements pollute your air, land, and water. We will remove these toxins and cure all illnesses. No child will ever again be born into sickness or pain."

He detailed their first actions: purifying the air, land, and oceans, starting with the poles and mountain ranges. In prisons, the worst offenders—death row inmates, lifelong criminals, rapists, and drug lords—would be removed.

"Our goal is peace," Morpheus declared. "We will educate the population on better ways to live, ensuring prosperity for all."

The people of Earth were divided. Some embraced the gods' vision, while others resisted.

Sadal Suud addressed the skeptics. "Did you ever fully trust your leaders? Did their promises bring you the peace and prosperity you deserved? We have cured your illnesses and cleansed your world of corruption. Now, we will guide you toward a harmonious existence."

Over the next six months, Earth thrived under the gods' rule. Crime disappeared, the planet was rejuvenated, and humanity prospered. Labrum approached Morpheus and Sadal Suud, pride evident in his voice. "You've succeeded in maintaining peace, law, and order on Earth. The people are happier and more united."

"Yes, Father," Morpheus replied.

Labrum smiled. "You kept your word. Humanity is better for it."

Sadal Suud added, "Life is easier for everyone, including humans. Peace will continue to flourish for the years to come."

Despite the thriving prosperity on Earth, a group of people remained dissatisfied with the new way of life. Morpheus and Sadal Suud, attuned to human thoughts and actions, detected their discontent. Over the next three years, they monitored this group while continuing their visits to humanity.

One day, the group called upon Morpheus and Sadal Suud, claiming they needed the gods' help. However, the two gods were well aware of their true intentions and prepared for an ambush. When they arrived, the group launched an attack.

Morpheus and Sadal Suud froze the attackers in place with a mere thought. Morpheus looked at them sternly. “What are you doing?” he demanded.

The group’s leader sneered. “We want Earth back the way it was—with our freedom and corruption!”

Sadal Suud shook her head in disbelief. “You already have freedom, along with prosperity and peace. Why would you yearn for corruption? You know the extent of our powers, yet you foolishly try to harm the gods who have safeguarded this planet for three years. Until now, we’ve had no need for executions, but your actions may change that.”

Morpheus’s expression hardened. “Your crimes leave us no choice. Why did you choose to attack us?”

The leader replied, “We want corruption back in the world.”

“That will never happen,” Sadal Suud said firmly. “That era is over.”

Morpheus searched the minds of the group, delving into their thoughts for a deeper understanding of their motives. After a moment, he straightened and spoke with finality. “I now know the truth. There’s no redemption for you. It’s time for you all to turn to dust.”

The leader, desperation etched on his face, begged, “Can’t you give us a second chance?”

“No,” Morpheus replied coldly. “I’ve seen your true intentions. Your time is over. Say your goodbyes.”

The execution was broadcast across the globe through the monitors. Morpheus addressed the world, explaining the reasons for the group’s actions and the necessity of their punishment.

When the execution was complete, Morpheus turned to Sadal Suud. “We must return to the ship.”

“What’s the matter?” she asked, concerned.

“I’ll explain everything when we’re aboard,” he said.

Back on the ship, Morpheus called a meeting in the Meeting Chamber. As the crew gathered, he began to explain the group’s attack.

“What do you mean, Morpheus?” Labrum asked.

Morpheus turned to Denab. “Pull up the recordings.”

Denab complied, displaying footage of the group’s behavior. The crew watched the scenes of defiance and aggression unfold.

Labrum studied the recordings closely before speaking. “They aren’t human,” he said.

Morpheus turned to him sharply. “What do you mean?”

Labrum leaned forward, his voice grave. "There are multiple universes, Morpheus. These beings aren't from this universe, nor are they from Caligula. They're intruders from another dimension."

Morpheus asked, "How can you be certain they're not from Caligula?"

Labrum explained, "We recorded all the nationalities and cultures during our time in the Caligula Universe. Denab, run a facial recognition scan to compare these individuals with those records."

Denab worked quickly and then replied, "There's no match, Labrum."

Labrum's expression darkened. "That confirms it—we're dealing with a new intruder in our Universe, possibly from Vishnu."

Morpheus nodded, his demeanor serious. "We need to search Earth for these beings and uncover their purpose here. Labrum, call the other ships to assist in protecting the planet. Pair up with your partners and begin a thorough search for others like them. We'll use our monitors and computer recorders to identify their presence."

Labrum added, "Shouldn't we notify the humans about the arrival of another race on Earth?"

Morpheus shook his head. "No. That could alert the intruders to our plans and compromise our operation."

As the *UNIV ORION* crew prepared to descend to Earth, two Achillesian ships entered the planet's orbit. The sight of the additional ships heightened their vigilance.

Labrum immediately contacted the other ships. "Maintain a sharp lookout for any additional intruder vessels. Protect our ship and be ready to assist us as we investigate Earth."

Captains Howse and Shrowd responded promptly. "Understood, Labrum. We'll patrol Earth's orbit and use a tracker beam to tow your ship for added security."

"Good thinking," Labrum replied. "Seeing three ships in motion will strengthen our presence and act as a deterrent."

With that, the *UNIV ORION* crew descended to Earth, determined to track down the intruders and uncover their intentions on the planet.

CHAPTER 37

New Intruders

Labrum had extensive knowledge of other Universes and the old gods and goddesses. However, the arrival of beings from a third Universe shifted Morpheus's perspective on the pervasive nature of evil across all realms. History, it seemed, would always repeat itself—regardless of the Universe, galaxy, planet, or people involved. Problems were cyclical, re-emerging to haunt civilizations over time. The patterns of existence, whether through the food chain, evolution, or societal structures, echoed across all Universes and dimensions.

Determined to provide clarity, Labrum led the *UNIV ORION* crew to the Hologram Hall. There, the crew and family watched vivid projections of the known Universes and their complex interconnections. As the holograms illuminated the endless possibilities of existence, Morpheus broke the silence.

"Father," he began, "Why didn't our records show evidence of other Universes when I was studying Achilles' archives?"

Labrum hesitated before answering. "The records were stored in a secret vault for safekeeping—or until a significant issue demanded their use."

Morpheus's voice grew stern. "Father, didn't I make it clear? No more secrets."

"Yes, Morpheus," Labrum replied quietly.

"Do we know what race of people we're dealing with?" Morpheus asked.

Labrum shook his head. "No, Morpheus. But I suspect they are from the Jarnsaxa Universe. It borders the Caligula Universe, which could explain the wars and chaos we witnessed there."

Morpheus sighed. "We've barely resolved one crisis, and now another is upon us."

"Welcome to your kingship, Morpheus," Labrum said with a knowing smirk. "But if my suspicions are correct, the Jarnsaxa Universe holds the answers to this new threat."

Labrum then suggested, "Morpheus, you and Sadal Suud must use your powers of the Tenth Dimension to jump between Universes. You'll find the answers there."

"And the Earth?" Morpheus asked.

"With three ships protecting it, Earth will be safe," Labrum assured him. "Besides, we'll monitor everything and keep you informed."

Wega chimed in, "You must go, Morpheus. The sooner you leave, the sooner you can return—especially if trouble arises here."

Morpheus and Sadal Suud agreed. Using their dimensional powers, they leapt to the Jarnsaxa Universe. Upon arrival, they were met with a staggering sight: a massive buildup of military forces.

"Sadal Suud," Morpheus said gravely, "We need to uncover their plans."

They quickly located the lead spaceship and, cloaking themselves in invisibility, infiltrated the ship's bridge. Inside, King General Aegaeon barked orders to his commanders.

"Prepare for flight!" Aegaeon roared. "Our mission is to conquer Earth—strip it of resources, enslave its people, and claim the planet as ours."

Morpheus and Sadal Suud captured everything on their monitors and transmitted the recordings back to *UNIV ORION*. Labrum received the transmission and immediately contacted Morpheus.

"Morpheus, you and Sadal Suud must leave now!" Labrum urged.

"Why, Father?" Morpheus asked.

"They plan to destroy Earth and enslave humanity." Labrum's tone was grave. "I know King General Aegaeon. His powers are unmatched—far more formidable than the Tarvosians."

"And what about us, Father?" Morpheus countered. "Sadal Suud and I are no strangers to power."

Labrum replied, "You are strong, but Aegaeon's strength is beyond anything you've faced. Do not underestimate him."

Morpheus turned to his wife. "Sadal Suud, what do you think?"

Sadal Suud's eyes burned with resolve. "We must protect the people, Morpheus. We hold our ground, no matter the cost."

Morpheus and Sadal Suud departed their ship and, while floating in the vastness of space, Morpheus said, "We will create a forcefield around all the enemy spaceships."

Sadal Suud nodded. "Keeping the battle confined to their Universe is a wise decision."

The two began to glow with an intense, otherworldly light as they channeled their divine powers. Together, they projected a shimmering forcefield that enveloped King General Aegaeon's fleet, rendering it completely immobilized. Morpheus then used his abilities to shut down the engines and electrical systems of every ship.

Addressing the fleet, Morpheus and Sadal Suud spoke in unison, their voices resonating through the silence of space. "Cease your attack on Earth and its people immediately."

King General Aegaeon's voice crackled over the comms. "Who dares address me in such a manner?"

Morpheus replied, “You are speaking to King Morpheus and Queen Sadal Suud, rulers of the Universes, Earth, and protectors of the Ancient Gods.”

Aegaeon scoffed. “I have never heard of any King or Queen of the Universes.”

“Now you have,” Morpheus said firmly.

Aegaeon’s tone grew suspicious. “Did you shut down the power systems of my fleet?”

“Yes,” Morpheus replied calmly. “My wife and I have rendered your ships powerless.”

The glow around the fleet intensified, catching Aegaeon’s attention. “Is that light in space… the two of you?”

“It is,” Morpheus said. “We are all around your ships, and you will find no escape.”

Aegaeon sneered. “We shall see about that.”

“Is that supposed to frighten us?” Sadal Suud asked with a hint of amusement.

One of Aegaeon’s captains interjected, his voice filled with fear. “Your Majesty, these are the ones who destroyed the Tarvosians.”

Aegaeon hesitated before asking, “Are you truly the ones who defeated the Tarvosians?”

"Yes," Morpheus and Sadal Suud confirmed in unison.

Morpheus continued, "We are aware of your plans to destroy Earth and enslave its people. We cannot and will not allow that to happen."

"How did you learn of our plans?" Aegaeon demanded.

"We are gods," Morpheus said. "As King and Queen of the Universes, we see and know all. You are about to learn just how powerful we are if you persist in your aggression."

Morpheus added, "Your ships are immobilized, and our forcefield ensures you cannot leave. You are at our mercy."

Sadal Suud extended an olive branch. "We offer you a chance for peace. Agree to talks, and you may yet survive to see another day."

Aegaeon, however, was defiant. "I am the King of this Universe, and you will see my strength soon enough."

"Go ahead and try," Morpheus said. "You are at a stalemate. You have no power, no escape, and no options. We could leave you within this forcefield to perish, should we choose."

One of Aegaeon's captains turned to him, his voice filled with resignation. "They have the advantage, Your Majesty. Our ships are powerless, and if we remain trapped, we will die."

Morpheus finally said, “We will leave you for now to contemplate your choices: peace or destruction. Choose wisely.”

As Morpheus and Sadal Suud retreated, they monitored the fleet, listening intently to the conversations among Aegaeon and his generals.

Within the fleet, the murmurs of discontent grew louder. Aegaeon’s generals admitted the harsh truth. “Morpheus and Sadal Suud have the upper hand. We have no way to retaliate or act. Their power is beyond anything we’ve ever encountered.”

The King declared, “Let me attempt to break the forcefield with my powers.”

Stepping into the void of space outside his ship, he unleashed all his might against the forcefield. Yet, no matter how hard he tried, the barrier remained unyielding. Defeated, the King returned to his ship and announced, “I couldn’t break the forcefield. But I have another plan: we’ll agree to the Peace Treaty, lure them in, force them to deactivate the forcefield, and then kill them both.”

Meanwhile, Labrum contacted Morpheus and Sadal Suud. “There are no other intruders detected on Earth or in its orbit,” Labrum reported.

Morpheus responded, “The intruders are from the Greip planet in the Jarnsaxa Universe. Their goal is to destroy Earth and reshape it into their vision of control.”

Labrum replied, "We cannot let that happen. Humanity has been nurtured with the principles of peace and cooperation. I've managed the humans' questions about your whereabouts, so there's no need to worry."

Sadal Suud interrupted, her tone sharp. "They plan to kill us under the guise of agreeing to a peace treaty."

Morpheus nodded. "Thank you, Labrum. Goodbye."

The two gods returned to the lead spaceship to confront King General Aegaeon.

Upon their arrival, the King addressed them. "Can we have a discussion first, Morpheus and Sadal Suud? I invite you aboard my ship. There will be no aggression against either of you."

Sadal Suud's eyes blazed with fury. "You lie! We overheard your plans to kill us the moment we set foot on your ship. We will speak from here, at a safe distance."

The King's expression twisted in confusion. "How could you possibly hear us?"

Morpheus stepped forward, his voice calm but edged with authority. "You admitted your treachery, King. We know your intentions."

Caught off guard, the King faltered, unable to find words to defend himself.

Morpheus pressed on. “What did you truly wish to discuss, King?”

The King hesitated, then asked, “Do you know the future history of Earth?”

“Yes,” Morpheus replied. “That’s why we are here—to protect and guide humanity.”

The King smirked. “We’ve seen glimpses of Earth’s future as well. In time, we saw your kind destroy the humans for their ignorance and refusal to follow your rules.”

Sadal Suud shot back, “We found your people on Earth sowing chaos and destruction.”

Morpheus added, “My people have safeguarded Earth for billions of years. We will not allow anyone, including humans, to bring about its destruction.”

The King tried to steer the conversation. “What is the status of the Peace Treaty?”

Morpheus answered, “Before we proceed, I want you to hear this recording.”

Sadal Suud played the audio of the King’s earlier statement: his plan to kill the gods after forcing them to deactivate the forcefield.

Silence fell as the King listened to his own words of betrayal.

Morpheus turned to him. "Now, tell me—what do you *really* intend to do?"

The King and his men looked defeated. Their bravado crumbled under the weight of their lies and aggression.

Finally, the King asked, "What will you do to us and our fleet?"

Morpheus's voice was cold and resolute. "You are imprisoned within this forcefield, where you will remain until your end."

The King's anger flared. "I will detonate one of my ships to break your forcefield!"

"Go ahead," Morpheus said, unfazed. "See what happens."

The King hesitated. "What would happen if I did?"

Morpheus explained, "Your ships are powered by nuclear engines. A detonation would trigger a chain reaction, destroying your entire fleet. The forcefield, however, will remain intact."

The King's face twisted in rage. "You are condemning an entire race to death!"

Morpheus's tone softened, but his words remained firm. "No, King. You are condemning your people. Your intent was to annihilate Earth and its inhabitants. Justice demands that your actions face their consequences." He continued, his voice ringing with divine authority. "Let this be a lesson to all Universes: the

King and Queen of the Universes are here to uphold justice and preserve peace for all time."

CHAPTER 38

The Gods Returning to Earth

Morpheus and Sadal Suud returned to *UNIV ORION*, but upon arrival, both felt unwell. Concerned, Labrum and Denab inquired about their condition.

"I'm not sure," Morpheus replied. "Could it be due to traveling through the tenth dimension?"

Labrum, uncertain, summoned Sirius and Terebellum to perform a full medical examination. After a thorough check, Sirius concluded, "Physically, you're fine, but the journey and use of your powers have exhausted you. You both need rest to recover your strength."

Family members escorted Morpheus and Sadal Suud to their Sleep Chambers, where they slept for five days. When they finally awoke, they strolled through the ship, greeting everyone warmly.

"How are you feeling now?" Labrum asked.

"Still drained," Morpheus admitted, and Sadal Suud agreed.

"Then rest some more. We'll handle matters with the humans and review the recordings and results later," Labrum reassured them.

Later, they met Giuseppe and Sophia. "How are you both feeling?" their parents asked.

"We need more rest," Morpheus said.

"We missed you," Sadal Suud added.

"Go rest, and we'll talk later," Sophia advised.

After a brief update on the ship's condition and how everyone was getting along, Morpheus remarked, "One big, happy extended family." His parents smiled in agreement.

Back in their chamber, Morpheus held Sadal Suud close, kissing her before beginning to make love. Their love sparked a radiant glow that enveloped the entire ship. As they healed themselves, the ship's systems also experienced remarkable improvements.

Sirius told Labrum, "Morpheus and Sadal Suud are healing themselves, and it's affecting the ship."

"That's obvious with the ship glowing," Labrum noted.

"The controls and systems are upgrading themselves," Denab added.

Labrum speculated, “The journey through the tenth dimension may have enhanced their powers, but it also drained them. Sirius, can you analyze their strengths on a medical level?”

“We can run tests,” Sirius confirmed.

Labrum suggested monitoring them closely for any lasting effects from their interdimensional travels.

Five days later, Morpheus and Sadal Suud emerged, fully recovered.

“How are you feeling now?” Labrum asked.

“Much better,” Sadal Suud said, with Morpheus nodding in agreement.

Labrum summoned Sirius and Terebellum to the Meeting Chamber, where the crew gathered to review recordings of their journey.

The footage revealed their invisible presence on the lead ship as they navigated the tenth dimension. It also exposed the Greips’ plans for a massacre on Earth.

Morpheus recounted, “We offered them a peace treaty, but they refused. Their refusal led to imprisonment, and they now face the consequences of their choices.”

“You gave them a chance, and they chose otherwise,” Labrum affirmed, supported by the others.

Turning to Morpheus and Sadal Suud, Labrum said, "We need to understand how the journey impacted you physically and mentally."

"It felt like time traveling but with a stronger pull on our bodies and minds," Morpheus explained.

Sadal Suud added, "Traveling through three universes drained us completely, especially the time we spent in their universe."

"Did you notice any lasting changes?" Sirius asked.

"Not that we're aware of," Morpheus replied.

The crew resolved to continue monitoring them as the ship thrived under the mysterious glow of their recovery.

"Let me explain what's happened since you both returned to the ship," Labrum began. "When we received you, you were completely worn out—weak, incoherent, and barely responsive. We had to carry you to your chambers. Sirius and Terebellum conducted physical exams while you were unconscious and ran extensive tests. Thankfully, there were no immediate issues. You slept for five days, briefly woke up, and then slept for another five. Do you recall anything after coming aboard?"

Morpheus shook his head. "No, just faint voices."

"I only remember being with my husband," Sadal Suud added.

"How are you feeling now?" Sirius asked.

"Okay, but still weak," Morpheus replied. Sadal Suud nodded in agreement.

Labrum continued, his tone cautious. "While you slept, something extraordinary occurred. Both of you began to glow, and the glow spread throughout the ship. Miraculously, the ship started repairing itself—every system, every part. It's clear something happened to you, either during your journey or in the other universe. We need you to monitor yourselves carefully for any changes, and I've scheduled weekly check-ups with Sirius and Terebellum."

Morpheus and Sadal Suud exchanged glances and nodded.

"You may be right about the effects of moving between planets and universes," Labrum noted. "We're already seeing changes in both of you."

"How are the humans?" Morpheus asked.

"And have there been any intrusions aboard the ship?" Sadal Suud followed up.

"We've conducted daily scans since your return," Labrum said. "So far, no intruders have been detected."

Morpheus suddenly recalled something. "The King General Aegaeon warned us about humans," he said, recounting the ominous tale. "He claimed humans were a lost cause, destined to destroy Earth through their greed and violence."

Sadal Suud nodded, adding, “He said our efforts to help them would only hasten Earth’s end.”

Labrum’s voice hardened. “Our mission is to prevent Earth’s destruction, no matter the cost. But if humanity refuses to change, they will face the consequences.”

At that moment, Morpheus and Sadal Suud simultaneously murmured, “Humans are still committing crimes.”

Labrum frowned. “How do you know?”

“It feels as though something has enhanced our awareness,” Sadal Suud said. “We’re certain of it.”

Acting swiftly, Sadal Suud instructed Kochab and Rastaban to use the ship’s monitors to investigate specific coordinates on Earth. The images confirmed their fears: humans exploiting others for their belongings and escalating weapon development. “The humans are muscling people for their belongings,” Morpheus said. “They don’t want to work for a living.”

Install additional monitors for Earth,” Morpheus ordered. “There’s more at play here with the weapons.”

“It’s a nuclear weapon,” Sadal Suud said gravely.

But the strain of their heightened abilities soon overwhelmed them.

“They’re weakening,” Denab observed. “We need to get them to the Medical Chamber.”

Labrum agreed. “Run them through the gamma X-ray machine for a full scan.”

The results surprised everyone. Sirius reported, “We found no abnormalities. They’re physically fine.”

Yet, as Morpheus and Sadal Suud recovered, they appeared revitalized, bursting with energy.

“How is this possible?” Labrum wondered aloud.

“The gamma rays must have recharged us,” Morpheus speculated.

Further tests revealed a startling discovery: the gamma radiation had altered not only Morpheus and Sadal Suud but also the crew and Morpheus’s Earth family, the Cappuccinos.

“Our blood tests all show traces of gamma radiation,” Sirius explained. “It’s enhancing our strength and vitality. The Cappuccino family, once ordinary humans, are now becoming more like Achillesians.”

“Is it harming them?” Labrum asked.

“Not at all,” Sirius replied. “They’re healthier than ever.”

Labrum’s focus shifted. “What about Morpheus and Sadal Suud?”

Sirius answered, "Their mental and physical capabilities have increased significantly. It seems the gamma radiation replenished their energy and powers."

Labrum instructed the team to remain vigilant. "Monitor them closely for further changes. Conduct strength and ability tests for everyone, including the Earth family."

Over the next few days, the crew and Cappuccinos underwent extensive physical evaluations. The results were consistent: enhanced strength, sharper minds, and improved overall health.

At a meeting in the ship's chamber, Sirius and Terebellum summarized their findings. "The crew is in excellent health. The Cappuccino family has undergone remarkable transformations, gaining strength and knowledge. As for Morpheus and Sadal Suud, their powers have advanced beyond what we thought possible."

Labrum addressed the group. "This is encouraging, but we must remain cautious. Morpheus, Sadal Suud, how do you feel now?"

"Strong," Morpheus said.

"Recharged," Sadal Suud confirmed.

Labrum turned to the Cappuccinos. "And you? How do you feel?"

“We’re better than ever,” Giuseppe replied on behalf of his family.

Labrum nodded. “Good. Let’s focus on our mission: protecting Earth and guiding humanity. We’ve gained new strengths, and we’ll need them for the challenges ahead.”

CHAPTER 39

New Criminal

The following day, the *UNIV ORION* crew prepared to visit Earth. "We'll take the time machine shuttles and set up camp around them," Labrum announced.

"We'll stock enough supplies for six months," Denab added.

Once the shuttles were fully prepared, Labrum gave the order. "It's time to travel to Earth."

"As we approach the surface, I want us to circle the planet," Morpheus instructed.

"Why circle it?" Labrum asked.

"Sadal Suud and I sense nuclear weapons being constructed underground," Morpheus replied gravely.

Labrum nodded. "Understood. We'll circle Earth and make our presence known."

As the shuttles orbited the planet, Sadal Suud used her telepathic powers to locate the perpetrators behind the secret weapons. The humans below gazed in awe and fear as the gods circled repeatedly, their craft gleaming like celestial beacons.

Sadal Suud identified three countries—symbolized by the Eagle, Bear, and Dragon—responsible for the weapons: the United States, Russia, and China. Her powers also uncovered whispers of corruption and crime festering in cities and towns worldwide.

Labrum activated the shield around the shuttles as they descended, landing on the White House lawn. The crew set up camp under the protection of the shield.

"Outside the shield, we must wear body shields for added safety," Morpheus instructed. "We also need to gather information from the people about their dissatisfaction with the laws we established for Earth."

Wega interjected, "We already know why they resist the laws, Morpheus."

"I want to hear it from them directly," Morpheus insisted. "Their opinions won't be judged—only their crimes. Kochab and Rastaban, review the recordings of the people and log key insights. Monitor for any threats while we're outside the shield. The team will pair off and visit designated locations: the United States, Russia, and China. These countries are violating our laws by developing nuclear weapons against us. Use the time rewind feature if necessary to trace the origins of these actions. Identify those responsible, and if there are issues, call for assistance."

With that, the team dispersed. Morpheus and Sadal Suud stayed at the White House, observing the grounds and its occupants. Their presence quickly drew hostility. Rockets and automatic weapons targeted them, the attack rattling the air.

"Shields holding?" Labrum asked over the communicator.

"Yes, they're impenetrable," Sadal Suud confirmed.

Amid the chaos, Sadal Suud instructed, "Locate the weapons factories and destroy them, along with anyone involved in their creation."

Morpheus called Kochab to reposition the monitors around the White House, ensuring full surveillance. Meanwhile, Sadal Suud's telepathic search revealed the President and military generals hiding in a secure underground vault. She relayed the information to Morpheus.

With a surge of power, Morpheus lifted the White House from its foundation, exposing the hidden vault below. Using his abilities, he unearthed the vault, exposing it to the world through the ship's monitors.

Broadcasting across Earth, Morpheus declared, "You are violating the laws of this planet. We know the countries building these forbidden weapons. Justice will come to them. But for now, witness how American politicians face accountability. Wars have always been the work of politicians—not the people."

He ripped open the vault's doors and seized its occupants with one massive hand, holding them up for all to see.

"Where are the weapons being built?" Morpheus demanded.

The politicians remained silent, their faces pale.

Morpheus's form expanded, growing to a towering fifty feet. He loomed over them and grabbed one man by the head. "Tell me, or you'll lose your head—and your life."

Terrified, the man stammered, "I'll show you where." Under duress, he led Morpheus and Sadal Suud to a secret base where forbidden weapons were being constructed. The base was hidden, yet now fully exposed to the wrath of the gods.

Meanwhile, Wega and Marcus journeyed to Russia, while Denebola and Maria headed to China. Both teams encountered similar resistance—attacks and outright defiance from the countries' leaders. However, unlike the American leaders who cowered in a vault beneath the White House, the Russian and Chinese leaders did not resort to hiding like children. Despite these challenges, the teams successfully located the secret bases in their respective countries and reported back to Morpheus.

"Bring the leaders to America and seal off the entrances and roads to the underground bases," Morpheus commanded.

When the teams returned to America with the captured Russian and Chinese leaders, they joined Morpheus and Sadal Suud at the White House. Morpheus summoned all the godly teams to convene, ensuring the events were broadcast across the globe via monitors, televisions, radios, and computers.

Standing before the world, Morpheus addressed humanity with unyielding authority. His voice resonated like thunder, carrying both judgment and truth.

"The betrayal of the gods will not be tolerated, just as it was not in ancient times," Morpheus began. "We came to Earth in peace. We healed your people, shared the secrets of space travel, and gifted you the knowledge to thrive in harmony. Yet, human ignorance persists, ruling over the potential for wisdom granted by the gods of the past and present—and the vast Universe itself."

Morpheus's gaze swept over the captured leaders and then pierced through the monitors to the billions watching.

"History is riddled with humanity's arrogance, believing you are greater than your fellow humans and even the gods who created you. You owe everything in your world today to the gods of the past. It was we who brought the human race to this planet and nurtured its beginnings. Yet, over eons, you have failed each other and failed the gods. The sacred texts of your Bible even recount the anger of the gods when humanity strayed. But today, your understanding of those lessons has faltered, replaced by cruelty, abuse, and ignorance.

"This punishment is not from Achilles, the home of the gods. It is born of your own sins, forged in the fires of your own destruction."

Morpheus paused, letting the weight of his words settle before continuing.

"Your weapons—no matter how advanced—cannot harm the gods in any way. But I will not stand idly by as you destroy the planet that has sustained you for eons. The world's population must now adhere to the laws of the new human race, or death will come to all. We entrusted new leaders to guide you in peace after dismissing the corrupt old politicians. Yet even they succumbed to the rot of power and deceit. Now, the world will witness the price of their betrayal."

With a commanding gesture, Morpheus ordered the execution of the leaders of the three nations. The scene was broadcast live, an unflinching reminder of the gods' unwavering justice.

"This is the fate of those who defy the gods and endanger Earth. Let this be the last betrayal, or humanity will meet a harsher end," Morpheus declared, his voice reverberating like the echoes of the universe itself.

Morpheus and Sadal Suud created a shimmering forcefield bubble, trapping the captured leaders inside. The gods gazed solemnly at the panicked men and women confined within.

Sadal Suud stepped forward, her voice calm but firm. "We will demonstrate the cost of your wars—how they destroy not only lives but the very fabric of existence."

She gestured, and one of the confiscated weapons was activated and dropped into the forcefield bubble. The leaders clawed helplessly at the barrier, their screams muffled within the glowing confines. Then, the explosion erupted. The forcefield contained the devastation, but the gruesome aftermath—the blood, scattered remains, and destruction—was visible to all.

Morpheus turned his gaze toward the cameras broadcasting to every corner of the Earth. His expression was unyielding as he addressed humanity.

"This is the reality of war. This is what you have created and embraced. Nuclear war will not only destroy your enemies; it will obliterate everything in your world."

Sadal Suud added, her voice echoing with divine authority, "The choice is yours: peace or death. Humanity must decide its own fate."

Morpheus turned back to the smoldering remains within the bubble. "This will stand as a monument—a stark reminder of the cost of war and the fragility of life. It will symbolize both the past mistakes and the potential for a peaceful future. Now, we will resume the path toward peace and the survival of humankind."

Sadal Suud addressed the world, outlining the new structure for humanity. "There will be no more currencies, no more taxes. Instead, people will work collectively for the resources and products needed to sustain life. Workweeks will be limited to forty hours, split into three shifts to ensure balance and productivity. Saturdays and Sundays will be dedicated to family and community—a time for joy and connection. Education will be mandatory for all, both children and adults, as knowledge is the cornerstone of progress. And crimes will be judged and punished swiftly, as they were in the past."

Morpheus then addressed the growing unrest and resistance among humanity. "You question these laws because you fear change, but my wife and I are the protectors of this planet and the Universe. Your destructive tendencies have left us no choice but to intervene. Humanity is on a collision course with its own annihilation, driven by greed, corruption, and unchecked power."

Sadal Suud continued, her tone filled with both sorrow and resolve. "Nuclear weapons, governmental corruption, secret societies, and corporate greed have pushed the world to the brink. These forces have infected not only your leaders but everyday families, trickling down into every aspect of life. There are more criminals than law-abiding citizens, and humanity's insatiable thirst for power threatens the very survival of your species and the Earth itself."

The *UNIV ORION* crew had given their all to aid humanity. They shared knowledge, healed the sick, and introduced new ways of living. Yet, the resistance to change persisted.

Morpheus and Sadal Suud exchanged a solemn glance. They had done everything in their power to guide the human race toward a better future. But as they reflected on humanity's stubbornness and self-destructive tendencies, a grim realization settled over them.

"We may have only delayed the inevitable," Morpheus said, his voice heavy with resignation. "Humanity's path leads toward its own destruction, not by our hands, but by its own."

And with that, the gods continued their mission, determined to give humanity one final chance to choose peace over ruin.

EPILOGUE

Earth has always been and will always remain a planet capable of supporting life in some form. Life is not unique to this world; civilizations from other planets exist throughout the known Universe and beyond. These beings—aliens—have played a role in shaping the worlds we know, including Earth. Far from being hostile, they have refrained from attacking Earth because they, too, have contributed to its creation and development.

The aliens remain hidden, not out of fear, but to protect their advanced technology from falling into the wrong hands. They understand that exposing their knowledge could accelerate the greed, corruption, and power struggles already rampant among humanity, ultimately hastening the destruction of the human race.

Morpheus, though a god born on Earth, is also an alien from the world of Achilles. His purpose on Earth was hidden from him during his early life so that he could experience humanity firsthand—its ways, its thinking, and its flaws. Growing up among humans, Morpheus observed the pervasive corruption, greed, and abuse in all its forms—physical, mental, and emotional. He witnessed the deliberate harm people inflicted on one another, the senseless destruction of lives, and the systemic flaws that perpetuated such behaviors.

Earth was meant to be a sanctuary for life, nurtured by the influence of alien civilizations. Yet, the aliens underestimated the destructive forces of human greed, corruption, and the lust for power. Over time, humanity has failed to interpret the truths encoded in its own history—truths embedded in artifacts, cave paintings, scrolls, scriptures, Egyptian and Mayan hieroglyphs, Nostradamus' quatrains, the Bible, and countless other ancient records. These accounts reveal a history that intertwines humans, gods, and aliens, but humanity has largely ignored or misunderstood these messages.

Governments and scientists, instead of uncovering and sharing these truths, have distorted history for their own purposes. They present a narrative filled with lies, suppressing knowledge about Earth's origins, its civilizations, and its connection to the broader Universe. The political backstabbing seen in elections serves as a microcosm of this deceit—proof of a world built on lies and manipulation. The fear-mongering about alien invasions, claiming they will conquer Earth, is yet another fabrication designed to maintain control through fear and ignorance.

Morpheus and Sadal Suud sought to bring balance and truth to humanity, striving to illuminate the path toward understanding and unity. Yet, they find themselves trapped in an eternal quest for truth, navigating through time itself. For time, infinite and unyielding, is the only constant in the search for meaning and justice.

The gods—whether humanity chooses to believe in them or not—are the architects of Earth and countless other worlds. Ancient writings bear witness to their influence, from the earliest days to the present. The gods have vowed to return, rectify the corruption, and right the wrongs that plague this planet.

They remind humanity of an immutable truth: nothing on Earth truly belongs to anyone. Land, homes, and even the human body are but temporary possessions borrowed for a fleeting moment in time. In the end, all return to the Earth, and all must face the legacy they leave behind.

www.ingramcontent.com/pod-product-compliance
Lightning Source LLC
Chambersburg PA
CBHW051522050726
47503CB00014B/429

* 9 7 9 8 9 9 0 5 9 2 1 0 0 *